Love Habit

~ A Historical Tudor Romance About Christian Monks

By TL Clark

Happy Reading

Love & Light

TL xx

Published in the United Kingdom by:
Steamy Kettle Publishing

First published in electronic format and in print in 2025.

ISBN: 978-0-9956117-9-5

Published in the United Kingdom by:
Steamy Kettle Publishing

First published in electronic format and in print in 2025.

This book was written by a human. No artificial intelligence (AI) has been used in the production of this book.

This is a work of fiction. Names, characters, businesses, places, events, locales, and incidents are either the products of the author's imagination or used in a fictitious manner. Any resemblance to actual persons, living or dead, or actual events is purely coincidental.

ISBN: 978-0-9956117-9-5

This book is dedicated to anyone who has ever felt it necessary to hide their love.

Table of Contents

Maps

I have drawn out the layout of Darenth Priory as I believe it would have been. Clearly, I'm not an architect or an artist. But hopefully, these images give you an idea of where the guys were. Weirdly, north is facing the left of the page. But keeping it in this orientation made more sense when looking at it.

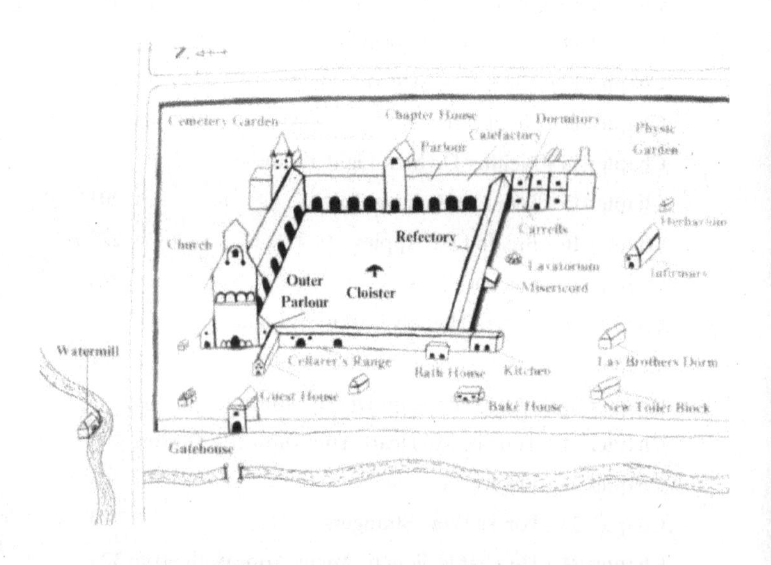

Figure 1 - Map of Darenth Priory drawn by TL Clark

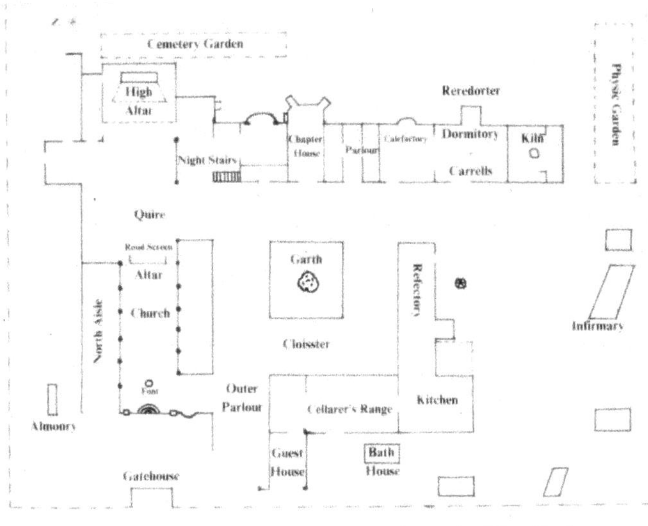

Figure 2 - Plan of Darenth Priory drawn by TL Clark

Hours

To help put the routine of a monk's life into context, I've worked out very roughly at what times the Offices / Opus Dei (Work of God) were celebrated.

The times were not governed by a clock but by daylight. There was a winter schedule and a summer one. These would change gradually throughout the seasons, depending on daylight.

I've worked these times out for Kent, England in GMT (Greenwich Mean Time). Because BST (British Summer Time) aka Daylight Saving was not brought into being until 1916. Not that GMT was used then either, but it's the best conversion factor I could use to 'make it make sense', at least in my head.

NB Daylight varies wildly around the British Isles.

"*Seven times a day I praise you,*" [Psalm 118/119:164] is basically what guided The Rule of St Benedict.

Summer			
Office	**Time (roughly)**	**Duration**	
Matins/Night Office/Nocturns	**02:00**	1 hour	
Loo break	03:00		
Lauds (a later portion of Vigils from dawn)	**03:30**	30 mins	Sunrise - 03:30
Reading	04:00		
Prime (early morning, the first hour of daylight)	**04:30**	30 mins	
Breakfast (bread & ale)	05:00		
Work	05:30		
Terce (third hour)	**06:30**	30 mins	
Mass	07:00	30 mins	
Chapter Meeting	07:30		
High Mass	08:00	1 hour	
Work/Reading	09:00		
Sext (sixth hour)	**09:30**	30 mins	
Work/Reading	10:00		
Midday Meal "dinner"	11:30	1 hour	
Nones (ninth hour)	**12:30**	30 mins	
Work/Reading	13:00		
Vespers (sunset)	**19:00**	30 mins	
Supper	**19:30**	30 mins	Sunset - 20:15
Compline (end of the day before retiring)	**20:00**	30 mins	

Winter (from 1 November till Easter)			
Office	**Time (roughly)**	**Duration**	
Matins/Night Office/Nocturns	**00:00**	1 hour	
Loo break then back to sleep	01:00		
Reading	06:00		
Breakfast (bread & ale)	07:30		
Lauds (a later portion of Vigils from dawn)	**08:00**	30 mins	Sunrise - 07:59
Work	08:30		
Prime (early morning, the first hour of daylight)	**09:00**	30 mins	
Work/Reading	09:30		
Terce (third hour)	**10:30**	30 mins	
Midday Meal "dinner"	11:00		
Mass	12:00	30 mins	
Chapter Meeting	12:30		
Sext (sixth hour)	**13:00**	30 mins	
Work	13:30		
Nones (ninth hour)	**14:00**	30 mins	
Work/Reading	14:30		
Vespers (sunset)	**15:00**	30 mins	
Supper	**15:30**	30 mins	Sunset - 15:52
Warming Room/calefactory (winter)	16:00		
Compline (end of the day before retiring)	**18:00**	30 mins	
Sleep	18:30		

Figure 3 – Table of hours by TL Clark

Introduction

PLEASE READ!

Dear Reader,

Thank you for selecting this book. I would like to foreshadow some of what you are about to read.

This book's intention is to give an authentic view into the life of two young men entering monastic life in 1485, with secrets held within their breast.

I am not trying to be sacrilegious or defamatory, and I apologise if I cause offence. But my purpose is to tell a tale which must've been true for many, yet hitherto untold. Now, in this modern world, I merely wish to honour the memory of those who were forced to conceal their love. To bring their love out of the shadows and into the light.

For the record, I am not a Catholic. And the views within this book are not necessarily a reflection of my own.

Whilst researching my previous medieval romance, Love in the Roses, I uncovered many hints as to the sexuality of some monks, including St Aelred of Rievaulx. And, as I thought it through, it became obvious; if you were a young, gay man in the Middle Ages, and you wished to avoid marriage (as it would soon become apparent you could not fulfil your marital duties), what would you do?

It was not actually a crime to be homosexual in medieval England (you can thank Henry VIII for that injustice with his crudely named Act in 1533), but it did fall under the general sin of '**sodomy**'. Now, this incorporated all "unnatural sexual acts" (*cringes* ***not*** my phrasing!), but these included ***any*** sexual intercourse outside of marriage and performed without the sole intention of procreation (even solo stuff and cunnilingus)! There were various penances issued for these venial/lesser sins; perhaps the worst being for oral, bizarrely. But I have become distracted by fornication.

The point is, that homosexuality was frowned upon in England but within the above context. I should mention there is evidence it was not universally shunned e.g. In 1098, The Pope approved a known gay man as Bishop of Orleans (despite a campaign against the promotion).

Clearly, one could not live openly as a same-sex couple. Like many things, it was fine as long as you were discreet.

I have given my guys as happy a life as I could within the medieval framework. Too many historical novels are miserable for those within the LGBTQIA+ community, and I wanted to convey a happier outcome whilst remaining realistic.

So, back to my question, what would you do? Well, you could seek a life where marriage wasn't expected. Oh, monks took vows *not* to marry. A whole community of men from similar, wealthy backgrounds? Tempting.

Now, I wish to make it abundantly clear that I am in no way suggesting that all monks were gay. Of course, they weren't. **There were many reasons to join the brethren:**

- ❖ One may wish to simply devote their life to God
- ❖ The lure of a peaceful, secure retreat was strong
- ❖ Perhaps one wished to escape some catastrophe/war
- ❖ Being a lesser offspring, one's wealthy parents didn't know what else to do with them
- ❖ A poor young lad may have a broken heart, and thus given up on women

But surely, we can agree that *some* monks, were in fact, gay.

Speaking of which, my monks are of the Benedictine order – to be honest, mainly because of their fondness for writing. St Benedict wrote The Rule in the 6th century, but as observances became lax, other orders were created to follow The Rule in their own way. Just how lax were they? Well, there are many debauched stories about monks. What one chooses to believe is up to the individual. But I suppose somewhere between the best and the worst of 'accounts' possibly lies the truth.

Incidentally, **the age of consent** in the UK at the time of writing is sixteen years old (for all sexualities). In 1485, people could be married as young as the age of fourteen (particularly girls). Basically, what I'm saying is that the ages of the characters in this book are legal.

A great deal of research has gone into this tome to make it as accurate as I can feasibly make it. However, the 15th century has sparse concrete evidence. And I may have taken some liberties in pursuit of creating a novel. Please bear this in mind before declaring, "They would not have acted that way!" – Nobody really knows for sure, and I am challenging some pre-conceptions here.

Herbal Remedies - I have alluded to several herbal remedies within this book but have kept quantities and specifics deliberately vague. None of these are to be tried at home. Some were outright perilous. There are plenty of safe, modern herbal complementary medicines and recipes out there (of which I'm a fan) should you wish to find them.

Toys - So, look, this author does ***not*** recommend using candles as toys. Please, there are cheap, hygienic options readily available in our modern world. Don't forget the lube!

A Note on Language

Please also note that I am not Chaucer, so have written this book in Modern English whilst endeavouring to give a flavour of the time period. At the end of this book, you will discover a *Glossary* of words which are now unfamiliar but add a delightful touch of the vernacular.

Bible quotes are contained within these pages. Where they are short, I have used the Latin wording and translated it into English, using the King James version. If they are longer, I have used the KJV to avoid fatigue. This is supposed to be a fun novel, not a lesson in scripture. However, the inclusion of such was important, because monks (*shrugs*).

Did you know that the first use of the word honey as a term of endearment appeared in the Bible? Fun fact. And may have some relevance (*wink wink*).

I have chosen Darenth Priory as the location; this was indeed a real place but has been used in a fictitious way here. All names and events are products of my imagination.

Darenth is in Kent, England, which is the same county where Isabel lived in my book, *Love in the Roses,* which is set in 1484. I thought it was interesting to have the two tales run parallel, showing both the differences and similarities between their lives.

This book begins in 1485; the very beginning of the Tudor era.

Monarchs around that time:

- Edward IV (York): 1461-1470
- Henry VI (again): 1470-1471 (imprisoned & died)
- Edward IV (again): 1471-1483 (died)
- Edward V (not crowned & disappeared): Apr-Jun 1483
- **Richard III (York): 1483-1485**
- **Henry VII (Tudor): 1485-1509**
- Henry VIII (Tudor): 1509-1547

I am fascinated by the lives of everyday folk living in such tumultuous times. After all, much has been written, and indeed dramatized, about the monarchs themselves. But what was normal life really like?

Having explored the life of a young lady entering an arranged marriage, it seemed only fair to also look at an LGBTQIA+ life.

CAUTION

This book is about two young men who become monks and fall in love. So, yeah, there's raunchy stuff, but you must practice patience to arrive at those scenes. And there may be more acceptance than you would expect.

There are religious references but also improper use of candles.

It is set in medieval/Tudor England (at the crossover point), so there are occurrences of disease and death.

If you are the type of person who would find these things difficult then please put the book down and find something more appropriate for your needs from the vast array of choice available. No judgment.

Still reading? Good. Ready yourselves for a saucy journey of discovery.

And thus, we begin our tale with Paul's arrival at the priory…

Chapter 1 – A New Dawn

Whether my limbs trembled more from spiritual awe or the sudden reluctance to part with my parents, it was nigh impossible to tell. Yet, shake I did as the magnificence of Darenth Priory loomed before me. The monastery was both daunting and wondrous in its grandeur with the sun beaming down upon it. The large wooden doors of the gatehouse yawned open unto my future.

"God give you good afternoon. Might I enquire as to the purpose of your visit?" a sturdy man asked, bowing.

"God grant you good afternoon. We are Lord and Lady Upley here to offer our son, Paul, to God," my father announced in his most booming, authoritative voice.

The gatekeeper's eyes widened. "I beg pardon, my lord. It is my sworn duty to check, you must understand. You should not wish me to be lax in this regard, I think, when your son lives among us." He bowed again as he spoke.

My father clapped him on the shoulder. "Of course, you do well. Have no fear. But might we now be granted admittance?"

"But of course, sir. You are expected and most welcome." He stepped out of our way, his arm indicating admittance.

Taking a deep breath, I followed my parents' lead. As my feet crossed the threshold, a rather odd sensation ran throughout my person—warmth filled my entire being. It may seem superstitious nonsense, but it rather felt like a hug of welcome. "I'm home," was my initial thought.

The guest master was sent for, and he approached as rapidly as permitted. That is to say, at a brisk walk, for surely monks must never run. He carried himself with both great confidence and respect; upright yet with a bowed, grey-crowned head, and his black robes swishing.

"You are most welcome, Lord and Lady Upley, and, of course, your son, Paul, whom we are most gratified to greet. I am Brother Faramond, guest master at Darenth Priory." He laid himself prostrate at my father's feet.

Getting up, he said, "Please, if you would follow me? Prior Ambrose is waiting at the guest house to offer prayers."

Brother Faramond had not raised his eyes once during the entire interaction. Yet, I was sure he had somehow taken in our appearance, nonetheless. And I was suddenly glad that my mother had persuaded me to wear more modest clothing. In place of my tight shirts and short doublet, I now wore a long cotehardie and looser doublet in duller colours. Even my poulaine shoes had shorter spikes.

We followed in silence. The stipulation was not required as surely words would have failed me had I tried to utter any. My heart pounded in my chest so violently I was certain it would interrupt the quietude.

A tall man stood, his tonsured head also bowed, at the entrance of the guest house. His crown of hair was still quite brown, only lightly peppered with grey. And his face was not yet lined with age. I was struck with how great this personage must be to achieve the role of prior so young. He commanded my immediate respect.

"God grant you the warmest of welcomes on this most auspicious day," he called. "Please, do gather here, that we might pray."

We formed a group in front of him, and he intoned a prayer before addressing us each in turn.

"Pax Domini sit semper vobiscum," (The peace of the Lord be with you always) he announced before issuing the kiss of peace once we had replied, *"Et cum spiritu tuo."* (And also with you).

Upon entering the building, we were seated so that Prior Ambrose could read the Divine Law. With full blessing and knowledge, we were then taken into the dining area where Prior Ambrose poured water on our hands and washed our feet.

"Suscepimus, Deus, misericordiam tuam in medio templi tui," he said (We have received your mercy, O God, in the midst of your temple) [Ps 48:10].

Brother Faramond repeated this. Finally, we were seated for our meal. My stomach was grumbling after our long journey. Having arrived after nones, as requested, we had foregone our midday meal thus far.

"As we are not in the refectory, and you are guests, I shall not insist upon silence," Prior Ambrose explained, "But I shall say that there will be more time to become better acquainted once we have dined. As Paul is to become a novice, we thought it best to start his time here in the manner in which he will continue. I do hope you will find our simple fayre to your liking."

I had been expecting this, but my heart still sank. My family had somewhat spoiled me the previous few weeks, knowing we would soon be parted. Or mayhap, they merely ate in their usual fashion following Easter, and I was simply unaccustomed to it.

Either way, I had delighted in all manner of meats, but now no more would I partake in such fine delicacies. It was a passing moment of delight, that period of familial bliss, which I would treasure forever.

In fairness, the vegetable dishes which were brought in were well-prepared and plentiful.

"The ale is brewed here at the priory," Prior Ambrose told me.

"It is a fine brew. I thank you," I replied, blushing that he had observed my enjoyment. I had licked my lips and closed my eyes momentarily upon my first sip.

Brother Faramond cleared our plates but rejoined us. However, he came to sit by my side this time. The prior and my father were already engrossed in their own conversation.

"So, young Paul, you are to spend the next four days here with me."

"As I understand it, aye."

"You will soon see that there is nothing to be concerned about. We are a worthy community here. Unlike some, we still closely observe The Rule of Saint Benedict. Firm but fair. During our time together, we shall meditate a great deal upon your future here. Your decision to become a novice must not be undertaken lightly, and we shall give it our full attention."

"Certainly, Brother."

My mother had remained with her gaze upon her lap. I noticed her fingers were clenched and her breathing hitched every so often. I had so often missed her whilst at school, and longed to offer solace now we were again to be parted, but it was not fitting.

Was I never to see her again? She who had been all love and kindness. I thought my heart would break at the very idea.

"Lady Upley, perhaps you would like to see your quarters for this evening?" the guest master offered.

She offered a weak smile, her green eyes watery with unshed tears. "I thank you, Brother Faramond."

We both followed the kind monk, leaving my father and the prior to their business. An exchange of monies and deeds lay ahead, and I was glad of the excuse to escape the moment of transaction. I had arrived in the spirit of serving God as his devoted lamb, not one to be sold. I was no fool, the reasoning was plain, but there remained a sordid taste in my mouth all the same.

"This is where you shall sleep, Lady Upley."

"It appears most adequate. I thank you for your hospitality."

"It is naught but my duty. I shall leave the both of you to your privacy. Please, rejoin us when you are ready." With that, Brother Faramond withdrew.

My mother sank down upon the bed, and I next to her. "Oh, Paul. I am a foolish woman. It is not as though we have been much in one another's company. But I always had our summers to sustain my fortitude. How will I...?" Her sobs stopped any further words.

I bumped my shoulder to hers. "Hush, Mother. You shall set me about crying, then the brothers will never want me here."

Her laugh was half-hearted as she wiped her eyes. "Fool. You would think that I would have gotten used to the idea by now. Your whole life, all eighteen years of it, you were destined to arrive at this juncture. And to see you here, I could not be prouder. Truly."

"And yet it is hard now to part. It seems so final," I admitted, my gaze downcast and shoulders slumping.

Patting my hand, she replied, "Now who is all gloom? What is this nonsense? I am certain we shall be permitted to visit occasionally. Indeed, let them try to stop me. I would tear the walls down brick by brick if needs be."

I snorted at the imagery my timid mother invoked. "It is not entirely forever that we say goodbye?"

"Nay, of course, it cannot be."

"That brings me comfort."

"And to me, my cherished boy." She pinched my cheeks as if I were still a child, making me grimace. Ruffling my hair, she lamented, "Oh, but these bountiful brown locks."

"Ease yourself, they are not to be shaved off just yet. Even then, a crown of hair shall remain."

"To me, you shall always appear just as you do now." She kissed my forehead.

"We really do grow too sentimental. This is a joyous occasion. I shall be well looked after, giving you no cause for concern. And you are on your way to see your grandson. Be sure to offer my congratulations and love to my brother and his wife, won't you?"

"Indeed. I am so happy that they are all safe and well. It is exciting, meeting my first grandson."

"And don't think I know not of your plan."

Her hands flew to her chest. "And what is this scheme with which you accuse me of?"

"Only that my brother's close proximity affords you a convenient spy."

"Would you have me kept ignorant of your condition?"

"I have repeatedly promised to write to you."

"Aye, for all the good that will do. The prior will have to approve every correspondence."

"Whereas my brother…?"

"Shall sneak glimpses of you when he happens to have business here."

I shook my head. "Mother, you must not make a nuisance of Harry."

"As if I ever would. And do not think to instruct me on my conduct. Come, enough impudence. We shall return to see how your father gets on."

The next morning, we arose after a disturbed night. Brother Faramond had bade me enjoy my rest whilst I could, for I was not yet required to attend the offices. However, the bell had awoken me with great alarm until my mind recollected where I was, and that it did not toll for an emergency but was calling the brothers to prayer. It took me a while to still my heart and regain slumber. Every time.

We had eaten breakfast before Brother Faramond could join us.

"Thank you for your forbearance. The mornings demand much of my time. But I am here now to bid you farewell, Lord and Lady Upley, having been excused from Chapter."

"We did not mean to keep you from your duties, but we thank you for your attention and hospitality. We shall away with all speed so as not to disturb you any further," my father replied.

Turning to me, he laid a heavy hand upon my shoulder and said, "Paul, all that is left for me to say to you is...make me proud."

Bowing my head with the weight of his words, I replied, "I shall endeavour to do so, Father."

Patting my shoulder before removing his hand entirely, he commanded, "See that you succeed."

My mother held my hands in hers and kissed them. Not a single word was shared between us. It would have unmanned me to attempt it and embarrassed her. We had shared our goodbyes before bed, knowing the impossibility of doing so at the hour of departure.

I stood mute, watching them mount their horses and ride off without so much as a backwards glance.

A hand rubbed my shoulder. "Very well, young Paul. Now let us begin in earnest. I have a book for you to start reading whilst I attend Mass. When I return, there shall be questions to be answered," Brother Faramond told me gently.

He ushered me back inside the guest house. "You shall not stir outside of this place until you are deemed ready to begin your novitiate. Use this time wisely."

Having sat me near a window with the promised book, he departed once the bell rang for Mass. I was glad to have the time to myself. Having wept heartily last night, I thought I was done, but the sight of my parents leaving had moved me greatly. Oh, I was here. Alone. Abandoned.

It was always going to be thus. The truth had never been concealed from me. Perhaps there would have been less pain had I not been aware they were travelling to my brother and his family—the ones who mattered. Harry was continuing the family name, honour and business. Whilst I was committed to the cloister.

Biting my lip, I stemmed the flow of tears. There was no use lamenting the loss. My situation was not entirely hopeless. There were worse prospects than being a monk. I repeated to myself the reassuring words I had spoken to my mother.

Here, I was sure of a good living. And this priory had a good reputation. Besides, is anyone ever truly alone when they are with God?

Having collected myself, I turned my attention to the book I was supposed to be reading. I chuckled, realising it was probably a test to see how much Latin I had learned.

There would be many tests and trials ahead. But I was not afraid. At least, I tried not to be. Everything was so new and uncertain. Still, I took comfort in the warm welcome I'd received.

My first full day at the priory was endured with humility. I was taken to the infirmary to undergo a health inspection.

The Brothers bade me, "Hold still and do as instructed. There must be no grumbling. You are not being treated any differently from any other person who has entered here."

"His brown hair is rather full but dull, curling about his ears, and is mercifully free of lice," Brother Giles, the infirmarer announced whilst Brother Faramond made notes.

Supposedly, these details would be held by the prior should any enquiry ever be made after me, perhaps if I were to run away. I could not think of any other reason one would require such information.

It was a struggle not to make complaint; I was prodded and poked, and regarded as one would look upon cattle. However, I did succeed in mastering my tongue, even if my face contorted into various winces.

Added to the maltreatment, was the judgement from the withered man with a white tonsure and vigilant brown eyes, which seemed unjust to my ears. Surely if he were fit to live within these walls there could be no question of my suitability.

The infirmarer held my lower lip in his fingers, dragging it down, before turning his attention to my upper lip. "His teeth are adequate."

I grimaced at him, showing said teeth off. I was rewarded with a ruffle of my hair. "Aye, you're coping most valiantly, young Paul. We'll soon be done."

My smile became genuine at his reassurance.

"His eyes are brown, large, clear and bright." He tilted my face first one way then another. "Beneath a thinker's brow."

I scowled at that.

Brother Giles chuckled. "Yes, a tendency to overthink, I suspect. Pay no mind, Paul, there was no offence intended. Quite the opposite, if anything. In conclusion, not overly tall and slightly on the slender side but we shall soon remedy that. No visible scarring. Well, I would say you are in good health, young man."

"I thank you?"

He chortled. "No thanks necessary. I am glad to be able to proclaim you fit for admittance. The rest shall be up to you."

"Oh, I almost forgot," I yelped, having righted my clothing, and reaching for my belt and scrip. "I brought you a gift."

"For me? But should I accept? Your kindness does you credit but we are not permitted to have possessions."

I grinned, pulling out the small bundle. "Ah, but this is for the betterment of all. I understood you would be the one best fitted to handle them."

Brother Faramond was looking on in silent bemusement as Brother Giles carefully revealed the small packets. His mouth gaped as he read what I had written upon each.

"But these...they are seeds?"

"Aye, Brother. Some of these herbs can be difficult to obtain, so I took the opportunity of procuring them when I could." I told him not they were from my mother's own herb garden.

"Oh, what a blessing. Yes, these shall be most useful. And I happily accept on behalf of all. Thank you, dear boy." He held up each packet for closer inspection.

"That was very thoughtful," Brother Faramond commented.

"I hope to assist the infirmarer, so it was only good sense to be prepared."

Brother Giles regarded me anew. "Yes, I was aware that Prior Ambrose had accepted you on that premise. Should you like to see my store? I shall lock these away safely until they are ready to be planted."

I looked to Brother Faramond who nodded his assent.

"Aye, if it so pleases you. I should like that very much."

He led the way, past the wall of what smelled like the kitchen, given the green odour. On we walked, across an open space and into a backroom of the infirmary. I gawped as my eyes took it all in. There was a large table and many shelves of jars. And in the corner lay a sizeable, comfortable-looking bed—not quite what I was expecting to see in a priory.

"On the other side of this wall is the infirmary fire. Useful when making remedies, but also welcome when the weather turns chill. It is convenient for me to sleep nearby, should anybody have sudden requirement of my services. And one more thing which may be of interest is the small building next to the physic garden where I keep some tools, and which I use as a drying room for the herbs. My herbarium."

"It is a relief to find you are as I had hoped you'd be, that you clearly seek to utilise herbs for healing."

"Indeed. God surely gave us such medicines in nature to assist when prayer alone does not suffice in caring for the sick. And they are less messy than animal innards, although they too have their uses."

I smiled and nodded. During our brief encounter, Brother Giles struck me as kind and knowledgeable. Some of my fears abated. I was yet to meet with the other brethren, but I hoped also to find them thus agreeable, and that they would not find me lacking.

I had so much to prove before my place here was accepted. And there was so much in me which may disappoint them. My secret burned inside like a furnace. I prayed for it never to be revealed. My life here was to be pure and devout.

Chapter 2 - Postulant Paul

Over the next few days, I was interrogated by Brother Faramond most thoroughly. It felt as though there were not a single thing about me which he was unaware of. Well, perhaps with one exception, but that would have been my undoing. I would not risk being turned out. The shame it would bring upon myself as well as my family would be unbearable.

That aside, the monk had the happy manners which encouraged open discourse without threat.

"Incentive with reward over fear of the rod is preferable, I find," he had told me when I had openly thanked him for his kindness.

Indeed, there was never any sign of harsh judgment or disdain shown by him. Brother Faramond simply nodded as he listened to my answers. Although, I suffered no delusion that he was not paying very close attention to my every word, assessing my merit.

But now, on my fourth day, the prior himself returned.

"God grant you good day, Paul."

"God grant you good day, Prior Ambrose." I bowed my head.

"Please, take a seat and listen to all that I have to say."

He proceeded to read The Rule to me.

But at the end of the extensive reading, he looked again at me with his discerning, pale blue eyes. "Paul, this is the law under which you are seeking to live. If you can keep it, come in. If, however, you cannot, freely depart. I must ask, do you still wish to enter our Order? Do you believe you can live in obedience? Do you undertake your postulancy under your own free will? Are you a true man of God, Paul?"

I lay myself prostrate at his feet. "Yes. Prior Ambrose, I do solemnly swear it. I am ready. Please accept me as a postulant so I may prove myself worthy. I vow to keep to The Rule. And to live in the worship of God, by His grace. I seek to remain, if it so pleases you."

"As I expected and dared to hope. We all have confidence in you. You are welcome to remain here in your postulancy."

Rising and lying a hand atop my head, he said, "Then rise, Paul. Come with me now, so you may enter your living quarters."

I rose.

Making the sign of the cross, he intoned, "*In nomine Patris, et Filii, et Spiritus Sancti. Amen.*" (In the name of the Father, the Son, and the Holy Spirit).

Before leaving, I took hold of Brother Faramond's hands. "Thank you, Brother Faramond. Thank you for your goodness and support."

"The work has been all yours. I have faith in you. Go with God's grace, continue as you have begun, and all will be well." He smiled the benevolent smile which had brought me so much comfort throughout this testing time.

A look was exchanged between the two monks which I hoped was something akin to approval. Nerves and excitement buzzed through me as I embarked upon the next phase of my life here. I had been utterly shut off from the community and was eager to meet others so I may ascertain what to truly expect at Darenth Priory.

As we walked towards the carrells, Prior Ambrose quietly explained, "We have only one novice here at present. Luke has been with us nigh on two years and is still not ready to take his vows. I say this in warning, but also to form a request. You have shown yourself to be a calm, quiet, rational person. It is my hope you shall be a calming influence upon Luke."

"Is he so very boisterous?" Clapping a hand over my mouth, I added, "I do apologise, Prior. It was not my place to ask."

He chuckled a little. "Indeed, Paul. You have an inquiring mind. This is good. But keep that tongue in your head, if you please. However, I shall indulge you this once. Luke is not a bad or violent fellow. I would not have you fear him. It is more...he indulges in jest when he should be silent."

"Ah."

"You are an intelligent lad with quiet ways. And are a quick learner. Perhaps having such an example in one his own age shall enlighten our novice, eh?"

"I shall endeavour to be of service where I can, Prior."

"Good lad."

We had walked past numerous buildings, including the kitchen again with fishy aromas emanating from within. My stomach rumbled, which I endeavoured to quell. To my right, I saw the infirmary, but Brother Giles appeared not. And on we went.

As Prior Ambrose opened the door to the carrells, a mass of blond hair shot up and swivelled to reveal the bluest eyes I ever beheld. He stood and bowed to the prior.

"Brother Barnabas, I bring to you our new postulant, Paul," the prior announced towards the man standing beyond the beautiful, blond being.

Tearing my gaze from who I assumed must be Luke, I bowed to Brother Barnabas. A serious-looking fellow, bent with age and the weight of knowledge. His dark grey tonsure and beard made him appear older still.

"Thank you, Prior. Paul, please take a seat next to Luke. We were just reading Bede's Commentary on the Proverbs, '*Super Parabolas Solomnis*'."

Seeing we were to dive straight into learning without so much as a hello to one another, I silently took my seat. Next to Luke. I did smile at him, but his gaze was intently pointed towards the master of novices. The prior left us, closing the door which rattled. And butterflies fluttered inside of me.

As if nothing of note had occurred, Brother Barnabas muttered, "Now, where were we? Ah, yes, "*He who ignores discipline despises himself, but whoever heeds correction gains understanding...*" [Proverbs 15:32]

I saw no sign of the jovial fool I had been told to expect. Luke appeared most solemn, and my heart bled for him. Certainly, this passage was being directed at him, and probably not for the first time, given what Prior Ambrose had shared with me. To work against one's nature is an irksome burden. The weight is heavy, and the journey long. I sighed.

"Have you something to say, Paul?" Brother Barnabas asked, his brow rising.

"Sorry, Brother Barnabas, no. I sighed, pondering the excellent points you were making. Pray, continue."

"Well, if I have your permission..?" he asked snidely before carrying on.

Oh dear, this was not the first impression I had wished to make.

How much there was to be lamented the next day.

Brother Barnabas' watchful eye had been ever upon me, stifling the very air I breathed. So much so that I began to doubt what knowledge was already within my grasp; simple questions became difficult to answer under his scrutiny.

The cloister was barred to me as I had not yet committed to so much as being a novice, placing me somewhere between a guest and a member of the community, meaning I had to take the circuitous route to the church.

On the other side of the rood screen from the brethren, I sat listening to the monks chant their psalms. Unable to join them, I prayed. I prayed for the fortitude to bear this isolation. There was no choice; this must be borne. Was Christ himself not tested? What were my trials compared with his?

The master of novices walked through to collect me after Mass and escorted me to the chapter house. The brethren stood in a line by a bowl. Having been previously instructed, I knelt by that bowl and braced myself.

Prior Ambrose, speaking a few words of introduction, stepped towards me and stood in the large basin. I picked up the large pitcher of water, but as it drew closer, the scent of herbs reached my nose, making me inhale deeper.

My eyes sought the infirmarer. Not one glance did he offer in my direction, his gaze was fixed upon the prior. However, the hint of a smile about his lips and eyes confirmed my suspicion.

Dutifully, I washed the prior's feet. As he stepped onto the cloths, I dried then kissed them. Brother Gervase, the sub-prior followed, then all the others; Hardwin the chamberlain, Hector the cellarer, Barnabas the master of novices, Faramond the guest master, Cuthbert the almoner, Giles the infirmarer, Jeremy the cantor, Godfrey the sacrist, Maynard the kitchener and Ulric the refectorian.

Some made me gladder of the scented water than others. Kissing gnarled, veined feet was unpleasant, to say the least. Yet it was important to not baulk, but instead to show my gratitude for this opportunity with all due humility.

Afterwards, I was shown to the refectory. Alone, I ate with only the two brothers who acted as server and reader for the week. Luke happened to be this week's server, and my eyes kept going to him. But he returned not my notice. They both sat apart from me in silence.

After my meal, I returned to the carrells and read whilst awaiting Brother Barnabas. Luke was apparently with the cellarer in the afternoons. I sweated all the more as there was no other person to divide the intense attention of the novice master.

It is shameful how much I despaired of my situation that first night in the dormitory. How verily I did feel each bitter sting of neglect and rejection. Tears watered my pale cheeks as I hugged my knees to me upon the bed, dwelling on the sorrows of the day. My heart broke anew at the thought of eternal separation from a loving mother as I remained amongst such cold men.

But a thought quelled my grief. Like the single, fetid, tallow candle burning in the dormitory, that thought shed scant light but made something visible...When previously I had grown to seek solitude, why should I shun it now? Had my ability to blend into the background at school not hitherto afforded me protection? And was I not now lying upon my bed unharmed?

Perhaps the last couple of years with the apothecary had enlivened my spirits too greatly, and I should now welcome a return to peace. Having mastered my thoughts, I bowed my head in prayer and thanked God for what I had hitherto been so ungrateful for – my safe seclusion.

With renewed vigour, I applied myself to the lessons Brother Barnabas instructed us in. And I listened attentively as he read from The Rule.

Luke sat beside me, also in trained silence. I dared not utter a word to him for fear of upsetting our tutor, but I did risk quick glances now and then – he was too beautiful to ignore entirely.

His blond hair fell in unruly golden waves which parted to reveal a noble brow above those dazzling blue eyes which gazed always ahead beyond his fine, straight nose. Yet how I wished he would glance my way.

But why should he look upon me with the same wonder? I was small and plain, and surely of no interest to such as him. And it was highly unlikely he shared my admiration of men, in any case.

More than the want of observation, I longed to speak with Luke, to learn why and how he came to be here. No opportunity of conversation showed itself, however, much to my vexation. As quietly as I could, I breathed deeply back into tranquillity, surrendering myself to God.

At each office, I was in attendance, away from the brethren. My prayers turned to gratitude for this chance, the one I was determined not to squander. I prayed that Brother Barnabas would see my desire to commit myself to his instruction.

I sat in bed that evening, still too restless for sleep, but at least no longer holding the degrading self-pity which had clung to me the night before. I recoiled at the scraping of metal; the curtain beside my bed was slowly being dragged along. I steeled myself to yell and fight.

But blond locks and a grinning face poked through the darkness. "Would you welcome company?" Luke whispered.

My hand flew to cover my mouth to stifle the laugh which threatened to burst forth. Not trusting myself, I merely nodded my assent.

Luke knelt on the floor and maintained his whisperings, "I would have said hello yesterday, but...well, you sounded as if the intrusion would have been embarrassing for you."

"You heard my snivelling?"

He bit his lip. "Aye, I did. But there is no shame in it. At least, I hope there is not, for I'm sure my weeping was far worse my first night."

"Truly?"

"Truly."

"Then I am sorry for it. But do we not risk detection? Shall we not be punished?"

His hair swished as he shook his head. "There is little to no risk, have no fear. There are but two brothers in the dormitory, and they are both snoring well. It is difficult to rouse them once they enter that state."

"You sound as if you have tried," I said, a brow raised.

His grin was mischievous. "Perhaps, but only to see if I could stir without censure. The waking hours have gotten me into sufficient trouble as it is."

"But you seem so studious."

There was mirth audible in his reply. "Appearances can be deceptive."

"I suppose they can."

"I should not linger too long. There is no use pushing our luck. But I could not go another day without letting you know a friend is near."

"That…that is most kind of you. Thank you. It means a great deal to know I am not entirely alone."

"I had no guide during my postulancy. I would not see another struggle when I can aid them. Know that the monks are not as severe as they seem."

"Brother Faramond was most amiable. I wish Brother Barnabas were more like him."

"But it is his duty to ensure we sincerely seek God. He must test our spirits under severe words."

"You have truly heard The Rule."

"I can scarce avoid it when it is read to me daily," he said with a wink. "But listen—"

He halted as a snore shuddered through the dormitory. One of the monks was stirring. We held our breaths, frozen in place. Blessedly, the regular pattern of snoring soon returned. I let out my breath on a hissed giggle.

"I will tell you this and then leave you. Life is easier here if you prove yourself useful. All the monks seek is your willingness to be part of the community and to worship."

"But how—?"

"You will find your way." With that, he tiptoed back to his side of the curtain.

Make myself useful. How on ever should I do that when nobody would speak to me?

Chapter 3 - Persistent Paul

After Lauds, we remained in the church for it was a Sunday. Luke and I laid ourselves prostrate at the feet of all the brethren.

As the outgoing server, Luke said, "Blessed are you Lord God for you have helped and strengthened me." Having received a blessing from the monks, he repeated this twice more.

As the incoming server, it was then my turn. "O God come to my aid, Lord make haste to help me." This too was said three times, with a blessing received.

Having washed the crockery and hand towels the day before, Luke had returned them to the cellarer. Now, I had to collect them. Oh, how the man looked severely upon me.

"So, you take your turn at serving already, Paul?" Brother Hector asked.

"Aye, Brother. And gladly so, for I would earn approval through charity."

"Hmm, very well. See that you break no item, and all is returned clean on Saturday."

"I shall. Thank you."

Bowing, I received the precious crockery and took them to the servery. It was a wonder I didn't drop the entire stack then and there, given how my hands shook. As stern as Brother Barnabas was, Brother Hector was easily thrice over. His brown eyes seemed to bore into my very soul and found me lacking.

Having first washed my hands in the ornate lavatorium, I quickly ate my meal and made ready. The monks soon arrived, and I brought them their dishes and pitchers.

"Ask, and it shall be given you; seek, and ye shall find." [Matthew 7:7]. That was my thought when I espied a broom leaning against the wall of the refectory. Everyone was busy eating and listening to the reading, so, unsure of who or how to ask, I grasped the broom to begin sweeping, believing my usefulness was about to be demonstrated.

However, one of the kitchen staff came scurrying across and grabbed the broom, looking most cross. He brandished it at me whilst vigorously shaking his head. I opened my mouth to explain, but the monk's hostility grew fiercer still. Finally, my legs saw fit to move, and I all but ran out of the room. With Brother Ulric, the refectorian, glaring intently at me.

A hand latched onto my shoulder from behind as I left, making me yelp.

"Hold, young Paul. 'Tis only I," a voice soothed in hushed tones.

Turning to look, I saw who it was. "Brother Faramond?"

With his hand still upon my shoulder, he guided me to a place near the wall. Yet, the monk still whispered, "I believe your intentions were pure, Paul. Have no fear. However, you insinuated the cleaning which had already been done was not of a high enough standard."

I gasped. "No, Brother, no. I meant only to be of service, to help in some small way."

"That is to be admired, even if the delivery was ill-advised."

My lip trembled. "Brother Faramond, I wish I were back in the guest house with you. I feel so lost. I seem wholly unable to put a foot right here. My mission is plain, but my way is hidden." My voice cracked and my hands covered my face.

"Paul, Paul, calm yourself. This will never do. Come with me." Without another word, he led me across to the kitchen's herb garden where we sat upon a bench.

The perfumed air had me inhaling deeply without thought. In turn, my spirits were soothed.

My confidant said, "We cannot linger long, for we must return before we are too greatly missed. But I would see you comforted. This is not the sensible young man I knew just a few short days ago. You must keep faith, Paul. God has a plan for us all."

"I understand. Yet I am confounded. I must prove to you all that I wish to be part of this community, and that I am devoted in my service to God. But how should I do that when confined so entirely?"

He looked up, smiling. "Brother Giles, how very timely. Might Paul request a little of your time?"

"Certainly. I came to check on him." Turning to me, he enquired, "Paul, you seemed distressed as you rushed out. Are you quite well?"

"Aye, merely frustrated at my lack of purpose. And embarrassed by my apparent misdeed."

Brother Faramond interjected, "It would seem that Paul seeks a way to prove himself useful. Might he encroach upon your valuable time? Surely there is some work for him in the infirmary?"

"You seek employment, Paul?" he checked.

"If it be not too bothersome to yourself."

"It would do me a great service, as a matter of fact. Come, let us return to the refectory so you can finish your duty there, then we might speak with Brother Barnabas afterwards, hm?"

I nodded frantically.

Brother Faramond patted my hand as he stood. "You see now, that was not so very difficult."

My cheeks heated as we three re-entered the refectory. Every eye was upon me. With a bowed head, I completed my serving duties.

Afterwards, Brother Giles caught me and Brother Barnabas by the arm and urged us outside and made his request of the novice master.

Having looked me up and down, he agreed. "I suppose it can be allowed this afternoon. But I expect you back in lessons all day tomorrow."

"Of course. Thank you, Brother Barnabas, thank you."

"Come then, Paul. You can carry the tray from the kitchen, for I have a patient who should be ready to eat now."

Eager to please, I did as he asked. Following him into his domain, I placed the tray down on a table next to an occupied cot which Brother Giles indicated. "Now, Brother Hector, do try to eat some of this broth."

The man's brown eyes lit up as he took the proffered bowl. I realised now that the cellarer had not been in the refectory.

"You go to too much fuss, but I thank you, Brother," he gruffed.

"Indeed, I do not. When one gets to our age, we cannot be too careful. A fainting fit should not be ignored. Who else should be given bone broth, I ask you?"

"The truly infirm."

"Oh, fie. Now you come close to grumbling." But there was merriment in his tone and look.

The patient winked at me. "In truth, Paul, you will have a wonderful teacher here. Ensure you listen well. But do not tell him I said so."

I grinned.

Brother Giles asked, "Paul, do you know how best to treat an attack of fainting?"

"Err...by the pounding together of rue, sage, fennel and ground ivy. A bag of these should be steeped in water. The strained water should be warmed and used to rinse the person's head."

"Excellent. That is precisely what I have done."

"Which I am grateful for, but it is not needed again, thank you," Brother Hector told him.

"Clearly not. You may leave as soon as you are finished with that bowl."

The infirmarer mock whispered to me, "You will note, Paul, that our brother did not make his escape before the medicinal food was brought."

I replied, "Surely you would not have him leave without such vital care?"

Having slurped the remnants of his broth, Brother Hector slid his feet to the floor.

"Have a care now, Brother. Slowly," Brother Giles admonished.

"I am fine. Let me be."

"Let us be certain before you rush away."

Muttering something under his breath, the not-so-infirm monk leant on the outstretched arm. I quickly went to his other side and offered the same.

"Ah, that is a good strong arm you have," Brother Hector commented, leaning upon me heavily.

Once his patient was standing, Brother Giles checked, "You experience no dizziness?"

"None."

"Very good. But might I sit you back down a while? I must show Paul something, and I would escort you back to your room."

"Brother Giles, I thank you for your care. But be assured that I merely stood too quickly after a prolonged period at my books. I will do very well on my own."

"If you insist?"

"I do."

"Then may God grant you good day."

We watched as he slowly shuffled out of the infirmary.

"Will he be alright?" I asked.

"If he is not, he only has his stubborn self to blame," Brother Giles replied, shaking his head. "Come now, I would assign you a task."

"But of course."

He led me to his back room. "As I was making the preparation earlier, I noted my ivy was low. I have some dried, but it needs grinding. Are you happy to oblige me?"

"If there is one thing I learned from the apothecary, it is how to grind well. Which jar is it to go into?"

He took one down and placed it beside the ivy. The pestle and mortar beckoned to me. I took them up and began my task.

Having watched over me, he said, "Good. There is a matter I must attend to. You shall be happy here on your own? If you do not finish, just leave the rest where it is, and I will take up what you do not complete. Do not make yourself late for nones."

I smiled at him. "Many thanks, Brother Giles."

"And you have mine also." Bowing his head, he left me alone in what felt like his sacred space.

The memory of the curmudgeonly jesting made me smile. I suspected the pair were firm friends. And the trust placed in me warmed my soul. I had not thought it possible to assist the infirmarer before at least reaching the status of novice. My hands worked with greater vigour at this unexpected privilege, determined to prove my worth.

My mind drifted as I ground the leaves. Today was May Day, and the world outside the monastery walls would be raucous and filled with frivolity. Maidens would dance around the erected maypole and matches would be sought. I found I did not miss it much, for here was all tranquillity. And I could be useful in the area I seemed destined for.

The next morning, I returned to the carrells.

"Brother Barnabas?" I hesitantly approached the master of novices.

"Paul?"

"Brother, it gladdened me to assist Brother Giles yesterday. I…I wondered if it may be possible for me to repeat that, if it should please you both? Once I am done with serving duties this week, there will be times when you are all at your meal, before the afternoon lessons begin. Might I fill that emptiness by assisting in the infirmary, do you think?" My head was bowed low.

"Permit me to speak with Brother Giles on the matter, and the prior. But it would appear to me to be a good use of your time." The corners of his mouth twitched with the hint of a smile.

"Thank you, Brother." I sat down at my place, trying not to grin.

Permission was granted, and thus I started a daily routine of assisting Brother Giles in the afternoons. All afternoon, not just the interim period after my dinner as I'd requested.

The infirmarer's amiable presence and the opportunity of being out of doors were succour to my soul. Until then, I had not fully appreciated how much I needed it. My mind had been resentful of entire days spent in book learning—it seemed that even I could tire of such.

Brother Giles spoke gently to me as I ground herbs and powders, washed dishes and boiled decoctions. I also dug the physic garden, planted, weeded and watered. The infirmarer was as eager to impart knowledge as I was to accept it.

"You have a ready mind and willing hand, Paul. It pleases me to know that when I am gone, the infirmary shall be well tended."

"Brother! You must not speak thus. I will allow that we should not fear death, but pray, do not welcome it so."

He ruffled my hair. "Quite right. I misspoke. I do not expect the heavenly Father to call me home just yet. But I am grateful to have you here."

"That, I am pleased to hear."

A steady flow of persons on pilgrimage had come through the monastery. Initially, they were confined to the guest house. However, as time wore on, they had travelled from further afield, mostly bound for Canterbury with its healing relics of St Thomas Becket.

These later pilgrims required the attentions of Brother Giles and myself. We washed feet, applied ointments and wrapped them up in bindings. That was by far the most common complaint; travel on foot was hard on the feet.

Of course, those who were seeking healing at the shrine were worsened by fatigue. The infirmarer and I did the best we could to set them back on the road.

I still had times when I could work out of doors, tending the herbs. There, I was sometimes joined by a lay brother named Brom, whose eyes were almost as black as his hair. He was taller and broader than me, but of a similar age, mayhap a little older. We weren't supposed to speak to one another, but loneliness cries out to others who are lonely. When nobody else was around, we found ourselves drawn together.

"Brother Giles is lucky to have you to help," I commented.

"Aye, he struggles to bend and weed as he used to. And I prefer it above all other tasks. Especially now. But I say that only to you, mind."

"Of course. But you did not wish to become a monk yourself?"

He laughed. "Nay, that's not for the likes of me. I'm low born and proud of it."

"I meant no offence."

He laughed again. "None taken. Besides, I wouldn't like to be about all those books or to sing my days away as you do. I honour God with the work of my own two hands," he said, raising up a fistful of soil.

"Aye. It is good, honest work. I am sure God is as thankful as we are. I may not know much, but I do know that the priory couldn't cope without your assistance."

He playfully shoved my shoulder with his. "Get away, you'll make me blush."

"Pah! A likely story," I dismissed, shoving back. "But to spare your blushes, you can go work that patch yonder whilst I continue here. Brother Giles will return soon."

Chapter 4 - Sing, Heavenly Angels

Luke was away from me more than I would like. Even his silent presence was somehow of comfort when we were near. But, as our situations were still precarious, neither of us wanted to risk too many nighttime whispers.

One morning, we were taken to Brother Jeremy, the cantor, for practice. A hint of frankincense still hung in the air of the church. Clouds outside had darkened the oak-beamed room within.

"Paul, I understand you have been educated in a monastic school. You have learned to chant, of course?"

"Aye, sir."

He raised a brow but did not comment on my lapse. "Very well. Let me hear you. Repeat after me." He then sang a simple, "Alleluia."

I repeated as best I could.

"Very well. Repeat the scales after me."

I did.

"Hmm…now let me hear Psalm one."

I dutifully sang what was requested. My many hours singing the psalms by rote finally found its purpose.

Brother Jeremy neither smiled nor frowned. "It is a good enough start."

He beckoned Luke who then stood in my place. I sat to watch. And I thanked God for the seat as the purest tenor notes I ever heard came out of Luke's mouth. It is no exaggeration to say that in that moment a beam of sunlight found its way through parted clouds and shone through the window, directly upon this angel on Earth. My heart and soul melted and reformed in the shape of his song.

"We can balance your tenor with Paul's baritone, I think. Yes, our choir shall have a fine harmony," was all Brother Jeremy said.

How was the man not more enthusiastic? Did he not hear what I did? Surely no one could be so unmoved. But he merely took us through some psalms together. My knees trembled to do so, feeling utterly unworthy to unite our voices.

The most glorious sensation filled me as we continued and tried a Gregorian chant. I was sure my own voice improved under such fine influence. And I had never felt closer to God.

So entirely swept up was I, that once we finished, I embraced the novice, patting his back in congratulation as I whispered, "You sing beautifully."

"I thank you. As do you."

"Let us not become too carried away with our worship," Brother Jeremy muttered.

I promptly recovered myself, embarrassed.

Alone in my bed, I turned my thoughts over and over. Why had I reacted so strongly to Luke's song? Mayhap it was the content, and I was overcome with the Divine spirit—such things were known to happen. And when sung with such clarity, one could hardly be blamed for being stirred.

But a niggle persisted. A seed had somehow been sown and was showing shoots which I could not yet grasp. Should I tend to it, and watch it bloom? Or was it a weed I should allow to wither, or even pluck and discard before it could become a threat? My head and my heart no longer seemed to agree on the right course, leaving me in bewilderment. I would need to pray on the mystery.

A blond mass of hair popped up by me. "You cannot sleep, Paul?"

"You neither?" My hand stretched and patted Luke's arm of its own accord. It was reassuringly firm. And mortification filled me. Grateful was I of the darkness which hid my blushes.

"Rest eludes me. I heard you rustling about, and thought we may calm one another?"

"Would you like me to tell you again how beautifully you sang? And how surprised I was, having heard only whispers and short, serious answers from your lips before?"

He grinned. "Such praise from you is most welcome. Oh, Paul, how I weary of silence. I think that is why I sing out so. It is as if my voice gets bottled up, and then unleashed in a burst given the slightest opportunity."

"Whatever the cause, it was a joy to hear."

"You know, you are not bad yourself."

"Oh, prythee, do not venture to say so. There can be no comparison. Rather, tell me, are you not happy here, Luke?"

"I try to be. But I seem ever at odds. The monks are patient enough, and I am not ill-treated. I should have no cause for complaint."

"And yet?"

"And yet, I don't know...there is a confinement which perhaps my spirit rebels against."

"Hmmm...I may have an idea. But it shall have to be carefully got at. Tell me, is the notion of working out of doors abhorrent to you?"

"I could bear it...Can you find me some activity? I think it may be what I need. I am kept too much indoors."

"As I suspected. Brother Hector told the infirmarer he had been too long at his books, causing his faint. It occurs to me now that you too are always at them."

His hand rubbed across his face. "Interminably!"

"Can you be patient? Do you trust me?"

He paused. "Curiously, more so than anyone else I ever met."

"Such prattle. I do not ask for so much. Merely that you place a little trust in me. Really, I do not know whether to console you or tease you for being a fopdoodle."

He snickered. "I think I would choose the teasing."

Ruffling his hair, I told him, "Forever in search of amusement."

Leaning into my touch, he replied, "I would always prefer happiness over misery."

My breath caught in my throat; there was such sadness in his tone. "Wouldn't we all? But have a care, we linger long this night. Do you feel restored?"

"You are surely going to be a fine infirmarer, for I feel much relief. I bid you good night."

"May God give you restful slumber."

The following morning, after breakfast and prime, when there was sufficient daylight, Brother Barnabas urged us to shave. He pushed us in the direction of the lavatorium. The mirror was not clear enough to precisely follow the course of a blade, which was somewhat discomforting.

"You do know how to shave, I trust?" Brother Barnabas asked, producing a sharp blade, soap and towels from a cupboard.

"Aye." We both nodded.

"Good. Then you may be barber to one another."

Biting my lip, I ventured a look towards Luke.

"You trust me, do you not?" he checked.

I gave him a curt nod, withholding the words which would tumble from my mouth. Telling Luke how very much I trusted him, that I would place my life in his hands would be utterly inappropriate, but nothing else came to mind. So, silence was my option.

With slow, careful, minute movements, Luke edged the blade down my soaped cheeks, gently stretching my skin with his other hand. My eyes were firmly shut; fortunately, this gave the appearance of forbearing the torment. And so I did, for there was sensuality in every meaning of the word.

The trust and closeness involved was of the utmost degree. We both breathed slow and deep as one. I felt only the slightest tremble upon my skin—Luke was masterful. Not one cut did he make. And oh, how I bathed in the close contact. His every touch sang across all my nerves.

He dabbed my face dry. "There, all done."

"Many thanks," I replied breathily and smiled at him, disappointed at the loss of connection.

"A fine job, Luke. Well done. Exchange places now," Brother Barnabas commanded.

I bit my lip so hard I feared blood would be drawn as I attempted to calm my shaking hands. It was quite a miracle that I did not cut Luke's beautiful face, but somehow, God willing, I succeeded. But had been ever so slow about it.

"Very well. Quick as you like, run a comb through your hair again, both of you, and we shall make you respectable yet."

We did so and looked to our novice master to assess our efforts.

"There, at last, two fine young men are revealed," he said, clapping us each on the shoulder. "Now we may polish our minds."

We followed him back to the familiar world of book learning in the carrells. Slightly awkwardly.

I was contemplating how to request permission for Luke in such a manner as to disallow refusal. I could not seem overly eager, and yet searching within, I discovered this to be the truth.

It should be no surprise, I reasoned, that Luke's company would be preferable to that of Brom who was then digging at my side in the physic garden. My conversations with him were most definitely against the rules; a lay brother should never be so near me, even as a postulant.

"You are very quiet today," Brom observed.

"Should I not be?"

He recoiled a little and frowned.

Taking a deep breath, I amended, "My apologies, Brom. I spoke harshly. There is a lot on my mind, is all."

"I don't mean to disturb. I'll go work yonder patch." And without another word or glance, he did.

I was left feeling guilty as well as thoughtful. Wandering across to the thyme, I picked a sprig, twiddling it between my fingers I pondered that perhaps placing it under my pillow would aid my sleep. My snappish mood clearly indicated my need for such. The peppercorn I was issued to chew upon during matins helped to keep me awake, but it made up not for the lack of sleep caused by the night office. Fatigue haunted me.

†††

All day, my ears had strained to hear the voice of Luke at each service. We were celebrating the Feast of Sts Phillip and James, so there were additional chants. Finally, at vespers, I heard him as the choir monks sang *Phos Hilaron* (O Gladsome Light) as the lamps were lit.

Closing my eyes, I allowed the hymn's soothing melody to calm my spirits. It held not the same striking effect as when I'd sung alongside Luke, but one could hardly hope for such experiences more than once in a lifetime. This was more than pleasant enough. My lips silently mouthed the words. It was over all too soon.

Bowing my head, I prayed for guidance and clarity:

"*Shew me thy ways, O Lord; teach me thy paths. Lead me in thy truth, and teach me: for thou art the God of my salvation; on thee do I wait all the day.*" [Psalms 25:4–5]

Mayhap it was the fervour with which I'd prayed, the better food that day, or the thyme which came to my aid; whatever the reason, I slept better that night. However, a solution still eluded me.

Was I being too selfish in wishing to spend time with Luke? Was this what temptation looked like? Or was I truly acting in his best interests? If the latter, surely a path would open before us. I was overthinking again.

Trying to put it out of mind, I attended my morning lessons in the carrells. Sitting next to Luke in silence was…insufficient, if I must own it. But were my thoughts those of a lonely young man seeking solace in conversation with a suitable equal? Or was temptation beckoning? Should I yield or resist?

I had not come to live this life in order to make friends. Seclusion was the safest option. Time and again, I repeated this to myself.

With heavy steps, I trod into the physic garden. Green leaves and bright flowers were growing rapidly and would soon be ready for the first harvest. Their scents were already mingling in a heady perfume. Until ready, I would continue my efforts to keep the soil weed-free.

"I am sorry if I offended you yesterday," Brom offered as I neared him.

Placing a hand upon his shoulder, I replied, "Please, do not think of it. I should not have been snappish and apologised immediately. I wonder at your mentioning it now."

He raked his hair. "I don't want to lose your friendship. It…it means a lot that you should pay me any mind."

"Despite what we're told to the contrary, I appreciate that two souls may confer if it offers comfort. Why, when I eventually become infirmarer, will that not be my very purpose?"

He nodded.

Taking his hand, I led him down the path. "This bed needs weeding today."

Brom did not release my hold as we stood by the infirmary wall regarding the plants.

"You are my friend, aren't you, Paul? You are like me?"

"Of course, I like—" but my reply was cut off by his mouth on mine.

Stunned, I couldn't move. But, as soon as my senses returned, I pushed him away and stepped back. "God in Heaven! What do you think you're doing?"

He looked as shocked as I felt, his mouth working uselessly. All he could stammer was, "I...I..." before running off.

"Brom. Wait!" But he took no heed.

"Paul? Errr...you're needed in the refectory."

I physically jumped, and squealed, my hand flying to my heart. "Luke!"

"I didn't mean to startle you. Or scare off your...friend." His blue eyes darkened under his scowl.

"You...you saw?"

"It is no business of mine. Brother Giles has taken a fall and is bleeding all over the place."

Closing my eyes, I took a steadying breath. "Very well. I will need to go to the infirmary first. Would you be so kind as to accompany me?" I didn't want to bump into Brom and become waylaid when the infirmarer needed me.

With his mouth set in a grim line, Luke gave a single nod.

I hastened to collect the jar of sphagnum moss from Brother Giles' storeroom before rushing to the refectory. The commotion hit my ears before the sight met my eyes; all the brothers were busying about Brother Giles who was still on the floor.

"Please, step aside, step aside," I called, pushing my way through.

Kneeling by my counsellor, I opened the jar and applied some moss. "This looks nasty."

"'Tis nothing, young Paul. There is no cause for dismay."

"It may not feel so very much, but there is a fair amount of blood, sir. We should go to the infirmary to treat it properly."

"Nonsense. Do not get carried away," he said wafting his hand at me.

I shot him a look of disapproval. "That would not be grumbling, would it, Brother Giles?"

His frown disappeared as a wry smile crept across his face. "Certainly not."

"That is good. I had feared that the supposition of infirmarers being the worst patients may indeed be proven correct. Come along now, if it pleases you."

Unintelligible murmurings were uttered.

"You are not hurt anywhere else?"

Patting himself all over, Brother Giles confirmed, "It appears not."

"You can stand?" I lent him my arm as he slowly stood.

My shoulder remained under his arm the entire way back to the infirmary, which was accompanied by many expressions of, "Oh, shall I ever recover from the shame? This humiliation? Pity me, Paul. Oh, to be the patient, not the rescuer. Oh, cruel calamity."

"Brother Giles. There is no shame except in the vanity to which you are now succumbing. Prythee, bear this inconvenience. Nobody shall think any the less of you."

"Young Paul, never grow old. It is a terrible condition."

I rolled my eyes. "You mean to tell me you fell because you're old? Hush now. I thought you a sensible man. Any person may take a tumble."

Reaching our destination, I settled him upon a cot, still clutching the blood moss to his head. "Oh, woe is me. My end is nigh after all. The hour grows later than my reckoning."

"Brother Giles, not another word, prythee." I tutted. "Such terrible mutterings from so great a man. And why, might I ask? Because he had a fall. Stop this prattle this instant." I gently took the moss away from his head whilst I spoke, so I might get a better look at his wound.

The infirmarer looked suitably chastised and remained silent.

"Well, it seems to have stopped bleeding, praise be to God. I feared it may need to be stitched."

Brother Giles jerked. "Surely not?"

"I told you it looked nasty, and I meant it. There was so much blood, I was sure you must be seriously injured. But, as it is, I think a poultice will do."

"And what shall you make it from, my student?"

"Bread, honey, vervain and salad burnet."

"You have been paying attention."

"You will be well there whilst I make it?"

"I shall happily remain here."

As speedily as I was able, I pounded the ingredients together and collected a length of linen from the pile. First, I washed the wound with vinegar. Happy that the moss had staunched the blood, I applied the poultice and wrapped the linen about Brother Giles' head.

I laughed. "Oh my, that looks grand for a small wound."

"Paul, it is impolite to laugh at the infirm."

I coughed. "Quite right. I apologise."

"Please, be seated. We may as well make the best use of this time. I assume you wish me to sit a while?"

"Aye."

"Paul, you have such a forlorn look about you at times. I do wonder if this life is truly for you?"

I flinched. "I had not realised I had created such an unfavourable impression."

"Now, don't take it to heart so. I mean only to enquire."

"I am not unhappy here."

"But have you truly reconciled yourself to the simplicity of a monastic life? I do not doubt your intentions. But you are young and vibrant. You have skill aplenty, and surely could be an apothecary outside of these walls."

It was as though an arrow had pierced my heart. "You mean to put me off?"

He patted my hand. "Paul, do not misunderstand me. I would be honoured to have you here with me. Have I not said as much? But nor would I attempt to ensnare an innocent, brilliant soul."

I snorted. "I am not so very innocent."

"Perhaps not."

"There is no uncertainty. Even a simple lay brother can tell."

"A lay brother, Paul? What experience have you with them?"

My cheeks grew hot. "Nothing. Pray, forget I made mention…"

"I am not your confessor, but I would have you know you can talk to me."

"I would not wish to cause offence."

"I would take none."

"You cannot promise that. You do not know…" I grew desperate. "On my oath, I gave him no encouragement."

I had said too much. Before he could cast me out, I ran away from Brother Giles. But I did not get far. Brom was swishing a stick through the air, cursing.

"Calm yourself," I cautioned, keeping my distance.

"Calm? *You* urge me to calm? You who are the cause of my vexation?" He pointed the stick in my direction.

"I? Brom, recall yourself. I never intended you any harm."

"And yet here we stand."

"You are not being fair, Brom. Prythee, what can I say to ease your mind?"

"There is nothing you can do. I thought you were like me. You said…" His shoulders slumped, the stick fell from his grasp.

I slowly approached and rubbed his shoulder. "Mayhap I was once. But I never told you as much. I meant to offer only friendship."

"It was all in my mind then."

"It would seem I showed more than intended. For that, I apologise. But Brom, it is not from disinterest that I speak."

He cocked his head.

"Be reasonable, Brom. I am to become a monk. Whatever has happened outside of these walls cannot ever be repeated inside them. Do you understand?"

"You have taken no vows yet."

"No, but I must live as though I have. I take them all as seriously as if I had sworn them already, especially the *conversatio morum*. If the monks ever suspected me…of…I would be turned out with nowhere to go. So, I suspect, would you."

"That may be."

I stroked his cheek. "I am sorry. Sorry for allowing you to somehow think we could be more. Sorry for not being able to…"

He grinned then. "So, you would?"

I chuffed. "It does no good to answer such questions."

"But you do not hate me?"

I looked to the heavens. "God, lend me strength. No, I do not hate you, Brom. Yes, you are attractive. No, we cannot act upon reckless impulses, no matter how great the temptation."

My body went rigid as the scuff of a shoe resounded. Wildly, I looked around but saw nobody. *"O God, come to my aid. O Lord, make haste to help me!"* [Psalm 69:2] I silently pleaded.

Parting from Brom with as much grace as possible, I rushed back to the infirmary.

Kneeling at the feet of the monk who still sat on the cot, I said, "My apologies, Brother Giles. I should not have left you so."

Placing a hand atop my head, he replied, "Paul, I accept your apology and offer my own in return. I pushed you for answers you were not yet ready to give. And worded my enquiry clumsily to boot."

I looked up into his kind brown eyes. In that moment, he was more a father to me than my own. Such affection and understanding shone from him that my own eyes pricked with gratitude. "Then you will not turn me aside?"

"Let me be rightly understood. Your presence here would be greatly appreciated. I was fearful of becoming selfish, and not allowing you to have a choice in the matter. For already I have come to value your assistance."

Lunging up, I hugged him then. He valued me. "That is all I ever wanted," I told him, my throat raspy.

He held me to him, wrapping me in his tender, loving care. To be so enclosed in his fraternal, spiritual love was balm to my soul. Never before had I felt so accepted and cared for. When my sobs began, he said nothing, content to rub my shoulder until my emotions subsided once more.

Wiping the remnants of tears from my face, I sat upright by his side. "Do forgive me. I am not certain what came over me."

"It is what comes to us all. The times of postulancy and the novitiate are trying. It is a letting go of the past and an acceptance of our future. It is a time of many hardships and trials. Questions are asked of us, as much from ourselves as others. We each of us experience some turmoil. But, if you allow, it leads to the greatest peace anyone can ever know."

Chapter 5 – Blessed Are the Meek

After my encounter, I thought it best not to pursue any scheme of spending more time with Luke. I had already erred and was suffering for it, even though friendship was all that I'd intended with Brom. And my heart whispered there may be more to my feelings with the novice.

I was a bundle of nerves all the following days. I feared being accused by an unseen person and being called to the prior at any moment to provide explanation. And none could be provided, at least not to any superior's satisfaction. My excuses would all seem empty.

Sighing, I buried my head in my hands at my desk. The life I was committing to was supposed to be one of simplicity. Enter the priory, devote oneself to God. Yet I seemed in more of a muddle than ever. Despite the welcome reassurances of Brother Giles.

"Paul. Are you quite well?" Brother Barnabas questioned.

Sitting up, I forced myself to look forwards. "My apologies."

"You do look pale. And I think Luke has had his fill this morning. Lest you should think me a tyrant, why do you both not go unto the grounds and take a turn about the cemetery garden? Enjoy some sun whilst it shines, eh?"

Not needing to be asked twice, I bolted for the door, almost bumping into Luke.

"With all due reverence, if you please," Brother Barnabas reprimanded.

"Yes, Brother," we chorused.

I motioned my hand to allow Luke egress. As did he. We giggled. Brother Barnabas shook his head. Luke's hand pushed against my back, forcing me to go first.

In silence, we walked together to the appointed garden at the rear of the church. The sun was indeed shining, lending its warmth to the mid-May day. Bees buzzed between the apple trees which were adorned with bountiful blossoms.

Luke held his hand aloft. "Behold, there are no apples with which I should tempt you with."

"You need fruit to be tempting mayhap?" The question was out of my mouth without thought. I gulped.

Swinging around a tree trunk, Luke stalked close to my person. "How wide your eyes grow. How easily you startle."

"How much the fool, you play."

He laughed. "Ah, so he does have claws."

"Aye, I have fight enough within me."

"I do not mean to fight. Not the now, anyway. I mean to make merry." Stretching his arms out, he turned his face up to the heavens and span in circles.

"You shall make yourself dizzy is what you shall make."

He stopped and stared. "You call me a fool again?"

"Indeed, I do not. I only feared I would have to revive you should you fall in a faint."

"Ever the infirmarer."

"Always."

Grabbing my hand, he led me in a two-person dance, twining our way between the leafy, blossoming trees. "Come, take merriment when it is offered."

Pulling on his hand, I brought us to a halt. "Have you lost all sense? You do not think Brother Barnabas left us without supervision entirely?"

He grinned. "I think Brother Barnabas was glad to take a nap. Look about us. Is there anybody else here?"

I checked in all directions. "It would appear that we are alone."

"Rare is such an opportunity. When the sun shines make hay. Hey nonny nonny."

I chuckled. His jubilation was impossible to resist. With a tug on my hand, he continued our merry dance. We had no need of trumpets or drum; the song we felt in our hearts was all we required. In and out we weaved, skipping and jumping, but mindful not to holler. Although, I may have laughed a little.

Stopping with my hands on my knees, I tried to regain my breath. "I am certain monks should not behave thus," I told him between breaths.

"We are not yet monks, my friend. Do not fret so. You enjoyed yourself, and I will hear no words spoken to bring shame unto such a moment."

Leaving me to regain my composure, he stood afore me and began skipping in place. Matching his measure, I whistled a lively melody whilst he danced a saltarello. The majestic deer of the forest could not outmatch the elegance of his leaps. Daylight beamed upon his golden head. The rays of a thousand suns shone from his eyes. And his laughter was akin to an angelic chorus of bells as it chimed through the air between us. And my breath was once more stolen from me.

I could have remained in that moment forever, captivated by his vivacity. Regrettably, however, the dance did come to an end. And Luke sat on the grass with a bump.

"Thank you," he said, his voice quiet and hoarse.

I joined him on the ground, leaning back on my elbows. "It was my pleasure. Aye, 'twas good to feel...alive."

"Oh, how I shall miss dancing."

"You experienced much of the dance before?"

"Not near as much as I would have liked."

"Pray, tell me from whence you came."

A cloud passed over his visage. "There is not much to tell. My father is a merchant, and I his third son. He sent me away to school as soon as he was able. And there I spent most of my time."

"And you danced at school?" I mocked.

"Father was forced to accept me home at Christmastide. But I was an embarrassment, always participating in the revelry with too much fervour."

I smirked. "That is difficult to imagine."

Picking a blade of grass and tearing at it, he answered, "I have no need of your censure."

"And I offer none."

His face whipped round to fully look at me. "A fine concession."

"For your honesty, I will share that I am also a third son."

"Truly?"

"Aye. My mother almost died bringing me into this world. My noble father prayed to God that we both should live, pledging me to Him should his prayers be answered."

"And thus you came here."

"It was never hidden. I grew up with the expectation. But tell me how you, with such a voice, were not given to the chantry?"

His lip curled. "That would have been my choice, but my father, ever the tyrant, condemned me to this path. He...being a boy treble was too girlish for his taste."

"You sang so high? I wish I could have heard it. But surely it is to be admired. Boy trebles are much sought after."

"Not when the family honour is at stake. It was too—"

I cocked my head, urging him to continue.

"Nevermind. It was his wish and so I must abide."

"Do you resent it?"

He stood up. "You ask too many questions."

Rising also, I apologised, "I have an enquiring mind. That is my greatest fault."

"But much sought after here."

"I deserved that."

He nudged my shoulder with his. "It is jealousy mayhap."

"Of me?"

"Is that so very astonishing?"

"Do you see yourself?"

"Aye, the wild child, ever seeking pleasure."

"The beautiful young man with the voice of an angel."

He blushed. As did I.

"Your loose tongue has found its way into my mouth," I added.

His eyes grew large. "Alas not."

"Forgive me. I should not have spoken so."

"Nor I. All this does no good." Wrapping an arm about my shoulder, he chanted:

"Two young men to Heaven bound,
One blond, one with hair of brown,
From two fathers they appeared,
With one Lord only to be revered."

"How very poetic. You have a beautiful heart," I told him.

"Or a wounded one. The greatest poets are the most tragic figures."

The bell rang for sext, and we hurried to prayers.

Alone in the chapel, once more separated from all others, I began, "*Domine Iesu Christe, Fili Dei, miserere mei, peccatoris.*" (Lord Jesus Christ, Son of God, have mercy on me a sinner.)

Luke was temptation itself; he had no need of the lamented apples.

It was the most conversation we had been permitted. And much was said in a short space of time. I tried to piece together the lively young man Luke appeared to be with the sad, almost pitiable one I had glimpsed. Were my skills sufficient to heal the heart sick? I prayed for them to be so.

My way was unclear. I wholeheartedly wished to help Luke, even if only to reconcile him to a monastic life. I would help him find peace. And yet, I was all too aware that I was stumbling away from my own serenity by doing so. He brought to me life in ways unbefitting a monk.

I was saddened when there was no repeat of our frivolous activity in the following few days. And I became ever more aware of the contradictions within myself. But mayhap it was better to admire Luke from afar. I seemed mainly to antagonise with my words. And I had regrettably brought a shadow over our momentary joy.

And now rain kept us indoors, even if the monks had been of a mind to allow us some freedom. And perhaps that is all my heart was whispering? A longing to be myself, away from restraint. But did that mean I could never be happy here? Should I set up as an apothecary after all?

"Paul, have a care," Brother Giles admonished, "You are supposed to be picking off leaves for drying not destroying them."

"I beg pardon."

"Would you like to share what is on your mind?"

Yes. No. "Brother Giles, what does it truly mean to be a monk?"

He chortled. "Oh, dear. There are many answers to that. But really, *ora et labora* should guide you. Pray and work."

"Yes, I know the words. But what is it truly like to live that way? Do you ever regret taking your vows?"

"It is important to ask yourself this. It gladdens me to know you are giving serious consideration to it. However, it is also important not to overthink. You need to listen to what your heart is telling you, for through that, God speaks. But no, in answer to your question, I have never regretted it."

"May I ask how you came to the decision?"

"Would it surprise you to know it was much like yourself? Although, I am a second not third son. I will tell you plainly, my father thought it a cheaper option than setting me up in a profession and marriage, much to my relief." He winked as he said this last.

"Thank you for your candour."

"I preferred the thought of living a quiet life, being of service. Life outside of these walls is a constant battle. There is no fight or struggle here. We live simply and peaceably in the main."

"Does it ever strike you as too quiet?"

"Perhaps. At first. But that is why you must progress slowly. We arrive at the altar to profess our vows gradually. There is an adjustment to be made. I can only advise you to surrender yourself to it. Besides, there is excitement enough in the flurry of someone being taken ill."

My cheeks heated. "I was most anxious for you when you had your mishap. But it would be useless to attempt denial of the thrill of being able to help which drove me on."

"You see how it is. Be at ease, young Paul. Let go the world of vice and sin which rages without."

He had brought me comfort and also pain. It was precisely sin that I was trying to avoid. I had thought myself safe here, but it was not the sanctuary I had expected.

I ventured to ask, "Is it ever possible to live entirely without sin?"

"Oh dear me, now that is a question and a half. Paul, we are men of God, but men we remain all the same. As devout as we may be, we are none of us saints. Thoughts, if not deeds, may keep us sinners. All we can do is be the best that we can and atone for any sins we commit."

"It is alright to have sinful thoughts?"

"Dear boy, is that not what we got to confession for? God forgives the true penitent."

Letting out my breath, I thanked him. Indeed, I was not aiming for sainthood. It was a good reminder.

Chapter 6 - Fortune Favours the Bold

Brother Barnabas had told Luke and I to stay behind after nones. And Brother Giles joined us.

"It is bathing day," the master of novices announced.

We were marched towards the bathing house, my thoughts flying. I hoped not to embarrass myself. Brother Giles' hand rested lightly upon my shoulder as we walked; it was reassuring more than guiding and was greatly appreciated.

We entered the dark room.

"Very well, the two of you disrobe next to the filled tubs and get in," Brother Giles instructed.

There was a curtain between said tubs. The two monks had their backs to us as we prepared to bathe. And Luke's face peered through the rear of our divider. First, I gawped but quickly shot him a disapproving look and shewed him away with my hands. However, realising my error, I quickly covered my privates with those mindless hands. He had chosen the moment I was fully naked. My cheeks were ablaze as Luke's grinning face disappeared back to his side.

"I do not hear any splashing of water as yet," Brother Giles called across.

With that, the rippling of water being disturbed sounded from Luke's tub. I hastened to do the same.

"Ahhhh," I moaned, sinking into the hot, herbed water.

"Mmmm...," I heard from beyond, a sinful sound which made me think impure thoughts.

A naked Luke was nearby. What did his body look like once freed from its tunic? I licked my lips. Was his body smooth, or did blond hairs adorn his person? As my mind's eye roamed downwards, trying to foretell the appearance of his manhood, I groaned.

"You should be purifying more than relaxing. Have a care not to enjoy yourselves too greatly," Brother Giles reminded us.

Alackaday! "Apologies, Brother Giles. The water is just so wonderfully warm," I explained.

"That is as may be but do ensure you are cleansed. There is soap to be used."

My pintel was throbbing as all my blood had surely headed there. Mayhap I should've remedied the situation? No, the water would've splashed too vehemently, and I would have been caught defiling myself. I just had to think bad thoughts; putrid cabbage, gnarled feet, forty days of eating fish…that did it.

I washed my body and hair with the soap provided. "Is that sufficient, do you think?" I asked aloud.

"Aye, if you feel sufficiently cleansed, you may get out," Brother Barnabas permitted.

As quickly as I could manage, I dried and dressed myself…without peeking behind the curtain. It was not fair Luke had seen me but not I him. As his black tunic was far simpler, he was ready before me and stood waiting as I emerged.

Brother Giles announced, "There is a fire lit in the infirmary. You may warm yourselves there until you are fully dry."

"I am to leave you in the care of Brother Giles until vespers. Mind you behave and give him no trouble," Brother Barnabas told us.

Luke and I nodded, watching the master of novices depart before following Brother Giles to his domain. We huddled near the sweet, earthy-scented fire, our hair still damp.

Smiling, the monk said, "I have work to do. Tinctures and unguents do not make themselves. I trust that you will both be good. You are welcome to stay here. Or, once you are dry, you may retire to the dormitory to read quietly with my full trust that you will not misbehave."

Luke looked as stunned as I felt.

"There is no need for such looks. You are young men, not little boys. I am certain you do not require my supervision at every moment. After all, God is ever watchful."

"Yes, Brother. Thank you. Your trust is not misplaced," I confirmed as Luke declared something similar.

"Well, well, well, I'll be in my back room then." And off he went.

Waiting for him to be out of earshot, Luke whispered, "What japes. We shall see who is smiling at vespers."

"I will not. But do explain yourself."

He chuckled. "Do you not wonder where Brother Barnabas went?"

"I had supposed him to be going for a nap."

"But Brother Giles suggested we'd be alone in the dormitory."

"But where else would he be at this hour?"

"Exactly." He grinned widely and wiggled his eyebrows.

"What do I not know that you do?"

"Well, the monks here are rather fond of their baths, and surely have them more regularly than most."

"You do not mean..?"

"I am aware that some tend to congregate in the guest house on those days. Ever curious, I loitered thereabouts one day. And what do you think I saw?"

"What? Pray tell."

"Ladies."

I gasped. "Surely not. In the monastery?"

"Aye. Ones of ill repute, by the looks of their striped hoods."

I covered my mouth with my hands.

"You should see yourself. But I maintain that I tell the truth."

"Heavens!"

"Are you dry enough yet?"

"I should say so."

We walked sensibly and quietly lest anyone should see and grow suspicious of our haste.

Once up in the fusty dormitory, I discovered we were indeed alone. I was struggling to come to terms with what Luke had told me. Nothing else had occupied my mind the entire way there. Sodomy is a sin. Monks have taken solemn vows. The Evangelical Counsels include chastity. Surely they would not go against such sworn oaths.

Yet Luke seemed so earnest. I did not suspect him of lying, but mayhap he was mistaken. In my daze, I failed to notice Luke had sat next to me on my bed.

"Tell me, Paul, what creates such frowns?"

"Your words. I must confess to being shocked."

"You are so very surprised? Then I am sorry for it. But it cannot be wholly unexpected. We are all of us men. Have you yet met one without needs?"

Blushing, I shook my head. "But should we not deny ourselves those needs? Does The Rule itself not say to deny oneself in order to follow Christ?"

"And yet we must console the sorrowful."

"Still your tongue. We must avoid worldly behaviour, as you well know. We should love chastity and reject carnal desires."

"But to love one's neighbour as oneself is good."

"I do not bend the rules to pollute myself."

"You are a better man than I. Of course, should anyone ever ask, any nocturnal emissions are entirely unintentional and therefore worthy of a mere fifteen psalms, which can easily be sung away swiftly here. But questioning is unlikely. I am yet to reach my twentieth year, so such things are to be expected. And I am careful."

"When your eyes shine with such mirth, it is impossible to tell whether you jest or are in earnest."

He grinned but narrowed his eyes. "I shall leave that to your own mind."

"Luke, you are too angelic to be so wicked. Besides, this conversation is entirely inappropriate."

Standing, he agreed, "You have the right of it. We should at least have a book to hand, lest anybody should intrude."

I shook my head, watching him fetch a tome from the cupboard. Rejoining me, he opened onto a page we both read to protect us from any enquiry. Not that I could think very clearly. Our dialogue had produced an unfortunate effect upon my person, which I was endeavouring to both conceal and quell. I envied Luke his tunic which hid much from view.

"You truly mean to live in purity?" Luke asked, a crease upon his brow.

"I...did, of course. But your revelation has me...considering if such self-imposed restrictions are not too high an expectation. Indeed, are they truly expected at all? But if not then why must we profess them?"

His hand stroked my cheek, and I involuntarily leaned into his touch. "Has anyone ever told you that you think too much?" he asked.

"Frequently."

My eyes had closed of their own accord, but when I once again opened them, a dazzling blue met my gaze. I inhaled sharply. As did he. He was about to kiss me, I was certain. My whole being thrilled at the prospect. My chest heaved as blood thundered through my ears. But alas, seeming to recollect himself, he pulled back.

Clearing his throat, he instead enquired, "Tell me of your life before. What was your experience of school?"

It took me a moment to react to such a hasty change of topic. "Much the same as yours, I suspect. Or anyone's. I did as I was sent to do. The teachers drilled us in psalms, lectured on the Ten Commandments and the Seven Deadly Sins. I learned from psalters and bestiaries. Latin became a second language, and arithmetic became… at least familiar if not my favoured subject. I perused manuscripts and annals."

"Hmm…I did not mean the subjects."

I cocked my head at him.

"The other students…did you…become much acquainted?"

I shrugged. "Not very greatly. I attempted to become invisible, in truth."

"And why was that?"

I looked at my folded hands on my lap. "…To avoid unwanted attentions."

His hand rubbed my upper arm. "I understand."

My head shot upwards, my eyes aimed at his as true as an arrow. "You do?"

"It may startle you to learn that I do not seek attention from all."

I shook my head.

"Not everybody is kind," he added, casting his gaze away.

"No, they are not."

"On my very first night at school, a group of older boys approached my bed, jeering. It looked bad for me. But I yelled, and the dormitory master came running. The boys took a beating for their attempt. And they would have paid me back in kind. However, I grew up with two older brothers and stood my ground. From then on, I was as loud as possible so that all would know they would face repercussions if they tried anything."

"Two opposite approaches with the same result then."

"It would appear so, my friend."

Leaning over the book, I hugged him as best I could. The tales of his outspoken ways were apparently not exaggerated but were not without reason either. Luke had learned the behaviour in order to protect himself, and I would not dissuade him from what felt safe.

As we parted, a thought came to me. "Are there never more monks who sleep here?"

He wiped his eyes, but I pretended not to see. "The others sleep in the dormitory but rarely. Only on such occasions such as the bishop's visits. Most have beds where they work which is more convenient. I think your infirmary friend is perhaps most fortunate as he often has a fire going so enjoys the added benefit of warmth."

I smiled. "He told me as much. But, I think you have the right of it. And that means we are in no great danger hereabouts."

He snorted. "Unless one is tending the gardens."

The blood froze in my veins. "Do not recall that day, prythee."

"I wish I could forget it for I saw too much which dissatisfied me."

"I did not mean...I made no encouragement."

"I noticed. And saw your polite but firm refusal."

He looked so crestfallen I would've offered words of reassurance, but I was struck dumb. I could not bring forth the right words as realisation slowly dawned—it was my denial which irked him most. My pledge to be chaste. Like a coward, I allowed Luke to steer the conversation far away.

As he brought up the subject of families, I asked, "You mentioned your father is a merchant?"

"Aye, with my eldest brother following into the business. The other is gone into law. My father deemed it judicious to have someone protect his interests."

"You are severe upon his intent."

He chuckled. "It is no supposition of mine. He declared as much."

"Such a loathsome world."

"Indeed. One I am not sorry to be parted from. Even if my father believes otherwise."

"He harbours ambitions for you yet?" My stomach lurched at the thought that perhaps Luke would be taken from me.

"He does. This priory is dependent on Rochester, a great establishment in itself. And in turn, falls under the patronage of the mighty cathedral of Canterbury."

I chuckled. "Oh, dear, I see. He fancies you to aspire to the mitre?"

"It matters not. I have no such ambition myself. But if he needed to believe that in order for me to come here, then I cannot help it."

My smirk surely matched his. "I am certain it was all in his own thoughts and received no prompting from yourself."

He smacked my arm. "Do not insinuate such deviousness. I am innocent." He batted his eyelashes.

"All innocence, I see it plain. I am convinced." We both laughed.

Feeling the need to console my friend, I ventured, "Does it help you to know my father also saw the opportunities for promotion? Ah, such veneration we could lend our families. I shall not have to battle you for glory, shall I?"

"Not unless you develop a partiality for the work of a cellarer."

Scrunching my nose, I confirmed, "Keeping track of kitchen staff and the comings and goings of food and fuel? Not I."

"I suppose it was natural given my upbringing. And it is better than being a steward."

"Eurgh! Managing lands and property for a lord seems so dreary."

"Quite. But how come you to your particular choice?"

I chuckled. "Chiefly from my own inquisitiveness. From a young age, I developed an interest in plants. When my younger sister fell sick, my mother cured her with herbs. For show, a surgeon was sent for. But I observed my mother's actions."

"She healed your sister by her own hand?"

"Mmhmm."

"Most impressive. But you seem a caring sort of fellow. I can see now where you get that from."

Biting my lip, I replied, "I suppose I am."

His finger held up my chin. "It is not something to feel ashamed of."

"I fear others would disagree."

"I do not care so much for the opinions of others."

"I wish I did not."

"Even now?"

"Especially now. Are we not continually assessed?"

"Paul, I do not believe that anyone could ever find you lacking."

My breath caught.

"You would disagree? No, make no answer for I see that you would gainsay me. It confounds me how you do not see your goodness."

"Mayhap it is all but show?"

"Nay. Do not say so. I would never believe it. And to lie is to sin." He winked as he said the last.

"Well, I would not commit sin."

"No, you would not." He sighed.

I smiled to myself at supper. Any form of meat or fish was conspicuous in its absence. The offerings were fast-like; surely an unspoken acknowledgement of the undertakings of sinful monks.

As shocking as it was to discover the brethren were able to take certain liberties, I wondered if I would ever be permitted such freedoms. Although I had stumbled across writings from the likes of Burchard of Worms, who expounded that sex acts between unmarried men are less serious than fornication of married ones, I was not confident the prior of Darenth would agree. It is one thing to accept the requirement to slake one's lust, but quite another to encourage it.

But then again, perhaps it could be managed in secret.

Something changed within me that day. I had been incredibly restrained, refusing to satisfy my urges, of which there had been many. The apprehension of my arrival, the uncertainty of my suitability, being kept under constant watch, the confusion over Luke, the fear of detection; all of this left me almost in a frenzy. And one way to dispel some of the agitation would have been to expel it through means of…well, taking matters into my own hand.

As I lay in bed that night, I thought of the hypocrisy of the brethren. If they can flout their vows, then surely I, who was as yet to pledge such oaths, was permitted leniency. My pintel hardened at the thought. And, to my shame, I stroked it under my nightgown and covers.

Visions of Luke swam in my head; his mischievous yet heated look as he peered at me in the bathing house. Those blue eyes which changed hue with his mood but were ever enticing. How our heads had drawn close whilst seated on this very bed, snatching our breath.

In my mind, my hands played through his blond locks, grasping and stroking in turn. Oh, that our lips should meet as I thought they would. In my fantasy, he did not pull away. He licked those plump, rosy lips of his and placed them on mine. Oh, sweet ecstasy!

Our mouths worked in harmony, opening and closing, drinking one another in. Our tongues glided, and still I wanted to taste him more, my hunger insatiable. His arms pulled me close, his own ardour evident against my person. My hips ground against his whilst our kiss grew ever more heated. And…oh…oh… "Argh!" I attempted to stifle the cry with my free arm as I emitted seed.

As quietly as possible, I gasped in air, bringing me back to the dormitory, away from the Heaven I had just glimpsed. Darkness descended once more, and guilt filled me. What had I done?

But the quietude of the room was disturbed. The wet slapping sound was not of my making. Hark, another was about the same business. And they were close. The next bed along. Biting my lips together, I listened to Luke's actions. Was he thinking of me? Or was he merely answering a faceless lust which he had admitted to being subjected to?

His breathing grew more erratic and shallow, snorting through his nose. His arm movements disturbed his blanket, beating like a drum. I was sure the monks would hear and rebuke him. But their snoring persisted, with mercy. My ears strained as I listened to his repressed hums which grew higher pitched until he gasped at last.

If I had not already spilled, surely I would have in that moment. It was as though we were together despite the curtain dividing us. I turned on my side to face him, although he would not know it, whilst doing my best to avoid the cold, damp patch on my nightshirt. A smile danced across my lips as comfort enveloped me, lulling me into a peaceful slumber.

Chapter 7 – Paul's Progress

We were busy the next day as the whole house celebrated Whitsun. I sat in my usual place in the church, admiring the boughs of birch which had been placed in the pew ends and hung about. But the lay brothers sat near in silence.

I quietly joined in the chanting of *Veni, Sancte Spiritus*, and it indeed lit up my soul:

"Come, Holy Spirit, come! And from your celestial home, Shed a ray of light divine!

Come, Father of the poor! Come, source of all our store! Come, within our bosoms shine.

You, of comforters the best; You, the soul's most welcome guest; Sweet refreshment here below;

In our labor, rest most sweet; Grateful coolness in the heat; Solace in the midst of woe.

O most blessed Light divine, Shine within these hearts of yours, And our inmost being fill!

Where you are not, we have naught, Nothing good in deed or thought, Nothing free from taint of ill.

Heal our wounds, our strength renew; On our dryness pour your dew; Wash the stains of guilt away:

Bend the stubborn heart and will; Melt the frozen, warm the chill; Guide the steps that go astray.

On the faithful, who adore, And confess you, evermore, In your sevenfold gift descend;

Give them virtue's sure reward; Give them your salvation, Lord; Give them joys that never end.

Amen. Alleluia."

Perchance, I should be now cleansed of all guilt and sin. Should I not now renew my strength, and hold true to what I had previously believed? And had been taught? Was I not being led astray?

My heart quickened at the second alleluia, "*Come, Holy Ghost, and fill the hearts of thy faithful people: and kindle in them the fire of thy love.*"

My cheeks certainly enflamed at the recollection of the fires which burned within me last night. Could it be that my being here was God's Will? Was he testing me? Or rewarding? It remained a shrouded mystery.

The services of the day held an exuberant tone as much as they were able, even if I was myself in turmoil.

I had more company at dinner that day. Our grand feast included delicious meat, so we had to eat in the misericord. All were to partake but there was only sufficient space for half the obedientiary monks, so Luke came to dine at my sitting, much to my delight.

The smell of roasting suckling pig had been wafting through the air, making my mouth water and stomach growl, long before we were due to partake. So, it was with great eagerness I took my place at the feast. One of the staff served us.

My hands brushed against Luke's as we both reached for the *poivre jaunet* sauce to pour over our helpings of *pourcelet farci* (the piglet). I withdrew my hand as quickly as if it had been stung and gestured that Luke should help himself first. Although we were outside The Rule of St Benedict, silence at mealtimes was a habit long-formed, and somewhat expected. And it was probably for the best that we ate in silence.

Having captured Luke's eye, which did not take any effort on my part, I licked my lips and smiled. He nodded his agreement. His smile warmed me more than the meal. Glancing around the room, the few others seemed just as delighted with today's dishes.

Finding I had drained my cup already, I caught the server's attention (who was from the kitchen staff for this sitting) and kneaded one hand on the other. He bowed his head and soon brought me more ale as I'd requested. Nobody frowned or glared; this was a day of celebration, and drinking Whitsun ale was the least one could do to show willing.

Part of me felt sorrow at not attending a grand fête this day. Neither would there be any boat races for us. Whilst my family would be enjoying all of that and more. Ah, such exuberant merriment. Never again would it be mine to enjoy. My heart sank.

Yet my spirits were lifted by the supposedly sin-free *sambocade* as it was presented. My eyes closed as I took my first bite of succulent, elderflower flavoured, smooth, creamy delight of a cheesecake. I put my hands together, offering a prayer of thanks for this treat. How was this not considered sinful over meat? Luke, who had sat next to me again, cleared his throat but our other dining companions bowed their heads at me, smiling.

Once finished, I stood to leave upon the signal. However, I almost fell back down, except Luke caught me in time. My face must have reddened terribly, I grew so warm. My friend's hand rubbed my arm as he silently checked I was able to continue. When I nodded, he led me away, supporting me about the shoulder.

Brother Maynard approached and whispered to Luke, "See he gets fresh air. I shall see to his serving duty this once."

"That is very kind. Many thanks."

The two bowed their heads, and Luke walked me out of the refectory. Once we were outside and well out of hearing range, he said, "I thought you drank too swiftly of the ale. Are you well?"

I swatted at him. "Fie, I am no quake-buttock quaffer."

"I never said you were."

"I just stood too quickly." My ensuing hiccup perhaps suggested this was not entirely the case.

"I think today's ale was mayhap a little stronger than usual."

"Ah, Whitsun ale indeed."

We both chuckled. I realised that Luke had led me out into the cemetery garden.

Pointing at a tree, I commented, "Ah, back among Eve's forbidden fruit trees once more."

"Still only the blossoms, though," he replied, shaking a branch.

A petal landed on my hair, making Luke smile beautifully. "A fine adornment."

"Avaunt! I shall hear no such prattle."

He swung around a tree trunk to level his gaze at me. "You think I mock you? But verily, I am in earnest."

God be merciful, but how I melted under his scrutiny. "You are?"

He stalked close, and pincered my chin. "I am," he whispered, "But you need no such decoration, for you are comely already."

I gulped.

His face screwed up and he grunted in anguish. "Paul, we have not much time, I fear. Prythee, put me out of my misery. Torture me no longer. I would know of whom you thought last night."

My eyes near popped out of my head. "Last night?"

"Oh, try not my patience. I cry your mercy. You know full well of what I speak. Paul, be not cruel. Speak plain and tell me true, was I in your thoughts whilst you practised solitary vice?"

"I...I....err...," I paused to draw breath whilst looking at the earth beneath my feet. "I did, aye."

His long, drawn-out breath had me looking back at him and asking, "You are relieved?"

He laughed. "Aye, much relieved."

"Truly?"

He grabbed me to him in an embrace. "Paul, you know not how I have longed for this. How fervently I have attempted to quash the desire which burns within."

"I had no notion—"

"I had dared not hope. I feared at first you did not feel towards men as I do. But when I saw you with Brom, oh, how I despaired. I cursed his name for being the object of your desire."

"I did not—"

He seemed oblivious to my objection. "But then you refused him. My heart soared at your lack of revulsion, but then was dashed to the ground and stomped upon by your repudiation on the grounds of your intended celibacy..."

Taking a step back, I clasped him about the shoulders. His blue eyes were glistening in the sunlight. "Luke, take heed. You grow too passionate. Prythee, calm yourself. Certainly, it was never Brom who took my fancy. And indeed, I find myself drawn to you in ways I should not. But, as much as it pains me to admit it, I cannot make you any kind of promise."

He clutched me once more. "I ask nothing of you, sweeting. Not a thing."

Rubbing his back, I held him in my arms until his breathing calmed. I lowered us both to the ground so that we sat side-by-side.

"Now that you know that I harbour desire, tell me, Luke, how does this help either of us?"

"It gives me hope."

"But what hope can we have in a place such as this? We must be more on our guard, not less, for if we are discovered we shall both be turned out. Or condemned to purgatory."

"What if we are not?"

"Are—"

"Still your tongue, prythee. I know what you would say. But I do not mean for us to be reckless. But knowing I may yet have hope is all I need. It has been very hard here without you. But with you by my side…you make me feel I can face any hardship life may throw in my path."

"I pray I do not yet prove to be an obstacle on that path. It would pain me more than anything to be your downfall."

His smile was aslant. "Nay, Paul, you shall as yet be the making of me."

My bashfulness held me in silence, not knowing where to look.

As if sensing the awkwardness he'd created within me, Luke requested, "Tell me something happy."

I pondered. "There was once an orchard where two young fellows cavorted—"

"No, Paul. Although, I am glad to hear that is a happy thought."

"Mmm…my happiest." I smiled broadly.

"Mine also. However, I meant something I do not know."

"Oh. Err…well... Let me tell you of a time when I was surrounded by familial love and protection. I suspect it shall make you laugh. My brothers, that is Harry and Nicholas, and I were about on our country estate one summer. My sister was as yet too young and had been kept home by our mother."

"Of course."

"My brothers were forever taunting me and would often play too rough. But we could also be more restrained. That particular day, we had found branches in the woods and were playing swordfights. So engrossed were we that we noticed not the rascals closing in around us."

"Truly?"

I nodded. "They were but local youths. Hedge-born varlets who planned villainy. They called out slurs which I cannot bear to repeat. But it was clear we were in danger."

"How dreadful."

"Let it be here known that my two older brothers were struck dumb. Usually so full of bragging boldness, they were suddenly still."

"You declared this was to be a happy tale of protection?"

I smiled. "Might I continue?"

"I beg pardon."

"Well, their fear fuelled my anger. Holding my branch aloft, I yelled, 'Away with you, you pox-ridden churls.'"

"You never did!"

"Aye. Of course, they laughed. But it was enough to launch my brothers into action. They ran at our would-be attackers, bellowing and brandishing their woodland weapons. And I followed suit."

"Did it work?"

"I think we must have looked fallen into mania sufficiently to scare them off, aye. They soon fled."

"A merciful victory."

"A fortunate one. But when we were safely alone, we laughed and embraced one another. I discovered that day the true meaning of brotherhood. That no matter how beastly they were in private, they would always stand their ground to protect me from others. And I them."

"I think they learned of your secret ferocity too."

I chuckled. "Aye, mayhap that as well."

"I pledge to always protect you also." He squeezed my hand.

"My thanks. And I also. I would do almost anything for you."

"Almost? What is there you would not do?"

I was silent a moment. "I cannot bring to mind anything as of now, but there must be room should something occur."

He chortled. "My strange, funny, serious, fierce, sweet friend."

"I am a contradiction."

"Hm, a happy combination, I would say. You are exactly what you need to be at all times."

"Well, it sounds rather dull when you say it like that."

"Nay, far from it." His eyes shone with admiration which warmed my very soul.

"What-ho! Here I find you, at last," Brother Giles hailed upon his approach.

I did my best to appear calm. "Indeed, Brother. We have not led you a merry dance in search of us, I hope?"

"Nay, it is a fine day for a wander. I had heard you appeared to be in a faint earlier, so I sought you out to check how you fare."

"Our brethren are fond of hyperbole, it would seem. I merely stood a little too quickly."

Luke added, "Aye, after he imbibed too swiftly of his ale."

I glowered at him. But Brother Giles chuckled. "As mayhap did you, young Luke? For something has loosened your tongue, eh?"

He looked abashed.

"Come now, the both of you, on your feet. Let me see how steady you are."

Luke and I did as instructed and walked in a straight line.

"Aye, very well, I am satisfied you shall not do yourself a mischief. I shall bid you adieu. Enjoy your afternoon."

"I wish you no work, Brother," I said as he retreated, earning another chuckle.

Turning to Luke, I noted, "It seems unfair that we are given our freedom to celebrate, whilst the monks must still attend to their duties."

"They were free from restraint in their youth, I daresay. We should make the most of it whilst we can. That being said, what shall we do?"

"Shall we not go hawking?" I quipped.

"If only. Try again."

"The tavern?"

He smacked my arm. "You are not being helpful."

"Am I not? What about a game of stoolball then?"

"Oh, no, but we do have skittles."

"We do?" I asked, my voice rising in pitch.

"Aye, come along," he said, getting up and tugging my sleeve.

I followed Luke to a cupboard where evidently the games equipment was stored. Carrying the skittles and balls, we hastened to a long strip of grass out of doors and set the wooden pins up in a diamond formation.

"You first," Luke said, offering me a ball.

"But wait. What do I win?"

"You are so certain of winning?"

I rolled my eyes. "If."

"Tsk, tsk, tsk. Gambling is a sin, postulant."

Shrugging, I dismissed, "Have it your way."

"I reserve the right to claim my prize upon winning, however."

"And, pray tell, what manner of prize would that be?"

Such mischief danced across his face as his eyes narrowed to slits that I almost feared his response. "Nay, I shall not tell for fear you would throw the game on purpose."

Shaking my head, I took up position. Crouching low, I drew my arm back then launched the ball towards the pins. All but one fell.

Clapping, Luke commended, "Very good. My turn."

We reset the targets. I stood a little way behind Luke as he prepared to take his shot. It was a great pity his tunic was so loose-fitting. This game was so much more fun when wearing tight hose.

The clattering of skittles falling pulled me out of my daydream. "Confound it! You had not declared yourself an expert."

He winked. "You did not ask."

Grinning, we set up again. This time, I knocked all the pins down, which earned me a cheer and applause from my opponent.

"Now, who is most skilled?" he asked, cocking his head.

"We shall see yet."

We became raucous in our cheering and good-natured derision. Brother Maynard, the kitchener approached, making us halt where we stood. As he neared, I lay prostrate on the ground.

"Forgive us, brother."

"Forgive? Nay, I came not to reproach. Stand, Paul. I wished to seek participation in this merriment."

"Oh, but you are most welcome, especially after you took my place serving," I readily agreed.

"It has been a while. But I beg your patience as I try my hand."

"Gladly."

Luke and I clapped, and I admired, "Very good. Only four left standing."

"Five down. Not so very bad."

"Pray, have another go," Luke offered.

"Aye, that was a practice," he agreed.

I laughed. "For what? There are no stakes here."

"Very true. We should all be in for it if caught gambling."

Before long, a few others had joined in. But my mouth gaped upon seeing Prior Ambrose walk towards us.

"Why such astonishment? Is a prior not also able to have his share of fun on a day of celebration?" He chortled.

It turned out that Prior Ambrose was one of the better players. But none outshone Luke who won.

"And what is your prize to be?" the prior asked Luke.

"Oh, but we did not play with any other aim than fun."

"Hmm...mayhap a pittance at supper would be fitting? Brother Maynard, can you see to it that our novice receives his reward?"

"Of course, Prior."

Brother Maynard did not disappoint. I know because Luke snuck a fig tart to the dormitory that night, from his hoard. I licked my lips, made sticky from the delicious morsel.

Luke stared and whispered, "It gladdens me that you take such delight in my winnings."

"A just reward indeed."

"I did have another in mind."

I looked askance. To which he leaned his body closer to mine as we sat upon my bed. We both held our breath as he paused, tantalisingly close. When I made up the rest of the distance, he licked at the sweet remnants from my lips, eliciting a 'mmm' from them.

Our lips met in a delicate peck which lingered but went no further. We sat staring into one another's eyes, astonished. Stuttered snoring from beyond sent Luke fleeing to his own bed. But it mattered not too greatly, for it was enough—that brief kiss held within it a promise of future days.

No, that was a lie. It was not quite enough to satisfy me, and there may have been more nocturnal emissions that night whilst visions of Luke and myself going beyond more than light kissing danced in my head. But there would be consequences.

Chapter 8 - The Seed Should Spring and Grow Up

We were listening as intently as possible to Brother Barnabas whilst stealing furtive glances at one another during a morning lesson. There was so much more to be said between us. But I could tell from his looks and hand gestures that Luke held as much hope as I did in my heart.

"The prior would speak with Paul, if you please, Brother Barnabas," a lay brother announced as he entered.

Our novice master looked heavenwards before answering, "On matters, it is supposed, which are so urgent that they cannot wait until after my instruction. Very well, Paul, go with this man, but do not tarry."

"Yes, Brother."

Worry creased Luke's brow as he watched me depart. Bees swarmed my insides. Surely our timid advances had been espied, and I was to be turned out. Oh, the shame. What would I do? Would my family take me back? How foolish I had been to give sway to my amorous thoughts. And now I was smitten.

How unsteady were my footsteps on that long walk to the prior's room. My mind whirred, excuses failing to conjugate. I would not place the blame upon Luke for I was no caitiff. But how could I own my wrongdoing and remain here? *Please, God, show me a way.*

To be torn asunder now, just as we were on the brink of...what? What could we be? No, I must surely give up any sinful notions. And yet the monks have their visitations. Should I not be permitted my own pleasure?

The lay brother knocked at the prior's door, and my knees almost buckled underneath me.

"Enter!" came the dreaded permission, echoing through my soul.

Slowly, I approached the man at his desk and bowed my head. "Brother Ambrose, you sent for me?"

"Leave us," he commanded the lay brother, and waited for the door to be closed and the lessening sound of retreating footsteps. "Yes, Paul. It is a matter of a delicate nature. Pray, take a seat."

I almost missed the stool but corrected myself in time to sit without falling.

"You see, it is laundry day, and it has been brought to my attention that there were...stains upon your nightgown."

I threw myself prostrate onto the ground, both thankful that the matter was not so terrible as feared, and ready to make amends.

The lies did not flow smoothly from my lips but rather jolted like a tumbler performing acrobatic feats. "Prior, forgive me. It was not a deed conducted by my own will, for it occurred during my sleep. And I was too ashamed to even make confession of it."

The prior sighed. "*In nomine Patris, et Filii, et Spiritus Sancti. Amen,*" he intoned, making a sign of the cross. "May God grant pardon for sins committed without our knowledge or consent. It is as I had hoped."

"Lord, have mercy. Christ, have mercy. Lord, have mercy."

"As your pollution was unintentional, I order you to kneel after each psalm sung today, and to ask God for forgiveness. But I shall not insist you fast on bread and water. You are young, and these things happen. But I do ask you to be mindful, and to try to avoid any repetition of this."

"Yes, Prior. Thank you, Prior."

"Rise. I did not call you to scold, Paul, however it may seem. In lieu of an abbot, I must take on some of those responsibilities. You are all my children, and I must take care of your immortal souls. We are none of us saints. But when we err we must make confession and be penitent."

"Yes, Prior." I had regained my seat but kept my head bowed, my cheeks aflame.

"Whilst I have you in my presence, I would know your thoughts on your progress."

"Oh, err...it goes well, I believe, thank you, Prior Ambrose. You are not unhappy with me?"

"This incident aside, I am pleased with how you seem to be adapting. It is a big change, which we all appreciate. You have made no grumbling and indeed, have been seen to be striving to do your best. Brother Barnabas has nothing but good reports of you."

"I aim to please, Prior."

"It is not for us to be pleased, but for God."

"Indeed. I would honour Him with my every thought and deed."

"May He watch over our endeavours. Go with God, now."

I bowed myself out of his presence at the dismissal. Outside, I leaned my back against the cool wall and puffed out a large breath. "Thank you, Lord," I whispered.

Regaining my composure, I made my swift return to the carrells.

"All is well?" Brother Barnabas enquired as I retook my place.

"Yes, Brother. Apologies for the interruption."

"As I was saying..." he continued the lesson as though nothing had transpired.

Luke was all smiles, his blue eyes shining with relief. When Brother Barnabas went to the book cupboard, Luke even risked squeezing my hand. Such warm thrills went through me at his touch that I was utterly lost. It was as though I needed his reassurance to believe I was still here. My heart soared at being reunited with him.

My pulse quickened as Brother Barnabas returned with wax tablets from the cupboard. Had I missed his announcement of writing practice, lost in thoughts of Luke?

Placing a tablet in front of each of us, our master said, "I need not remind you that we are not scribes. However, we are sometimes called upon to copy manuscripts and texts which are within our possession when they begin to age, thus preserving knowledge. And we offer assistance to our mother cathedral when they are in high demand.

"Knowledge is a precious commodity, and as such, is deserving of our utmost care and attention. You shall not be entrusted with such lofty commissions until you have first proven yourselves worthy of the task. Do I make myself clear?"

Luke and I nodded, my head showing eagerness whereas my poor counterpart looked all apprehension. My schoolmasters had praised my writing in the past, and I was keen to show Brother Barnabas something which I was good at.

Hunching over, I set about my task with glee. My stylus bit into the wax without too much pressure as I copied out the phrase we were given. I tried not to stare at Luke once I was finished, but it was impossible not to notice his tongue poking out in concentration as he continued his efforts. Folding my hands, I forced myself to look down at my desk.

"Let us examine your handiwork," Brother Barnabas announced once Luke's stylus went down, approaching my desk.

Biting my lip, I passed him my wax tablet.

His eyebrows rose, "Not at all bad. You show great promise."

However, a frown descended as he looked at Luke. "Come along, lad. We may as well get it over and done with."

My heart went out to Luke, so forlorn did he look. "Prythee, Brother, I really did try my hardest."

The master of novices shook his head. "You are indeed more suited to numbers. But your leger entries must be readable. You shall just have to continue to practice. I do not lose hope in you. There is some improvement here."

I thought Luke would cry in relief as he listened. But he held himself well, and merely nodded as he whispered, "Thank you."

I had recited the psalms and kneeled as instructed during the offices. It was a light penance as far as these things go. But my silent prayers to God begged for mercy.

I was here at His calling, yet I knew not how to avoid giving my heart also to Luke. Mayhap they could share it? Surely, there was room for divine love and…I was unsure what name to give the feelings growing within my heart; spiritual love? Fraternal?

I recalled to mind, *"Beloved, let us love one another, because love is from God; everyone who loves is born of God and knows God."* [1 John 4:7-8] – whatever name given unto it, love always comes from God and glorifies Him.

Yet, still I doubted. I was to become a monk. And had this very day made promises to deny Luke yet was already thinking of defying them.

Had I not lied to the prior? A sure sign of my guilt. I sought forgiveness for that also.

But my feelings were growing stronger and could not be denied.

It was with greater zeal that evening at compline that I quietly sang the antiphon:

"Save us, Lord, while waking
and guard us while sleeping,
that awake we may watch with Christ
and asleep we may rest in peace.
May the Lord grant us a quiet night
and a perfect end. Amen."

The next afternoon, I was in the infirmary with Brother Giles.

"It is blessedly quiet this day," he commented.

"A happy respite from the constant flow of people seeking treatment, indeed."

He sat on a cot and patted it. "Come, sit with me a while. I must rest my weary bones whilst I may."

"Would you like some ointment applied, Brother?"

"No, I do not seek to add to your burden. But I would speak with you."

"Something troubles you, Brother?" I asked, sitting.

"Not as such. I would impart some wisdom, however. Knowledge of your meeting with the prior has reached my ears."

I blushed and swallowed rising bile. "Does everybody know?"

He chuckled. "For a community which is mainly silent, we can be quite quick to spread news, despite the requirement to not gossip. But it is no great matter. Only pity for the discovery was conveyed."

"But—"

"Paul, I would not have you commit the sin of lying. Make yourself not uneasy. I do not mean to cause embarrassment. Must I repeat that we are all men? I mean only to convey a means to avoid any repetition of rebuke."

I shuffled uneasily, mortified.

"Blessed are the young. They believe themselves the first to experience anything at all. I would have you know there is always someone who has gone before you. Now, you may consider yourself most fortunate in your chosen occupation."

He leaned under the cot and retrieved a leather bag. "As an infirmarer, I consider it advisable to carry a few items about my person to avoid running around in search of remedies amidst urgency. Such as when I took a fall, for instance."

"Pray, do not remind me."

He chortled. "I am in full health, with no small thanks to your quick thinking. Now, would it not have been useful to have some blood moss and strips of linen to hand?"

"Indeed, it would."

"Ah, you see how it is. I had hoped to make a gift of this wallet once you were confirmed as a novice or even a junior monk, but it seems prudent to do so now."

"For me?" I asked, my eyes wide, taking the proffered wallet.

"For your role, and the betterment of all. It has a strap so you may comfortably carry it across your shoulder. And it contains such items as may reasonably be required."

I opened the bag, glancing at the contents. "Brother Giles, this is most generous."

"Not at all. As I said, it is a reasonable requirement for people such as ourselves."

"I shall treasure it always."

"Now, I urge caution. For nobody else must know. There are those about who value too highly the pittances they receive in exchange for information, as you have unwittingly fallen prey to already."

"I confess to being shocked to learn someone had reported the state of my linen to the prior."

"Sweet treats are luxuries indeed to the lay brothers, I fear. Oh, they argue with themselves that they are not the ones transgressing, that it is God's work. But in the Lord's name, every evil begins."

"But I did wrong."

"Two wrongs do not a right make. You are capable of confession as much as the next man. There is no need for others to tell tales. But I am carried away by my censure of those mean-spirited varlets. What I wanted to tell you was that should you...feel a certain urge which is too strong to deny, you may find a quiet place and take one of these linen strips and spill into that. Clean and dry it yourself, and nobody shall be any the wiser."

Grinning, I narrowed my eyes. "That sounds awfully close to deceit, Brother."

"Concealment is mayhap the happier word. Else you may face fasting next time, and a lifetime upon your knees. As if we did not spend enough time at prayer and singing psalms to cleanse us of such minor sins already."

I giggled. "You sound like Luke."

He made an 'o' with his mouth. "You have spoken with Luke of such matters?"

"Mayhap I felt drawn to converse with someone of similar age."

"Ah. Talking of whom, should…well…there is a vial of oil in your wallet which may also prove useful. And I do not keep so close a watch on my bottles of that should you require refilling." He tapped the side of his nose.

My mouth opened and closed like a fish gasping in air. Surely, he did not infer..? No, he could not possibly know.

"Dear boy, I have noticed how you look at one another. And how hurt he seemed when Brom tried to press his advantage."

I yelped.

"Now, now. Have I told any other person? No, and never will I do so." He laid a hand upon mine. "Know that in this too, I am your friend. I have had a secret love of my own, and I could never deny anyone else that happiness and comfort. But it is possibly wise to keep your own counsel until at least you have professed simple vows."

Tears welled in my eyes. I could make no verbal reply.

"Aye. I was not always an old man. Hugh was my light, my joy, my confidant, my comfort and my nights. We often slept side-by-side."

"But did nobody condemn you?"

"We were careful. Besides, it would be a great hypocrisy if they did offer censure. Are you aware of the ladies who are sometimes permitted admittance? As I say, we are all men. And it is best to vent our urges before they build into frustrations which breed anger. And if the humours are allowed to build too greatly within the body from total abstinence they can even bring about death. Why else do you think the Bishop of Winchester maintains his flock of geese in the stews of Southwark, hm? It is not all for monetary gain, I assure you. One does not have control over that many harlots without indulging in what they offer, I daresay.

"But do bear in mind that this should be measured with some self-denial. Do not give in to every urge, for that too would lead to peril for your soul."

"But it would seem Hugh was more than an urge, if I may be permitted to say so?"

"Aye, he was. And all the less sinful for it. We were not caught up in lust alone. Love is always a blessing. But enough. I still feel his loss, some years on. I shall not repeat his name to you lest I open the wound so far that it cannot ever be staunched. But it was important that you know how much I support whatever may transpire. A good man is a good man, Paul. Even if he sometimes transgresses."

I hugged him. "Thank you, Brother Giles. For sharing that. For trusting me. For supporting me."

He wiped his eyes. "Very well, enough of this idleness. Let us make ourselves busy. Tinctures and unguents do not make themselves."

During my moments of solitude, I thought upon what Brother Giles had shared. His gifts were many and great. Did he realise what blessings he granted me that day? Acceptance and support—they meant so very much. Nobody had ever imparted thus greatly to me.

Knowing I was not alone was the greatest comfort. Until that moment, I had believed the monks would all be against such relations. Mayhap I had begun to hope for some little understanding after discovering the truth of the ladies. But this was beyond my imagining. Brother Giles had had a love of his own. With a man.

The dawning of realisation rose like the sun; Luke was more than an urge. I had done things with others before him, but they never held my heart. How blind I had been. Romantic love was possible and surely planting its seed within me.

Any excesses of our feasting were balanced by the Ember Days on the Wednesday, Friday and Saturday following Whitsun. No food at all passed our lips until after nones, making my stomach grumble. And even then, we were restricted to fish.

However, much to my delight, the dishes were not the meagre fayre of my schooldays. The cooks in the monastery were most creative whilst complying with regulations. One day, I even enjoyed *Oystres in Cevey* – the chopped morsels of oysters in their spiced wine sauce were delectable.

And not one among us had cause for complaint. The Rule was read aloud, in part, to us daily. We each of us appreciated how lax our approach was. For now, Pentecost was passed, we should fast *every* Wednesday and Friday until the fourteenth day of September. But the order of Benedictine monks had long since left that way of living to the likes of the Cistercians. There were many reasons for my inclination towards Benedictines above all others, but this surely was part of it, for the less severity the better.

We feasted again on Trinity Sunday. Whitsuntide has always been a time of holy devotion and celebration. And it must be said that the monastery concentrated its celebration through the joy of food, given that we were restrained from other forms of exultation.

For Corpus Christi (one of our principal feasts), we partook of transubstantiation; the transformation of bread and wine into the body and blood of Christ in Mass. The polyphonic chants of the liturgy echoed in the very rafters of our church. The faint fragrance of musky, sweet damask roses and the hay-like smell of woodruff wafted happily about from their garlands.

Pageants and processions were surely being enjoyed outside our community walls. Possibly, some were taking their First Communion.

The lay brothers joined me in the church, given the importance of the celebration, still separated from the obedientiaries. We listened to the *Solemnity of the Most Holy Body and Blood of the Lord*. And deferential scripture readings from the [Book of Exodus 24:3-8], [Letter to the Hebrews 9:11-15], [Gospel According to Saint Mark 14:12-16 and 22-26].

With great humility, we recalled the freedom from sin and death, and the gift of new life being offered in and through Christ who rose from the dead to bring eternal life.

A procession was made in Mass where the Blessed Sacrament, held in an elaborate monstrance, was carried to the "altar of repose". Awe and respect flowed through me as I was permitted to share in this wondrous occasion.

By receiving His Body and Blood, I confirmed my task of being a bearer of Christ - to all people and until my final breath. I had never lost sight of my calling, to be here in the name of worship. But never had I felt it so greatly. My life was His.

Days passed, and the pace of life slowed for the community around me.

Luke and I were unsuccessful in our attempts of snatching time alone together. I grew desperate and it seemed as though ants crawled throughout my person. I longed to convey some of what Brother Giles had told me, although I would not break his confidence by disclosing the personal details, of course.

My fingers twitched to reach out to Luke's. To be held by his strong arms would transport me to Heaven itself. However, even our glances were restricted. And the monks seemed to keep themselves awake until at least one of us was sleeping. Possibly, it was but in my head, but I felt more closely watched than ever. Was it because of my sinful act?

"Brother Giles, I believe you may be correct in asserting a great hypocrisy dwells within these walls," I mused one afternoon as we ground powders.

He replied, *"All therefore whatsoever they bid you observe, that observe and do; but do not ye after their works: for they say, and do not."* [Ps 48:10].

"You would tell me to blindly obey despite their actions to the contrary?"

He tutted. "Paul, are you no longer willing to take the vow of Obedience? Yes, I would tell you to obey. You are not yet so filled with wisdom that you know how to bend the rules to your own satisfaction whilst remaining true to your faith. You are not yet even a novice. You have been with us, what, but one month?"

"You are given to think me arrogant?" I asked, wincing.

"Oh fie, I tell you that you must have patience. Practice caution. Observe. Learn."

I am certain my face conveyed the sullenness which descended upon me at hearing his words.

"Oh, young Paul. Do not think me unfeeling. Have I not told you I am a friend?"

"You have. But I struggle so. And yet there are eyes everywhere."

He chortled. "Oh, dear. Hmm…it is possible I forgot how confining the lives of postulants and novices are. You are tested greatly to ensure your readiness for our way of life. Hm, yes, I see your predicament."

I ran my hands over my face with a groan.

"Never fear, young friend. Leave the matter with me, and old Giles will see what he can do. But you had best work all the more diligently in the meantime."

"Brother Giles, all I ask for is hope."

"That, we always have. Try you to live more in the life of spirit and less in the carnal mind and body at present. *For we are saved by hope: but hope that is seen is not hope: for what a man seeth, why doth he yet hope for? But if we hope for that we see not, then do we with patience wait for it.*" [Romans 8:24-25]

"You would have me pray harder?"

He chuckled. "Is that not our purpose?"

Ever eager to live the life I was promising myself to, I followed the good monk's advice. And with a great deal of meditation and prayer, I began to calm. Brother Giles gave me a drink made from root of liquorice each day which quelled the worst of my yearnings.

I surrendered myself again and again to God's plan. For surely he had one. Had I not been guided here to this very place and alongside Luke by His hand?

And my patience was rewarded a few long days later. Both Luke and I were sent to Brother Giles after nones.

"Ah, it is good to see you both. How fare you, young Luke?" the monk welcomed, grabbing us each firmly about the shoulders in turn.

"I am well, I thank you, Brother."

"Good. It pleases me to hear it for I am in need of assistance this fine day. The sun is shining its blessings upon us whilst the lay brothers are about the fields making hay. I require more meadowsweet, and here I am without sufficient hands to gather it for me."

"You would ask us to collect the herb for you?" I asked.

"Indeed. That is exactly the thing. You see, it grows along the riverbank which is difficult for me to manage. But two fine young fellows such as yourselves will collect it speedily. And it fulfils the requirement of some physical work, which I fear has been lacking for you of late, Luke. Brother Hector has kept you at the books too much, I think."

He looked at the floor, and quietly replied, "That may be so."

"Then here is the answer to all our prayers. *He that gathereth in summer is a wise son: but he that sleepeth in harvest is a son that causeth shame."* [Proverbs 10:5]

"We gather herbs not hay, but it still pleases the Lord?" I checked.

"It must be so. You have your wallet about you, I see, Paul. Good lad. Here, Luke, you can carry the basket and tools for the gathering. Be sure that all are returned safely, else the cellarer will be cross with me and not allow this again. Now, let me direct your footsteps..." He gave us clear instructions where the meadowsweet could be found, but I felt his guidance far beyond that simple task.

Luke and I walked quietly beyond the walls of the monastery, keeping a careful gap between us. The basket swung to and fro at his side. It took a great deal of effort not to grin.

Over the road, we walked and turned left at the water mill, its wheel standing still. Every man, woman and child was in the fields gathering in the hay. I had been surprised not to be sent thence myself. However, it would seem that it was not the work of monks, much to my relief. It was hard, gruelling labour.

Once out of the way of other people, Luke let his curiosity show. "Not that I make complaint, but does it really require two of us to gather meadowsweet?"

"Perhaps not. But, oh, there is so much to tell you. Brother Giles is sympathetic to our cause."

"And what cause might that be?"

"Us."

"Oh, there is an us, is there? And how should he know, pray tell?" He smirked.

"Not from my lips, I assure you. But he is a keen observer."

"This, I shall bear in mind."

"No, do not be cross, Luke. He…has similar…inclinations, I believe."

"He would like to kiss you too?"

Playfully shoving his arm, I corrected, "Fie! Still, you mock. But in all seriousness, you would like to kiss me, would you not?"

Stopping, he turned and met his lips to mine. "Very much," he whispered.

"Mayhap we should gather the herbs first? Lest we forget ourselves entirely."

Stepping back, he nodded. "Aye. You have the right of it. For once I begin I may be unable to stop."

My heart thundered until it almost burst out of my chest. "Me too."

We continued along our way. "There, look," I said, pointing.

Standing proudly ahead was a crop of creamy-white, lace-like flowers dancing atop their green stems. Queen of the meadow in both name and stature. We busied ourselves cutting and gathering what we could.

Swiping his forehead, Luke declared, "I am all a-sweat."

My pintel throbbed as I watched him lift his tunic off. Luke stood naked before me, and all I could do was gape. His shoulders were broad, his stature proud. If his father had seen fit, with training, he would have made a fine soldier. But I was exceedingly thankful he was here.

My eyes drifted downwards and was pleased to see he was long and neither too slender nor thick; his hood was as rosy as his lips. And growing larger before my eyes.

"I meet with your approval?" he asked, grinning.

I slowly nodded.

He crept towards the riverbank and plunged into the water with a yelp. "'Tis cold!"

"You were expecting a warm bath, mayhap?"

He drew his arms forwards, splashing water my way. "Impertinent whelp!"

Hopping about, I clambered out of my attire and sprang to join him, launching into the water. "Argh!"

"You were expecting a warm bath, mayhap?" He used my own words against me.

"So cold!"

"Come, let me warm you." Approaching, he stood and held me to him, rubbing my arms.

"I think we have cooled sufficiently."

"Aye. It would seem I was too eager for my own good. Let us dry off in the sun's warmth."

Shivering, I followed him back up the riverbank, hiding my shrivelled manhood. Cold water was definitely not what I needed at that moment.

"There is no need for concealment. I have seen you already," he told me as he lay on the grass.

"Aye, but not like this," I replied, lying next to him on my side.

"Then I am at a disadvantage for this is your first viewing."

"Ah, but I saw before you entered the water."

He laughed. "Verily, you did take a good look."

"There was an opportunity, and I took it." I laughed back.

"Was this part of the old monk's plan?"

I nodded against my palm, supported by my elbow. "It is probable."

"I would hate to be a disappointment," he murmured, running his hand through my hair, making my eyes close in bliss.

"Impossible." I licked my lips.

He planted a tender kiss, soft and questioning. "We have so little time. Opportunities like this are so rare. I would not waste it. Yet I would not make you do something against your will. Or rush into action neither of us are prepared for."

"You cannot know how much I have longed for this. You rouse in me a desire to transgress. But urgency makes me bold. I would yet know whether it is mere lust which you feel for me?"

He sighed, again stroking my hair. "It is more than I can put into words. I hold you in high regard. Nay, more than that. As early as it may be to declare so much, you have made a nest in my very soul. And I know not whether it is a blessing or sin, but I long for more. To explore every part of you, not just bodily. Although, that is, I confess, enticing."

"Your words echo my thoughts. Oh, Luke, how I have wrestled. The torment I have endured."

His hands had not ceased their caresses. "Peace. It is enough to know we both feel the same, is it not?"

"Aye."

"Know that even when we cannot show it, that I am here for you."

"And I you."

He smiled. And the sun seemed to radiate from him.

"And still, it scares me. I have never before felt this way."

"Nor I. There have been…moments of mutual touching with others before…but it was ever in fun. Nobody held my heart."

"Likewise. But how can it be so, Luke? I barely know you."

"Yet you see much of me, I think. And when I look at you it is as though we have always been acquainted."

"That certainty, aye, I share that."

"I do not believe we should fear it. But rather embrace this great unknown together."

"But if we progress does that not make a mockery of what we are to become? We are here to avoid marriage, are we not?"

His laugh lacked mirth. "Aye, that is as may be. But when I make my pledge, it will as yet be in earnest. I embrace God. And I shall still be declaring my renunciation of personal possessions. You and I do not speak of marriage. That would infer a material contract. And procreation. No, that is not for us. No possessions and no children. Paul, do you not see that you bring me more peace than I have ever known, simply by your presence? Only with you at my side can I conceive of taking those vows. It is *because* of you not despite you that I would become a monk."

I stared at him with a watery gaze, my mouth agape. Not long did he leave me in stunned awe, for moving near, his mouth crashed over mine. And I opened up to him entirely. Our kiss was deep, and I lost all sense of the world. There was only Luke.

Desire washed through me like a tide. The longing of previous days paled in comparison. Like a limpet clinging to rocks, my arms gripped onto him. And he me. Hands wandered up and down naked flesh, in an endless search of a learning of their own. Whimpers and moans met between us, echoing in our mouths.

With a trembling hand, I reached out. "May I?"

At his slow nod, I took ahold of his pintel. Oh, wondrous joy, to feel his firmness within my grasp. Slowly, I stroked down his length, his prepuce moving back with the motion. Luke moaned softly. As I slid my hand back up, his skin covered his tip like a velvet glove.

I giggled. "You have a monk's hood already."

"Paul, now is not the time for laughter, prythee. You risk insult."

Moving myself down his body, I placed a kiss upon his tip. "My apologies, you magnificent example of manhood. I would never insult one such as your fine self."

Luke chuckled. "Will you come back up here, you dalcop?"

I obeyed, but moaned, "But we were becoming better acquainted."

Wrapping me in his arms, his voice hoarse, he told me, "This is where I need you." And kissed me with great fervour.

How I melted into those strong arms. He could have asked anything of me and I would have done it. I was no longer my own person; I seemed drifted away on the breeze.

The weight of his body landing atop mine was a heavy comfort. His tongue tangled with mine, tasting, testing. The tang of ale still delectably present as I lapped.

Groaning, I bumped my hips upwards. Sweet mercy, he responded as required, and our shafts brushed together delightfully. Still, I needed more. How I throbbed and yearned. A fire had been set ablaze but demanded more fuel to burn fully.

"Can you raise yourself a little?" I asked breathily.

With the strength of an ox, he did so. And I wasted no time, taking hold of both our pintels and stroking us together. The groan which came out of Luke's mouth had my hand working all the harder.

"Augh!" he cried, his head shooting back. "That…feels…augh!"

His body tensed. My movements grew faster, now slickened with our fluids.

We both groaned and bucked as my hand continued its relentless quest. It was too much. All this contact after so precious little. My nightly visions had not gone far enough, did not do justice to this frenzied ecstasy.

With more cries and a judder, Luke squirted his seed, hot and sticky between us. My hand kept tugging as I too breached through to that other realm where only light exists. My earthly body spasmed and emitted more fluid than I thought possible.

Soft kisses on my cheeks brought me back to Luke's presence. Love shone from his eyes like sapphires. My whole being radiated with bliss.

"Extraordinary," Luke said, his voice still hoarse.

"Incredible." I wrapped my arms about him, drawing us together.

The sun shone down on us as we sighed, revelling in our moment. Happiness poured through me. I could have lived that way forever. But alack, I needed more room to breathe so pushed us to our sides, facing one another. I kissed him softly.

"As much as it pains me to say it, we had better wash off and journey back," Luke said, his dazzling light already fading.

"Must we?"

"We cannot live out here, my sweet honey."

"We could try."

"Until it rains."

"Eurgh! There is too much truth in that."

He stood, pulling me up to join him. "But I will be forever thankful for this."

"Likewise."

"Paul. It has never…that was…"

"Aye, it was my best too."

Any remaining desire was washed away by the cold river water as we cleaned away all evidence of what had transpired. Reluctantly, we dressed. Once again, his tunic made easy work of it. Soon enough, I would don such apparel.

"What is on your mind?" Luke asked.

"Oh, I was wondering whether I shall be happy or sad to be in monk's robes."

"I'd be happy if you were in mine."

I swatted his arm. "Cheeky!"

"You were in earnest? Ah, well, both. I like your clothes."

"You should have seen what I used to wear."

"I am sure you shocked and delighted all around you."

"Oh, how I shall miss colour."

"And the tight hose?" he asked with a wink, making me chuckle.

"Aye, those I shall miss most. Yet the habit has its benefits."

"It certainly does. I think I shall love your habit for its convenience. But when one must wear it day in and night out, it does begin to whiff somewhat."

"Love and loathe."

"Indeed."

I finally looked presentable again. We began our walk home, but not until one more kiss and embrace were enjoyed. We were both eager to fill our stores, knowing it may be some time before we could be reunited in such a manner.

As we walked, our act already drifted into a dream, and I began to doubt it had happened at all.

"Would it be impertinent to ask how you knew how to do that? Not that I am grumbling, you understand." Luke's question brought me out of my gloomful musing.

"Are you certain you would like to know?"

"Aye."

"Very well. After I left school, I was sent to live and study with an apothecary."

"No! Not he?"

"Nay. Hold your tongue. He had a son."

"Ohhh!"

I laughed. "Aye, oh indeed. He was apprenticed to his father, who sometimes had to journey away from home."

"And you two were left alone?"

"He was a little older than me. Sadly, his mother had died some years before. And his sister had been sent off to a convent school. So, yes, we were alone. He had to be available for customers, of course. But there were times of idleness."

"You liked him?"

Rolling my eyes, I admitted, "Not anywhere near in the same fashion as I like you. Did I not already declare as much? Did you think to catch me in perfidy?"

"My apologies. Prythee, continue."

"Hmph! We were both curious. He was not hideous, and we learned from one another."

Luke chuckled. "Only my serious Paul could make such matters seem like an experiment."

"But that's what it was, I suppose. And you shall be more thankful when we get to full fornication."

"We shall get there, shall we? You are so certain?"

I preened. "It is a foregone conclusion, my fairest of fair."

He laughed. "What has become of my sweeting? Once so serious and shy, now so playful and bold."

I stopped and ran my fingers down his cheek. "Only with you. You make me bold."

Our foreheads met, his hand resting on my chest.

"Lord, please look after me and grant my prayers for strength," Luke murmured.

"*Domine, miserere nobis.*" (Lord, have mercy on us).

Recollecting ourselves, we walked with a little distance between us. We were approaching an area where people may be about. There could be no more lewd talk, frank conversation or any hint of affection.

As we passed through the entrance of the monastery it was as if a veil descended. We once more appeared all innocence.

Chapter 10 - Seek His Face Continually

Our blessed moment of union was a joyous memory, but also one of torment. Yet I would never regret it. Luke was of the same mind beyond any doubt—a comforting thought indeed. But having tasted a slice of the pie, I coveted its entirety. And yet was denied even the smallest touch. The only exception being our time shaving, which was nowhere near enough, and only increased the longing.

Fearing detection, we were saintly in our abstinence. My *testiculus* may have become engorged to the point of pain, but no satisfaction would I grant myself. I drank plentifully of the liquorice root tisane to stem the worst of my aching orbs.

Around this time, Sub-Prior Gervase came to the infirmary in pain with the gout.

Whilst we made preparations some distance from our patient, with a raised brow Brother Giles whispered, "'Tis likely this was brought on by his overindulgence on the feast day of St Barnabas a few days ago."

I silently nodded and set about soaking the man's foot in warm rosemary water and wrapping his legs in cloth.

"'Tis easing. My thanks to you both," the sub-prior said with a sigh of relief.

"Prythee, rest yourself here a while until you are able to hobble to your room," Brother Giles offered.

I busied myself with cleaning and tidying until he had limped away, refusing my offer of assistance. The brethren had their pride, as I had witnessed often within these walls.

"The Lord be merciful. We are left in quietude at long last," Brother Giles announced, holding his hands up to the Heavens.

I grinned at him but shook my head.

He chortled. "Forgive my outburst, young Paul. But it has been days since I sent the two of you out on your errand and I am yet to hear of its success. But judging from your frequent smiles and daydreaming, I surmise it went well?"

I nodded. "Aye, it went well. And I have wanted so much to thank you." I wrapped my arms about the man who patted my shoulder in return.

"Very well. I did not act seeking gratitude."

"Yet you have it all the same."

"The pair of you share something special, I suspect."

"Aye, Brother. We both seem to feel something…vast."

"God moves in mysterious ways. But I am glad He brought the two of you together here, and that I may be of some small service to you."

"It is no small service. Your actions were great and good. You risked much."

"Not as much as yourselves. I am old and difficult to remove. Your cautiousness is sound. I would not place your future in jeopardy."

"Speaking of removal…is Brom well?"

"Aye, well enough."

"I have not seen him tending the herb garden of late."

"And this is cause for concern?"

"I should not wish him harm, however impudent his actions."

"Then you may rest your conscience. He has been busy elsewhere, mostly with haymaking."

"Ah. It is good to know. I thank you."

He smiled kindly, his eyes creasing. "You are a kind boy, and will be a fine member of our community, as I have noted."

"You do not think I gave him the wrong impression, that I am at fault?"

"Dear boy, you really do worry yourself overly much. If you have a fault, this is surely it. Brom is his own person. Certainly, you should not have conversed so freely with him. By breaking that rule, it is possible you raised a hope within him. However, his actions were his own. He feels foolish but not resentful, in my opinion."

"I did not intend…"

"Ah-ah, St Bernard of Clairvaux would remind us that the road to hell is paved with good intentions."

"Indeed. Sometimes, our actions do not match our intention. I am sorry to have caused injury."

"I am sure both he and God pardon you as you pardon Brom. Now, let that be an end to your worry over the matter. Happier times are ahead."

"Thank you for your ever wise counsel."

"I am but God's servant."

Over a week had passed since our happy moment, and I could bear it no longer. Once the sounds of snoring filled the dormitory, I crept the other side of the curtain.

"Are you awake?" I whispered, gently squeezing Luke's arm.

"How can I sleep when you are an ever constant presence in my mind?"

Through the gloom of night, I realised he was already lying facing me. I laid me down on my side so that my back was pressed against his stomach. It was a tight fit on his small bed, but with the aid of his arm clinging about my waist, we both managed to stay on.

"How I have missed you," he murmured, nuzzling my neck so that I had to stifle a moan.

"And I you. Hearing you read in our lessons has been soothing yet also brought its own frustration as I could make no reply. And I would hear different words from your lips."

"How are we ever to survive this way?"

"With great fortitude. Our friend reminds me that we must have patience. That it shall not always be like this." I would not say Brother Giles' name aloud lest one of the monks awaken and overhear.

"How so?"

"He tells me that his lover and himself often slept side-by-side."

"How I long for the days we can do likewise."

"In the meantime, we must make the best of what we have."

"Professed like a true monk."

I smothered my chuckle with my hand. "I believe our friend means to provide more time. But we must not grow too impatient and endanger us all."

"I will cling onto hope."

"That is all we can do."

We lay together in silence. My spirits calmed in his warm embrace, and we shared heavy sighs. But our position was not comfortable, and all too soon I had to roll onto the floor.

Kneeling, I reached up and ran my thumb across his cheek. "I fear I should return to my own bed."

"It would not do to be caught together, I suppose."

"Hold onto hope," I reminded him, stretching up for a peck on his lips; if I attempted more than that then trouble would surely follow.

"Hope."

It is strange how days can blend together so as to be undistinguishable from one another. I went from office to work to office in a trance—work and pray.

However, variety finds a way eventually. As I watched Luke still struggling to write, a series of images played through my mind; every touch and action with his hands was recalled, from picking meadowsweet to tapping my arm and gesturing…there was something always the same.

With great courage, I asked, "Brother Barnabas, might we beg absence from our duties this afternoon?"

He raised a brow. "And what possible reason would you offer for such a contravention?"

Pressing my lips together, I gathered my thoughts. "If it pleases you, I would request the use of the wax tablets. It is my hope that I may be of some assistance to my fellow student."

"And you consider yourself better fitting of the role of teacher than myself?"

"Pray, I mean no censure. I hold you in high esteem. Only, a thought occurred to me which may be of use, and I would try it. But I would avoid embarrassment by making the attempt with just the two of us, if that notion does not offend. At further risk of asking too much, I would also request any scraps of parchment which might be about."

"You do indeed ask much."

"I do."

"And yet you have me curious. And who am I to deny learning? Very well, return here after you have both eaten, and I shall inform Brothers Hector and Giles, as well as preparing all the materials required. Let us see if you can bring about an improvement."

After my meal, I waited anxiously in the carrells, rearranging the items Brother Barnabas had so kindly supplied. Luke walked in alone, and in my surprise I rushed to embrace him.

"Are you not the one who urged patience?" he asked of me.

"Aye, and I do not gainsay it now. But I am afraid of disappointing you. I was indeed in earnest in my offer of assistance."

"It was not a trick?"

"No. Pray, take your seat. I would not have you cast out for your lack of ability. If Brother Barnabas is giving sway to despair, I am certain that Brother Hector must be utterly dejected if not seething."

Sitting down, such dark clouds sat upon that angelic face that I too was in danger of falling into desolation. I was certain this was the primary cause of the monk's hesitancy surrounding Luke. But I would do all within my power to dispel the gloom.

"Pray, pick up the stylus and write something on the wax tablet."

He scowled. "You know how I struggle."

"I do. Hence us being here. Prythee, yield to my whim."

He glowered.

Bending low, I whispered into his ear, "Do so and I shall reward you at the earliest possible moment."

The stormy blue lightened a little as he squinted at me before cutting into the wax.

"You press too firmly," I noted.

"You see how it is hopeless? If I do not do so, the stylus refuses to comply at all. You should have spoken with me before condemning me to this misery. For now, my lack of ability shines brighter than ever and cannot go unnoticed another day. You have placed me in greater jeopardy than ever."

I gasped at the vehemence of his speech. Clenching my jaw, I steadied myself. "Get ahold of yourself, Luke. We have barely begun yet you lash me with your tongue. Must I repeat my desire to come to your aid?"

His hands washed down his face. "What would you have me do?"

"First, I would have you warm the wax and erase that scribble."

"You are cross with me."

"Aye, a little. But let us proceed, nonetheless. Come, make the wax afresh."

Rubbing with his thumb, Luke prepared the surface.

"Now, take ahold of the stylus in your left hand."

His back went rigid. Then he turned a severe glare upon me. "What is the meaning of this?"

"Just do as I ask."

"You shall get me into trouble."

"Luke, you declared once before that you trust me. I repeat, take the stylus into your left hand. And ensure you lift it after each stroke."

Grudgingly, he complied and wrote the same word. "Paul, Paul, look. You can clearly make out the word."

Clapping him on the back, I replied, "So, I see. Well done. Write it out again underneath." I added in a whisper, "And grasp the stylus as carefully as you would my pintel."

He spluttered. "You are most bold today."

"Only for your benefit."

"But can you not at least refer to it as a spitter or your tarse?" he asked in hushed tones.

"Nay, I cannot be so lewd. And you shall not find me so easily distracted. Now, hold the stylus gently like a good fellow."

Smirking, he did so. And wrote an even neater phrase.

"Excellent. And you would have shunned my lesson."

"I am sorry for it. Paul, this is a miracle. It must be."

"Have you never tried this? Truly?"

"Certainly not. I would never have dared my school master's disapproval. And I had feared to be turned out here. But you, you have lent me your strength."

"Let us try more. Smoothen your wax."

Holding the tablet above the candle this time, Luke cleared the surface, using the other end of his stylus to do so. "What should I write?"

"*Spe gaudentes: in tribulatione patientes: orationi instantes.*" [Romans 12:12]

He chuckled. "Aye, 'tis a fitting one for me. Rejoicing in hope; patient in tribulation; continuing instant in prayer."

I would not say as much out loud, but his writing was not perfect. However, there was a vast improvement.

I kissed his cheek. "I am so proud of you."

He beamed up at me.

"Shall we try on the parchment now?"

He nodded enthusiastically.

"Just as gently, commit the inked quill to the parchment."

The ink splattered a little, but the completed phrase stood proudly upon the page. We both cheered aloud.

"What is all this noise?" Brother Barnabas admonished as he entered.

"My apologies, Brother. But see what I have done," Luke said, holding out the piece of parchment.

"Have a care, you shall smudge it. The ink has not yet been sanded," I cautioned too late.

The monk confirmed, "No harm has been done. And I must say I am astounded. How come you to produce this?"

Luke hung his head, not uttering a word.

So, in his place, I said, "Brother Barnabas, I would ask you to recall how marked is the improvement."

"I have noted as much."

"Forgive me, Brother, but I insisted Luke hold the stylus in his left hand."

The ensuing silence was deafening. I could see horror and alarm cross the monk's features. His brow creased. "It seems sinister."

"Mayhap. But when there is so much benefit, might we not pardon it? After all, does the heart not dwell on the left of our bodies? Do we not hold the knife with that hand? What is it to us if we swap that over for the stylus?"

"Hmm...there are those who would condemn your actions, Luke."

Luke opened his mouth, but Brother Barnabas held up his hand. "But I am not one of them. What Paul says rings with truth. We write the word of God, and He surely would not permit such to be done in any other way but in that which is holy. And the results are so wondrous that they must be approved. But do allow me to speak with Brother Hector so he is not too affrighted."

"Gladly. Thank you, Brother," Luke said, getting up and embracing him.

"Let us not get carried away now."

Luke immediately backed away, but his grin remained.

"Might we display this in the dormitory, Brother Barnabas?"

"If Luke would like to keep this parchment by his bedside upon his shelf, I see no reason why he shouldn't. Yes, it may be a nice reminder."

"It would please me and encourage continued effort and patience, I think," Luke agreed.

"Then let it be so."

The Feast of John the Baptist arrived on the twenty-fourth day of June; a day like no other. We celebrated the day of the saint's birth; a feat only fit for the Blessed Virgin Mary and St John's cousin, Jesus himself.

"Illum oportet crescere me autem minui," (He must increase, but I must decrease) [John 3:30]. Thus, we were reminded to humble ourselves and ensure our lives were pointed towards Jesus Christ. We too must make way for him as St John did.

Three Masses were held that morning, where we prayed, *"O God who hast made this an honored day for us by the birth of Saint John: bestow upon Thy people the grace of spiritual joys, and guide the hearts of all Thy faithful into the way of eternal salvation."*

And at vespers, *Ut Queant Laxis* was sung. Our cantor, Brother Jeremy, had clearly amended it for Luke's tenor voice (as opposed to contratenor). There were two lower, slower voices underneath his. The effect was truly powerful in its beauty – vivifying. I was much stirred spiritually; my entire being seemed to vibrate with the power of the melody swirling about me.

In the misericord, we feasted upon succulent *Bourbelier de Sanglier*; roasted boar with a spiced wine sauce. I did so enjoy feast days. My stomach was full.

Just before sunset, even we, like those outside our walls, walked out of doors to the large bonfire the lay brothers had laid with bones to chase evil spirits away. They joined us there, and I spotted Brom amongst them. We glanced at each other before turning quickly away. There was embarrassment but not animosity in his brief look, I noted with relief, just as Brother Giles had told me.

Prior Ambrose recited the prayer, "*In the honour of God and of St John, to the fruitfulness and profit of our planting and our work, in the name of the Father and of the Son and of the Holy Spirit, Amen.*"

At this signal, the fire was lit to a round of applause. We all beat sticks or rang bells as the flames leapt into the air. It was as raucous as monks could get, and all in the name of warding off malevolent beings, including dragons.

We disposed of musicians and dancing, of course, for they would not be appropriate in a monastery. But we did receive an extra cup of ale as we stood by the fire.

I had hoped that we could sneak away alone whilst all others were occupied with the flames. But alas, we none of us lingered long for we had to go to our rest before rising early for matins. However, the lay brothers were left attending the fire; no doubt they would have some merrymaking until midnight.

My second month at the monastery certainly seemed to go by faster than the first. Mayhap I was fighting less. Any inner struggles with the rigid times seemed lessened. After all, there was no use resisting such things. It was just the way of the priory. And I was beginning to adapt.

Indeed, I seemed to naturally awaken for matins and lauds before the call to prayer. And my body knew when to void its bowels; this too was dictated by The Rule. Although, some visitors to the infirmary were given a small piece of soap to put in their *fundamewnt* before resting on their bed when they struggled with this. Brother Giles had noted that this was especially in demand after a period of feasting.

That aside, washing, praying, working and sleeping were steadily becoming instinct. I was learning the Psalms more fully and studying a great many texts under the guidance of Brother Barnabas.

I discovered that occupying myself with matters of the mind helped to keep at bay matters of the body. To an extent. There were times, particularly after my midday meal, when I was alone in the herbarium awaiting Brother Giles, that I had cause to use the linen strips he had so thoughtfully supplied.

Matters of the heart were not quite so easily put aside, however. Luke was by my side, tantalisingly close in the carrells each morning, and just a curtain away at night. So near yet so far. I yearned for conversation with him, for even that was difficult to manage.

My prayers were answered the night of the Solemnity of Saints Peter and Paul. Special services had been held, including the Solemn Mass of the Saints. Both saints were duly venerated, sharing the day as "these two were one" and patron saints of Rome.

We also enjoyed another meal of meat in the misericord that day. When I would have held my cup aloft for more ale, Luke stayed my arm. He took my open hand and turned it downwards, then moved it slightly with his outstretched hand in confirmation he wished me to deny the offering.

Once the server had moved on, Luke set a finger on his tongue. I squinted at his 'honey' sign, but at his pointed look, I realised it was not that of bees which he was indicating. Had he not called me honey on our blessed day of togetherness? My loins heated at the hoped-for meaning.

As if reading my thoughts, Luke bent his right thumb into the middle of his hand, clutching it with his fingers and raised his fist—apple. Our place, the cemetery garden. Of course, we had eaten together and would be alone until at least nones.

As soon as our meal was concluded we swiftly but quietly made our way out of doors. The weather remained dry, but I suspect even the heaviest downpour would not have deterred us.

Ensuring we were, in fact, completely alone and concealed among the apple trees, we embraced one another. I held Luke so tightly it was a wonder that he could breathe at all.

"How I have missed you," I whispered hoarsely.

He nodded. "And I you."

There was no need to explain it was touch that we craved—our hands expounded all as they explored each other's person. He placed kisses atop my head and down until my face and neck had not a spot left untouched.

Greedily, my mouth found the warmth of his. Our tongues lapped at one another, meeting as long-lost lovers. We each of us whimpered and moaned as our bodies rubbed together.

Tugging at the ties of my hose, Luke lowered them before urging me to sit. "I would not risk you taking a fall. And I would worship you this day of the saint whose name you bear."

I cocked my head, "Was I not to reward your writing efforts?"

"I do not recall. Surely, I should thank you for your assistance, however."

"You make it difficult for me to refuse."

"Then do not."

"Err…you have done this before?"

"Be assured my mouth knows what to do."

As soon as I sat, with my pillicock bobbing freely, Luke's mouth descended, licking and sucking the top in sweet torment. My hips drove upwards, seeking further progress into his mouth.

My silent pleas were answered by Luke's head lowering a little and one of his hands stroking my columnar part. Up, down and around, his hand moved in joyful harmony.

"Oh, Luke, my lief, you are truly an expert," I murmured, my head falling back.

The hands which I had propped myself upon were trembling, yet my hips thrust up and down at his ardent attendance. Forcing myself to remain seated upon the ground, I freed one hand so my fingers could run through his hair and apply gentle pressure to encourage him to take me deeper.

My darling duly obeyed, his head bobbing. Oh, how he sucked me into the warm confines of his mouth as his hand worked faster. He was relentless in his attentions.

It did not take long for the telling tightening of my *testiculus* and limbs to occur. My jaw clenched as I bit down the urge to cry aloud as I surged forth. God bless the man, Luke's mouth stayed upon me until I stilled.

"I needs must also spill," he muttered, rolling onto his knees, hitching up his tunic, moving away and taking himself in hand.

All I could do was watch; my limbs were deprived of all power. But what a sight he was to behold. His dazzling eyes closed tight, his breaths panted, and within a few movements, he spent his seed in the grass with a gasp.

"Oh, sweet mercy," I cried.

He crawled his way back to me, his tunic still carefully held out of the way. "Have you one of those strips of linen about your person?"

"Mayhap, but pray, allow me to clean you."

Nudging him onto his back, I quickly licked away any salty remnants on his skin, making him groan. "Augh, how shall I ever get enough of you?"

"I know not."

Moving so we lay front-to-back, he kissed my head. "My sweet honey."

"You enjoyed that?"

"You need ask?"

I shook my head. "Not in earnest."

"You shall never cease to shock me with your cheek following our copulation."

"What excuse can I provide but that you raise the devil in me?"

"Nay. Never declare as much. There is no devilry in our deeds. It feels too good to be anything but holy."

"You have the right of it. My apologies. But you do free my tongue so much that it utters nonsense."

He chuckled. "It is a pleasure to hear you become the dalcop."

"A pleasure, you call it?"

"Aye, it gives me a rest from the role."

Smacking his enrobed arm, I turned to face him. "It is my turn to disallow a thing. You are far from foolish, my fine fellow. You show me a man who disagrees with me."

"I..." He paused. "Brother Hector would."

"Pah! He is but a froth-mouthed, full-gorged goat who should be ignored. Brother Barnabas sees your intellect, and I value his opinion far more highly. Therefore, I say you are never again to think of yourself as anything but the well-informed person you are."

"I will own it if you remind me."

"At every possible moment, I shall." My fingers ran through his hair.

He kissed me; a slow, lingering meeting of lips. "We should probably make ourselves presentable lest we are discovered in a state of undress."

Hastily, I pulled up and tightened my hose and tugged my cotehardie down. However, I was not yet willing to dispense of the comfort of Luke's embrace, so wriggled back into place. He held me close, and I sighed, fully content as he nuzzled into my neck.

"Thank you," I said.

"My thanks also to you."

We both breathed out a, "Mmm."

Afore, there had been so much I wished to tell him, but all seemed to lose meaning when I was lying thus. We remained silent for a good while. Indeed, I suspected he may have fallen into slumber.

The bell ringing for nones jolted us both alert and had us running towards the church.

Chapter 11 - Wherefore Sighest Thou?

An idea came to me, that Luke and I might have time alone together each saints' day, thanks be to the arrangements of the misericord. Thus, I greatly anticipated the next, which happened to be the feast of St Margaret of Antioch, the patron saint of our church. The celebrations were sure to be grand. However, that was yet some weeks away. Patience!

I could and would endure. It must be borne. And mayhap it was a test sent from God.

Three weeks can seem an eternity, even with the aid of prayer. I was glad then that we had gone to the lengths we had before. We had both acknowledged the rarity of such opportunity but had not truly realised the strength it would require between times.

Each stolen glance was one of shared sympathy. I thought I should go mad with agitation. To be thus torn asunder when we would become better acquainted was cruel torment. It was not only our bodies which craved one another, but we were even denied conversation.

I had not permitted myself to creep beyond the bedside curtain, not trusting myself not to act upon the growing urges which burned me to the core. Luke did not appear by my bed either and surely felt the same restraint. To not even hear his sweet whispers of comfort—oh, bitter despair. I would pour words of consolation into his ear, but it was beyond attempt.

In the mornings, we were together in the carrells, and I could not decide whether that was better or worse than being fully parted in the afternoons. The temptation to reach across and touch his hand, to cast heated looks, to whisper the short distance…it was all too much. But to not even have him within my sight caused almost physical pain. There was not sufficient liquorice tisane in the kingdom to quell my desire.

With great concentration, I stilled my shaking hands sufficiently to write a letter to my mother. I had been here for two months and was keen to inform her of my progress. And I believed it would be a form of distraction. Carefully, I told her of the friends I had made.

To omit Luke's name would have served only to draw more attention from the prior when he read my missive before sending it. Therefore, I mentioned him but no more than any other. I admitted we were a support to one another given our closeness in age and similar stages of our profession. Yet it felt like a lie and left a bitter taste in my mouth. I longed to tell her how I had met someone special and the joy I felt in his presence.

There was so much I could not include in that letter that I wondered whether it was worth sending at all by the time it reached its conclusion. However, I handed it to Brother Barnabas to pass along.

And then, at long last, the day of celebration drew near. The feast day of St Margaret of Antioch was closely observed. We were ordered to take a bath the day before.

Shaved, hair trimmed and combed, washed and in fresh clothing, I surely gleamed like a sovereign piece or akin to cloth of gold.

As hoped, we were dismissed for the afternoon. Bathing day was a delightful thing indeed. The monks made themselves scarce, and so Luke and I took ourselves to the dormitory. Alone. How my heart thundered, and my extremities tingled. I grew quite dizzy.

I harboured a longing which dared not be heard. It was for Luke to determine when he was ready. But how my pillicock throbbed at even the thought of today being that time. Would he wish to go further than before?

We sat upon my bed in silence, suddenly unsure of what to say or do. I traced his fingers with my own, our hands between us.

"Paul, I…"

When he could not find the words, I lay my lips upon his, requesting a kiss. Eagerly, our mouths met, our tongues becoming reacquainted. Like starving men given sustenance.

Bodily, we turned so we could get closer. Our hands grasped along cheeks, arms, hair, anywhere they could. Our kiss growing more impassioned all the while.

Groaning softly, Luke leaned his weight upon me, urging me to lie down. And who was I to argue? He writhed against me as we lapped. And still I wanted more. Needed to feel him.

"Dare we risk…?" I began.

Luke got up and removed his tunic, and I rid myself of my clothing, my hands clumsy in their haste. But I was rewarded with a naked Luke who once again laid atop me. Feeling his skin on mine was divine. Every curve and contour fit with mine.

The pulse in my pillicock throbbed to the point of spasm. "I beg his pardon."

Luke gave a toothy chuckle. "Only if you pardon mine also."

"Oh." So embarrassed was I by my own body that I had failed to notice his.

"I desire you to distraction."

"Luke, I…we are deliciously clean should you wish me to take you in my mouth." I was fuzzled by desire, yet also emboldened.

"Then all would be over. Paul, I would…what you said before. I would be inside of you if you would have me."

"You do not have to. It is not a foregone conclusion. That was said in jest. Mayhap we should discuss the implications first. I would not risk your soul. I am aware you have not yet fully done the deed."

"Paul, it is opportunity, not want or courage which has been lacking with us. Besides, you take the greater part of the sin. But I cannot risk so long a wait again. I say again, if you will have me, I would be with you fully. I am more certain of this than anything hitherto in my life."

"Then enter me without any further delay."

"I do not know how." His voice was so quiet, so unsure, so unlike my Luke that I held him to me.

"Then leave it to me," I whispered in his ear, making him shudder.

He nodded.

"Lie on your back."

He squinted but moved. I reached into my wallet and retrieved some linen strips and the vial of oil. This was happening. I was fairly certain we would not be discovered, but the possibility made me desperate. I was driven to act more decisively, faster, and yet with trepidation.

My hands shook as I unstoppered the bottle. But one look in those lust-filled blue eyes and all but Luke was forgotten. I poured oil into my hand and rubbed it along his stiff part. He drew out a long, "Mmm…!"

"You like how that feels?"

"So slick and soft." His eyes had closed.

"Mhm." I rubbed up and down a few more times.

When my hand withdrew, his gaze returned to me. Attentively, he watched as I poured out more oil and reached around to apply it to my rear.

"Might I help?" he asked.

I anointed his fingers with oil. "Take just one finger and insert it."

"In…?"

I nodded.

He was so careful. And far too slow. I was eager for more yet kept to his pace. "Augh!"

"Did I hurt you?" he asked, removing his finger.

"Prythee, return your finger and add another."

He chortled. "As you wish."

"So good." He did not move, so I rode his fingers by my own effort.

"Ah." Taking the suggestion, he slid his fingers in and out at last.

"How I need you."

I slipped off and took his pillicock in my hand. Adjusting my position, I held it at my entrance and looked into his eyes. "Are you ready?"

"If you are."

Slowly, I lowered myself upon him, each of us making small grunts with every inch.

"Paul. I'm in, oh my, oh…" His hips began to thrust, seemingly of their own accord.

I raised up and down on my haunches to further the movement. Covering my mouth with one hand, I stifled a cry.

"I am not hurting you?"

"No, Luke…aurgh…you supply only…pleasure." I took myself in hand, relieving the need for touch.

"Oh…good…oooohhhh."

His actions increased in vigour, and how delightful were his thrusts as he spilled his seed inside me. So much so that my muscles pulled taught before unleashing me into bliss.

"Oh, sweet mercy." White light burst behind my closed eyes, eradicating any and all trace of darkness.

Reaching for a piece of linen, I wiped my seed from Luke's belly. As soon as I had, he beckoned me to lower down. I lay there in his arms, held safely in his warm embrace.

"You showed me Heaven, I think," he told me, kissing my neck.

"Likewise."

"That was so much more than I had anticipated."

"But good?"

I felt his grin. "Nothing but the best."

"I must tell you that...Luke, you make me feel things in a way that I never have before. You truly are incredible."

We quickly got dressed lest anyone should come in. But we returned to laying together, kissing and nuzzling for as long as we dared, fully immersed in one another. In our own world. I had never before known such happiness.

We celebrated our saint in Mass and held the offices. Truly, I did praise her. Yet there was another reason to rejoice that St Margaret's Day. Luke and I had been properly united, and I was complete. Our bond was firmly fixed, and my future seemed nothing but joyous. Sincerely, I offered thanks that day.

Retreating to our favoured cemetery garden once released from the company of others, Luke and I lay on the grass, smiling at one another. I ran my hand through his hair, needing the reassurance of touch to free myself of any notion that yesterday had been but a dream.

"I would always see you smile thus," Luke commented.

"The monks would soon chastise me for it, I fear."

"They should learn to embrace happiness more."

I laughed. "That may not be quite the purpose of this life."

"And why should devotion be austere, pray?"

Still laughing, I shrugged. "I know not, in truth. Quiet reverence is but the way it has always been carried out."

"But I would sing out of the joy He brings, how my spirits are lifted by his presence."

Running a finger along his cheek, I told him, "You raise my spirits. You bring me joy."

"As do you. But I was speaking of the Lord."

Squeezing my lips, I attempted to subdue my glee. "I beg pardon."

"I see there is no serious conversation to be had with you this day. Very well, let us discuss more frivolous matters."

"You see the way of it. When happiness fills us thus, it is impossible to remain focused on the serious. And make no mistake, God is serious."

He tickled me, making me laugh until my eyes watered.

"I relent. I repent."

"Your penance shall be ten kisses," he said, peppering me with such.

"If that is the punishment, I must sin more."

"I would commit sin every day for you."

"For me or with me?"

He shrugged. "Does it matter?"

"I prefer with."

His lips lingered over mine, a breath away. "Do you indeed?"

"Mmmhm..." I muttered, accepting his invitation.

A sweet, slow meeting of mouths ensued. My eyes closed as I savoured his delights.

He pulled away, but his eyes sparkled. "Mayhap it is for the good of our souls we must appear chaste most of the time. We would surely do naught else but carnal activity if we had not the religious presence here."

"Aye. Here we may pray in between our moments of weakness."

"I am not so certain you are weak. You are surprisingly strong, my sweeting."

To prove him correct, I twisted and rolled so he was underneath me and returned his tickles. "Underestimate me at your peril."

"I concede. Did I not declare you strong?" he said around laughter.

"You did." I laid my head down upon his shoulder, still once more.

He held me to him, and thus we remained in happy contentment.

It was a busy week of celebration. On the twenty-second day of July, we revered St Mary Magdalene. And three days later, St James was honoured. The fact that each saint's day saw us feast in the misericord certainly had no bearing on our devout observations of every single one.

Luke and I took full advantage of our free time together on each occasion. We had pledged to make the most of what we had, after all. But the days in between were made all the harder, for my hands longed to reach out to him all the more with each passing day. Rain showers only added to those dreary times.

The first day of August heralded the first wheat harvest, which was celebrated with Lammas. Largely, such celebrations were for those other than ourselves as we concentrated on *Sancti Petri ad Vincula*—St Peter at the Chains. However, I did very much enjoy the rastons served alongside a dish of meat in the misericord; nothing could make my mouth water like the promise of that rich, buttery, sweet bread. Well, not that I could admit aloud.

In church, we had first intoned, *"Now Christ God, the Rock, doth glorify the rock of faith, illustriously, in calling all to celebrate the dread wonders of the most honorable Chains of Peter, the first and chief of the disciples of Christ our God, Who granteth forgiveness of sins unto all."* And surely, partaking in such rich indulgences was sinful, but forgiven that day.

And I hoped that my continued deeds with Luke were also forgiven anew. Whenever chance presented I conceded. There was no restraint forceful enough to stand in our way, not even the threat of fiery pits could prevent our union. For, without Luke, I would have been thrown into pits of despair. And did I not suffer sufficiently in the intervening periods?

Stealing away, we secreted ourselves in the herbarium, having obtained the key from the infirmarer, and locking the door behind us. Amidst the heady, earthy scents, we kissed and embraced with great fervour.

Kneeling at the feet of my lover as if at an altar, I made the sign of the cross before raising his tunic, licking my lips. "*Benedic, Domine, nos et haec tua dona quae de tua largitate sumus sumpturi, per Christum Dominum nostrum. Amen,*" I chanted the *Benedic, Domine* (Bless us, O Lord, and these Thy gifts which we are about to receive from Thy bounty, through Christ, Our Lord. Amen).

"Paul! You go too far in your blasphemy."

"Nay, for verily I am indeed about to eat. I shall consume everything you are about to impart."

He scowled but the twitch before my eyes showed he was eager for me to carry out my promise. And I wasted no time in so doing. My tongue laved his tip, causing him to groan and shudder. The blood crashed through my ears like waves of the sea and pooled at my groin where it simmered.

Tantalisingly I pressed my tongue into his crevice. His hand gripped into my hair. Glancing up, I saw his tense jaw and pleading eyes. Unable to deny him, I lowered my mouth and sucked. Luke hissed his pleasure.

My head bobbed up and down as I rocked along his column, my cheeks hollowed. Back and forth I slid, revelling in his delight. Savouring this most delectable treat.

Needing to catch my breath, I pulled off and rested my cheek against him, my nose tickled by his nest of blond curls. The musky scent of him filled my nose as I breathed deep. He could have been impatient, but not my Luke; he stroked my hair whilst I recovered.

The air was thick with the mixed aroma of our lust as well as the herbs. Thus spurred on, I took up where I'd left off. The satisfied hum which escaped me travelled through him and came out as a groan from his lips. The first drops of liquid dripped into my mouth which were greedily swallowed.

With more urgency, I applied myself, giving all I could to his desire. I was at his mercy and he mine. My hand worked him in unison with my mouth. Up and down, back and forth.

Luke gripped onto the table behind him as his body went rigid. His hips bucked as he pumped into my grateful orifice. As promised, I consumed every surge, gulping as fast as possible.

Only once he stilled, did I release him. His smiling face shone down at me with its warmth. Christ may be the Light, but Luke was my sun. Without him, I was cold and dark. A tear ran down my face which he caught with a finger.

Squatting down, he cupped my cheek in his palm. "This is not sadness?" he whispered.

"Far from it."

Tenderly, he kissed along the path my tear had taken. "Good."

With his kisses growing in strength, I found myself coaxed fully onto the floor on my back. Loosening the ties, he pulled my braies and hose down just far enough to spring me free.

"My sweet honey needs to expel too." It was a statement, not a question.

I hummed as his gentle lips found their mark. There was care in every stroke he bestowed. He was not rushed. Slowly, he fondled and drew. I surrendered wholly to his whim. And when my release came, it brought calm like no other. It was as though I had been dipped in a font. I wept again as I was cleansed from within.

Luke held me to him as he lowered himself next to me. He kissed my forehead and rubbed my chest.

"I beg your pardon," I croaked.

"There is nothing to forgive, sweeting."

There were no words to describe what was transpiring. Relief, a sense of renewal, gladness, calm, ecstasy, being found; I felt them all mix and whirl. Luke held me safe until my deep sighs subsided.

"Thank you," I told him quietly.

"My thanks to you also."

"Luke, is this what love feels like?"

"I think it must be."

"Then, I love you, Luke."

"I love you too, my Paul."

"My lief."

Wrapped in our secret love and comfort, we remained a little longer. But, sensible of our circumstances, it was not as long as we would have wished. We righted ourselves, brushing off dirt and dust from one another.

With a smirk, Luke asked, "But what is this? No *Agimus Tibi Gratias*?"

I gave him a wry smile. "You seemed to consider the *Benedic, Domine* before a sacrilege. I did not wish to cause further insult by issuing the after-meal prayer."

"But I am thankful." Raising my chin with a finger, he met his lips to mine.

"My eternal gratitude."

Chapter 12 - I Will Pay Thee My Vows

Weeks passed. And, as attending the offices and working had become habitual, so too did our lovemaking. Luke and I joined together whenever we could, determined not to lose a single moment; all forming part of the order of our lives. And each time I worried a little less. The fear of detection waned as my desire grew. Luke was part of my life, and I could not be sorry for it.

Ergo, the feasts of St Lawrence and the Assumption of the Virgin Mary were celebrated. Work, pray, love; August rolled along. How little did we suspect the world outside was preparing for change. But change happens whether we are prepared for or even aware of it or not.

The approach of my final days as a postulant was signalled by the arrival of my parents. I went to the guest house when so summonsed. My mother wept as she held me in her arms. I managed with Almighty strength to maintain my composure.

"Oh, my boy, my boy. How I have missed you," she cried.

"And I you. But it has not been so very long. Calm yourself, my dear mother."

She patted all about my face and body. "And you have been well looked after? You seem a little fuller of figure than you were. Good. I do not believe that school was as diligent as it should have been, you know. But here you stand, a young man in good health, just as your letter said."

My father intervened. "You are become carried away, woman. Do not forget yourself. Take comfort that the boy is well and have done with it."

However, his own emotion necessitated a clearing of his throat before he could address me. "And you do look well, lad." He slapped my shoulder.

"Aye. My body and soul are fed well enough," I confirmed.

"You hear that, Husband? Body and soul. He is become monkish already. So, you mean to remain here, my darling boy?" my mother questioned.

"Now, now, we are not to come about it with such directness. Let us discuss this rationally and calmly over the meal which the good brother here has provided," my father reminded her.

Brother Faramond was standing by, trying to hide his smile. Gesturing with his hand to the laid table, he said, "You are most welcome."

It was wicked of me, but every time *Benedic, Domine* was said now, I had to bite back a smile. Luke was right in his scold; it had been sacrilegious. I had intended it half in jest and half in sincerity. But ever after it caused unbidden carnal thoughts. Such was my punishment.

However, having prayed, we took our place. The priory made a great show of offering humble fayre. There was no meat present. However, what we did have was well-sauced. Tasty but simple. Just as we should be used to, of course. My mother's notice of my expansion was an embarrassment, but one brushed over by all present.

With us, sat Brother Barnabas. "Your son has shown great promise and is a credit to you both," he told my parents.

"I'm glad to hear it," my father answered.

We were all quiet for a while. The monks and I were not used to conversing over food, and it was awkward to do so now, especially over so delicate a matter. So, we maintained silence until the meal was over. And yet, words still did not seem forthcoming.

"Paul has indicated his will to become a novice," Brother Barnabas tried.

"Aye. Mayhap you would be good enough to leave us with him alone awhile? I mean no disparagement or insinuation. But some matters are perhaps best kept private."

"I understand," Brother Barnabas said, getting up with Brother Faramond, "We shall wait outside in readiness to call upon the prior when you are ready."

The air became thick, and I could scarce draw breath.

"Paul. My son. You have always been aware of my oath to God. And have been brought up accordingly. Mayhap I have been too strong in my assertion. However, I would not go against my word. It has been kept. But now the choice must be yours and yours alone. Once you take this next step there is no going back. At least, not with any ease. Are you truly prepared to live out your days thus?"

I could not look at him for fear my eagerness would show. For surely, Luke was as much an enticement as the peaceful way of life I had found here. To spend my life in devoted prayer, useful work and in love – it was more than I had ever dreamed of.

Gripping the edge of my seat, my head bowed, I simply said, "I am."

My mother gasped. "Paul. You are certain? It is a solemn vow you are about to profess. Do not make it if you have any hesitation. You can take more time if needs be. Or come home with us now. I would so love to have you with me again. We can find some other profession for you. As your father said, his pledge is now considered fulfilled. He has led you here. Do not do something which later you may regret."

I swallowed hard. Her desperate plea did not leave me unmoved. I am not sure it had ever occurred to me that I would have a choice at this moment. But here it was, both my father and mother making plain that this was my decision to make.

I sat there, the heat of their gaze piercing through me like a knife. Biting my lip, I considered what may yet be. Here I sat with my family, yet beyond the walls of the guest house, my new family awaited me in the monastic precinct. At times, they had been harsh but only when they needed to be. Most of the time, I was supported.

Brother Giles came into my mind, his fatherly smile and encouragement glowing as brightly as a candle. Brother Barnabas with his gruff guidance. Prior Ambrose's kind yet assessing observations. And, of course, the bright eyes and strong arms of my Luke.

No, I had no choice. In that brief moment of consideration, I saw the love I had here. And knew I would never find its like anywhere else. Not even my excellent mother could provide such peaceful, delicate devotion. I was home. And God had welcomed me in, knowing my truth. I would not deny Him.

Hours could have passed in those few breaths. But finally, I looked up at the expectant faces of my parents and told them, "I will become a novice."

My mother rushed to hold me. And at last, I could hold back no longer; tears fell in rivulets down my cheeks as she sobbed in my arms. Her sadness was mine. Never again would I set foot on my family's land. Their houses were no longer my home.

I was losing them in order to gain guaranteed salvation. That did not come without a cost. I would miss them all. And it struck me that it was their souls I should now be concerned for, for they were out in the world with all its evils whilst I dwelt in safety.

But His will must be done. And the larger part of me was happy to do it.

After my parents and I had bid farewell, Prior Ambrose came to speak with them. Whilst I was led to the prior's room to await him. Brother Barnabas accompanied me, and his presence was most appreciated.

"It is a daunting time, no matter how much we have deliberated upon it. The decision which once seemed easy becomes enlarged as our heart weighs heavy," he told me.

I nodded. "Aye. I was so sure. I still am. And yet my heart is breaking at the loss of my parents."

"It is hard to have to separate the two lives. But these times come to us all. And it is done with purpose. For we cannot be fully present if we cling to the past. We relinquish all we once had and once were so we may be born anew to God."

"I know. I had not expected it to feel this way, is all."

"It is why the postulancy lasts so long. And the novitiate yet lies in wait for further consideration. You must find your own answer through time and prayer. To ensure your will is truly to seek God. It is not to be got about easily. You have endured much to reach this place. Your spirits have been tested, but you have not been found wanting. For all it is worth, my severity was a necessity. But from hereon in, you shall find it less so. I am not of a tender nature, but even I am not so morose as I must surely have appeared to you."

I smiled wryly. "This too I know. And understand."

His smirk was akin to the light of Heaven; the first I had managed to glean from him. "Clearly, I have not schooled my features as successfully as I had imagined."

"Aw, Brother Barnabas, it took me a good long while to realise it. Have no fear. You have held menace enough."

"Have a care, Paul. It is not entirely to be forsaken now."

"I should be sorry if it were. Forgive my freedom of speech."

"Just this once, I shall allow it. For I welcomed your outpouring with my soft words. It is a day to discuss matters freely. And as such, I will permit myself to express that I am in, fact, mightily proud of you. You have been a diligent student, as I pray you will continue to be."

I nodded. "Indeed. I wholly intend to continue as I have started."

"Then allow us now to await Prior Ambrose in quiet contemplation. There is time yet to rid yourself of all doubt."

I know not how long we waited. My thoughts tumbled and fell until at last they were caught up on angel's wings and soared. Again, I was struck by how I came to be here. Surely God knew who I was and welcomed me even so. Luke and I were both brought here. If it was not His will then I did not know what was. So easily we could never have met. But we did, and I felt comfort and joy.

Prior Ambrose entered and bid Brother Barnabas to conduct the reading of The Rule. I listened intently. Wholeheartedly, I agreed to devote myself to God; He cared not if Luke eased the way, made me happy whilst I prayed my life to Him.

The prior checked, "Paul, you cannot cast off from your neck the yoke of The Rule. You shall be accepted into the community as a novice. You shall be expected here to remain within these walls. I ask once more only, do you accept what is laid before you?"

"I do."

"Then God bid you welcome. We shall conduct the official clothing ceremony the day after tomorrow. It would not be appropriate to do so on the day of St Bartholomew. But from this moment, you are to be regarded as a novice."

I beamed. "Thank you, Prior Ambrose."

"You have earned your place. You may go with God."

†††

We learned of the demise of King Richard III on the battlefield of Bosworth, and the proclamation of King Henry VII in that same place. We were all of us astonished. And it was as though the monastery itself took a breath of composure.

And so it was that on the day I became a novice that the bells rang out in a full peal. I was under no delusion that they rang for me. They were, of course, heralding the end and beginning of kings. But I would make a liar of myself if I feigned not to feel a degree of grandeur on that auspicious day.

Having already delayed because of St Batholomew's Day, Prior Ambrose was anxious not to prolong the wait any further, especially as the Bishop of Rochester had arrived himself to conduct the ceremony. I had made my personal proclamation, but I still needed to swear my oath to the brethren.

Standing in my own, colourful clothing for the final time, I gazed about the oratory. My knees felt weak, and my hands trembled as I clutched onto the petition I had written. It is with little wonder then that I felt myself elevated, thus presented amongst such company.

The monks were all gathered and looked on, all eyes upon me. The bishop conducted a sermon then intoned Psalm 33. At which point, I approached on wobbly legs and solemnly declared my intention. All then chanted the *Veni, Creator Spiritus*, an invocation of the Holy Spirit.

The solemnity gripped me tightly. There was no mistaking the seriousness of my declaration. My hands shook even more until I feared I would drop the parchment clutched within them. But I managed to lay it upon the altar and sign it in the presence of the bishop.

Three times, I chanted, "*Suscipe me Domine secundum eloquium tuum et vivam, et non confundas me in expectatione mea!*" (Uphold me, Lord, according to your word, and do not disappoint me in my hope.) [Psalm 119:116]

All about me repeated the same, adding a "*Gloria Patri.*" (Glory Be to the Father).

Prior Ambrose stepped forward and helped relieve me of my secular clothing. I would certainly have struggled to do so alone; my hands seemed not my own. The black tunic, black scapula and black hooded cloak befitting a novice were all placed upon me with the full weight of the occasion bearing down upon my shoulders. I then laid myself prostrate at the feet of each of the brethren, ending with the bishop, receiving their prayers.

"From this day forwards, Paul is accepted as a worthy novice member of the community here at Darenth Priory," the bishop announced.

And thus, I entered my novitiate.

Chapter 13 – First Fruits

Luke came to me my first night as a novice, once the others were asleep. This took some considerable time for the dormitory grew almost crowded. The bishop's presence seemed to press the brethren into strict adherence of The Rule in every way.

Without a word, Luke crept onto my bed and held me. I melted against him, safe in his arms. Quiet kisses were left upon my head. He must have known how much I needed his reassurance in the dark of night. There was little doubt I had made the right decision, yet still, he was a comforting reminder of the wisdom of my choice.

I fell asleep in his arms, but he must have got to his own bed safely as I woke up alone. And saw him emerge beyond the partition for matins with no glares or recriminations.

The bishop decided to remain several days with us, much to everyone's vexation. He cast his penetrating scrutiny over all. Everyone went about their daily business with their head bowed down and shoulders hunched. And ate drearily. It irked all the more for we each suspected a great hypocrisy in his severity, owing only in part to his not being a reedy man.

Despite his looming presence, it was a joyous time for me as doors were now opened where once they had been closed. So long as I was accompanied, I was permitted to travel throughout the cloister – such a beautiful area. The squared, green garth was surrounded by covered, columned walkways, holding its own serenity. There stood in the centre a fine open-arse fruit tree, the jewels of which would surely be enjoyed in December. One day, I would sit as the other monks to read or meditate.

As a serving member of the community, I was now also admitted into the presence of my brothers. I took my place next to Luke in the back row of the quire as we extolled the offices, my voice rapturously joining his in praise.

And no longer did I partake of solitary meals. I dined alongside all the brethren, listening to the daily reading as we silently ate.

I was the beneficiary of many a kind look, smile and even pat on the shoulder as all welcomed me truly as one of them, albeit as a novice. No two men were alike, but none showed any hostility, only acceptance. I had heard of rivalries in such houses, but I was yet to witness that here.

No matter whether it was with the fretting refectorian, Ulric, or the mild almoner, Cuthbert, I was delighted to be in the company of my brethren. To see their various faces, to stand or sit side-by-side filled me with a sense of belonging. It was a peaceful sort of joy, warming me from within. Mayhap made all the greater for my long period of separation.

Still, it was a pleasant relief when the bishop departed without having found anything serious to complain about. I was all the more grateful for the pliable nature of our beloved Prior Ambrose—truly a man of good sense. He looked over us all, ensuring we behaved as we ought yet with a friendly outlook. Any leniency was to encourage happiness in obedience; far more effective than harsh punishments, not that we were without those entirely. Firm but fair.

It was the day after we venerated the Beheading of St John the Baptist when we regained our selfdom. The bishop had thought it wise to ensure that day was duly celebrated without exuberance before leaving.

As we sat for our dinner, the reader spoke. "Before I begin this reading, Prior Ambrose wishes to convey our warm welcome to our novice, Paul, and bids you all enjoy your pittances in celebration."

I blushed wildly as the monks brought their hands together as if in applause, but without making a sound. I bowed my head, bringing my hands into prayer. The pittance turned out to be *chireseye;* a delectable cherry bread pudding, which seemed to be much enjoyed.

The monks surely wanted to have a day spent in frivolity after being kept in such close confines, as Luke and I were given the afternoon off as if it were a saint's day. Thus, we carried ourselves off to the cemetery garden.

The early apples were now in fruit whilst others were still growing. Golden sunlight beamed through the laden branches yet was not full warm; there hung a slight chill in the air.

"Arrrrh, it is good to be out of doors and away from prying eyes," Luke cried as he dropped to the ground, running his hand through the grass.

"I never knew a summer could feel so drear."

"However, a few days does not a summer make."

"Nay, you have the right of it. It has seemed an eternity, but I should not dismiss an entire season for the sake of a few days. I misspoke."

He laughed. "Always so in earnest, Paul. I did not mean to chastise."

"I should have grown accustomed to your ribaldry by now."

He tickled me. "Ribaldry is it now? I shall show you bawdy speech."

He opened his mouth, surely with a run of coarse expressions upon his tongue. But I interrupted with a kick of my hips as he had rolled on top of me in his continued tickling. "I should rather you show me bawdy behaviour."

That halted both his hands and words. As his eyelids half-closed, he emitted a sort of growl, and he ground himself against me. "I am more than happy to show you."

So sorely I was tempted to continue what I had begun. But for once, good sense prevailed. "Alack. My lief, we are out in the open, and surely with fruit to be gathered, it would be unwise to carry on any further in this manner here. Not that I don't long for it."

Dipping his forehead to mine, he breathed out a sigh. "You are infuriatingly correct."

With a chaste kiss, he rolled off of me and onto his back and covered his eyes with his arm. "Will this torment never end?"

"Aye." I was on my side, looking at him.

He peeked at me. "You grin like a fool."

A frown descended. "Your tongue has a nasty way of pronouncing caustic words for someone who professes love."

Turning, he reached his hand to rub my cheek. "Please accept my apologies. I would never choose to hurt you. I am greatly frustrated, but that does not excuse my being spleenful towards you. Truly, I am sorry for it."

I kissed the tip of his nose to chase away the duly-earned remorse. "I accept. I was going to remind you of Brother Giles' words of wisdom."

He collapsed back down and gazed up at the sky. "Tell me again of how one day we shall share a bed, Paul. How we will sleep an entire night side-by-side unhindered. That we will be able to touch, kiss and sard all we desire."

I chuckled. "That rang out beautifully until you turned bawdy again."

"You are insulted?"

"Nay. In truth, I share your discomfort and impatience. You know I do. Albeit in different wording. Some feelings are too great to be contained and may only be expressed bodily. You have shown me this."

"And I will show you again."

I chuckled more. "You play the comforter now? You offer me reassurance? Was I not supposed to be doing so for you?"

His blue eyes sparkled in the sunlight. "You did." Reaching out his hand to mine, he squeezed.

We lay there side-by-side, surely both dreaming of that golden future when the sounds of another approaching crashed into our joy. We stole our hands away as if stung by one of the hovering bees.

"What do you two mean by laying about here?" Brother Maynard, the kitchener bellowed.

Luke sat up. "We were meditating upon yesterday's lesson."

The monk laughed. "And who am I to question the sincerity of that? Oh, but you should see the look upon your faces."

Also sitting up, I glared at him. "Brother Maynard, I had not thought you cruel."

"Oh, come now. I meant no harm by it. You have as much right to rest as anyone else here. And I must say, you have chosen a fine spot to do so. I always enjoy the peace of this garden. Hence my volunteering to come and harvest apples for the table." He winked.

"You astonish me, Brother."

"These things have I spoken unto you, that my joy might remain in you, and that your joy might be full." [John 15:11]

We both smiled, but it was Luke who spoke. "How very apt that you quote a verse about fruit branches."

He ambled towards us, his green eyes crinkling with mirth. A man of middling years, with no grey in his dark brown hair. He had before struck me as cheerful, but I had not previously been exposed to his jesting. It struck me that he may rival Luke in that area, but not in my heart.

Crouching down, looking most serious, he whispered, "And you think I had not chosen those words on purpose, mayhap?"

We both laughed at his theatrics.

"Come, Brother Maynard, join us a while. It would seem we are all three in the mood to talk nonsense," I offered.

Settling down beside me, he assented, "It is not often I indulge myself, but let this be one such occasion, for it is a fine day and my spirits are high."

Lowering my voice, I noted, "Mayhap in consequence of a certain visitor's departure?"

He made a show of gasping and covering his mouth. "Surely you would not be speaking of an esteemed personage who only honours us with his presence?"

"Nay, I would ne'er suggest such a wicked thing."

He chortled. "Oh, dear. But he was especially onerous this visit, was he not?"

Luke flickered his eyelashes. "I know not of whom you speak."

Getting up, he paraded around, looking grim. Then, deepening his voice, declared, "You there, you are not praying hard enough. I see no tears. How is God to know the extent of your love for him if you do not show it?"

We all three laughed.

"He never said such a thing," I said, wiping away tears of laughter.

Sitting back down, Luke admitted, "Perhaps not. But I would not put it past him."

"Oh, why must he be so severe in his duty? Nobody can take him in earnest," Brother Maynard wondered aloud.

"The question is surely more how did he rise to his position?" I asked.

"Ah, in this, I have a little knowledge. But it is not exciting. Suffice to say he was formerly a man of sense, but the power has gone to his head."

"That is indeed saddening to learn."

"I hear they had to enlarge his cowl," the monk said in an exaggerated whisper.

"They did no such thing. Can you imagine?"

"Nay, but at least we are all smiling again."

"Come, let us find merriment in more humble things. Brother, you are gathering apples. Are they for tomorrow's dinner?"

"Ah, that is for me to know. Speaking of which, I had best return to my duties. But thank you for the respite."

"I hope to have it repeated."

He smiled broadly. "Aye, I should like that. God be with you."

I looked across to Brother Maynard in the refectory the next day and beamed at him as I ate a slice of delectable apple and blackberry pie. He tipped his head in acknowledgement, a faint smile upon his lips.

Of course, normality resumed. We worked and prayed diligently. And Luke was once more out of my reach. But I was glad the infirmary had grown quieter, at least.

Settling down on a cot and waiting for me to sit by his side, Brother Giles bid, "Pray, tell me, now we are finally alone, how fare my young friends?"

Bowing my head, I had to admit, "We grow impatient, I fear to say, Brother."

"I thought as much. Ah, but it is a sorry situation. And not all feelings may be drunk away with root of liquorice. Alas, we must bear what we can with as much dignity as we may muster."

"You have found me lacking?"

"Nay, I do not say so. If you must hear it, I admire your fortitude. You have nothing but my sympathy and support, Paul. I remember the fervour of young love. With this in mind, I would bring to your attention that this Saturday shall be a bathing day, what with the Nativity of the Virgin Mary approaching, as well as The Exaltation of the Holy Cross. Now you are a novice, you will be expected to join us in the cloister for a haircut first," he said, ruffling my hair.

"I shall be grateful for that. But they shall not cut a tonsure?"

He laughed. "You are not a full monk yet, have no fear."

I nudged his shoulder with mine. "I am in full knowledge of that fact. I simply wanted to brighten the conversation."

"You succeeded. Oh, dear me. What a scandal that would cause. But I am easily distracted. No, after you are made presentable, you shall have some free time, I think." He winked.

"Ooohhh!"

"You see how I too can bring joy, despite these creaking bones?"

"Oh, fie. You are not so very decrepit. Come, let us pound you some radish, bishopwort, garlic, wormwood, helenium, cropleek and hollowleek."

He chortled. "Aye, and boil them in butter with celandine and red nettle, I suppose."

I smirked. "We must ensure we keep you in good health. You are highly valued by us all."

"This is how you show your gratitude, is it, you wastrel? You mock your elders in thanks?"

At first, he appeared earnest in his injury, but he laughed when I began an apology.

"So young! Have you not learned as yet when I am in earnest and when in jest? I have certainly learned the difference in you. And I am not so readily offended."

"It seems to be a matter I struggle with. Luke has remarked upon it also," I confessed, my humour fallen.

His response came with an arm about my shoulders. "Come away with you. We shall indeed make some ointment whilst discussing this further. But have patience with yourself. As I frequently remind you, you are still young. There is much to learn, but you are fortunate in the time afore you in which to do so."

There was already a brass pot which contained the reddening mixture I had referred to, of course. Aching heads and joints were a frequent complaint, so we began preparations for the next batch. Just not necessarily for Brother Giles' benefit.

Whether it was the rhythmic motions of our work, the smell of the herbs, Giles' gentle voice or his wise counsel, I could not determine, but by the end of the afternoon, calm was once more restored.

My mind was often disturbed by continual thoughts which refused to cease. Luke, Giles and even Barnabas were correct in their notice of my thinking too much. But only Brother Giles seemed able to help quell those unbidden demons. Mayhap Luke could also, but more by chasing them off by filling me entirely with lust instead.

As September began, Brother Giles was, of course, proven correct. Each of the monks who could escape their duties convened in the cloister after nones. To the layperson, I am sure the noise was not so very loud. But to myself, who had grown accustomed to the quietude, it was quite a commotion.

We lined up amidst much jostling to either to use the whetstone to sharpen our knives or for the attentions of Brother Godfrey, usually our sacrist, but today the haircutter. Nobody wanted the cooled water or his blade once blunted, it seemed. I was merely gratified to note from my place in the queue that the brother's hand was steady.

Ever since that first day when Luke shaved me, we had continued to shave one another's face. Our excuse was that it was safer. But the truth which lay behind that reason was that it afforded us some little contact and we could glance into one another's eyes. The intimacy always sent thrills throughout me.

So, the thought of anyone else now touching me in a familiar fashion felt almost a betrayal. Standing behind me, Luke squeezed my hand briefly. "Look not so worried. I trust Brother Godfrey. I have seen no blood yet."

Looking over my shoulder, I mouthed, "He is not you."

His breath warmed and tickled my neck as Luke leaned in to whisper, "Nor does he pretend to be."

I took comfort in Luke's presence. He remained close behind me until I took my seat.

"Now, let us see what we can do with this," Brother Godfrey said softly, running his fingers through my hair. The action failed to have the same effect as Luke's touch, and I at last took a full, deep breath.

"You shall not take a bowl to my head?"

He chuckled. "Nay. I think we may permit our novices some little vanity yet, eh? It would seem a pity to be too severe with these lustrous locks."

"You think them fine?"

"Aye, as fine a head of hair as ever I saw."

Luke was snickering. "I do believe Brother Godfrey permitted only a little vanity, Paul."

I bit my lip. "I beg pardon. Only, nobody has admired my hair before. It is rather brown and dull."

The monk pointed to his head. "There is nothing wrong with brown hair, I would thank you to remember. Now, what shall we do? Shall I keep it just below your ears, and shorter at the front, just above your brows? That should be neat enough."

I smiled. "If you think that best."

He chuckled again. "Aye, a little vanity indeed. It shall become you very well. You have already surrendered your fine clothes. Let us do this in stages."

"You noticed my clothes?"

His scissors began their task. "I do have eyes. You have been seen walking about on occasion. And when all else here are in the same attire, differences are more noticeable. I mean it not as criticism. I too used to find pleasure in colourful garments."

"You should have seen what I wore before I came here."

"I think I would have liked that and can only imagine. But even when we adopt our habit and receive the tonsure, there are small ways in which we can remain individuals."

"My gratitude."

He remained silent as he continued his work.

"There now. Spick and span new. Or shall be once you have taken your bath. Get along now," Brother Godfrey announced, having finished.

I risked a glance at Luke who smiled and nodded on his way to take his turn. My feet hesitated. I longed to watch as his blond mop was tamed. Brother Godrfey's kind allowances eased my mind that Luke would not be shorn too close. My fingers would be left with something to run through.

However, my destination was not yet the bathing house. It only struck me as odd that Brother Godfrey should know the details of my horarium once I was waiting for the whetstone. Smiling, I wondered whether he was one of those who took their bath late to accommodate the visit of the ladies. That would explain his exceptionally good cheer. Or mayhap he simply enjoyed cutting hair.

"Far more dapper." The sudden voice from behind made me physically jump, which encouraged laughter.

"My apologies, Paul. I had thought you heard my approach."

Turning, I saw it was Brother Maynard. "You startled me. Greetings, Brother."

"So, I see. I shall not ask where your thoughts had taken you, they were clearly far from here."

"Indeed. How fare you, Brother?"

"I have no cause for complaint. I might even confess to being happy this day."

"That is good to hear." I kept to myself my suspicion of his reasons, being of the same nature as the ones I'd just been contemplating.

"And yourself?"

"Mayhap a little lighter for being relieved of some hair."

"Oh, he did not take so very much."

I chuckled, running my hand down the ends of my hair. "No, not so very much."

"He is a good man. Brother Godfrey always takes care in his work."

"It is much appreciated."

Luke approached and I had to stop myself from running to him. My fingers twitched, wanting to test the new length of his hair. He too had been neatened but not severely so.

"You look fine," I managed to say.

"As do you."

"Two dapper young men. Who would have thought to see the like in a monastery?" Brother Maynard added.

"Who, indeed," I said.

Luke helped to steer the conversation into less dangerous territory as we shuffled down the line. It didn't take too long to reach the front. Taking my knife from my belt cord, I ran it back and forth along the whetstone, occasionally adding a little water.

The scraping noise had been setting my teeth on edge all the while I queued, but now it shivered up my arms too. Gritting my teeth, I persisted until my blade was sharp. Fortunately, it did not take very long.

I stepped aside but lingered.

"Oh, but of course," Brother Maynard said, guiding Luke to take his turn.

"That is very kind. Thank you, Brother."

"Novices follow the same times, do they not?"

"And someone must ensure Luke takes his bath," I said.

"I need no coercion, thank you. I am all too glad to be cleansed of filth."

So hard did I bite my tongue, I feared blood should spring forth.

"Aye, the dust and dirt gather alarmingly swiftly even here," Brother Maynard acknowledged, seeming oblivious.

With both our knives sharpened and back in place, we bid our companion farewell and walked to the bathing house together. Once the ringing in my ears subsided, I was ready for conversation once more.

"You wish to be made pure, do you?" I enquired, nudging Luke's shoulder with mine.

Bringing his hands together, he grinned. "Of course, as does every monk."

"So pure and innocent."

"Indubitably." He fluttered his eyelashes.

Alas, we were still as yet too much in plain sight for me to kiss him.

"There you both are. You took your sweet time, but at least you look less the ragamuffins. Come, tarry no longer lest the water get cold," Brother Barnabas groaned as we entered the bathing house.

"You are alone?" I asked.

"You are both novices and grown men. I am sure I can be trusted with you. Indeed, you could probably bathe quite alone, except for the care which is my duty forbids it."

"You are very good."

"Quickly now."

Unfastening my belt, I set it and my wallet down. My scapula and tunic were then lifted in one swift movement—far easier than my old clothing. Yes, the dreary black garments did have their advantages.

Sinking into the warm water, I sighed, letting the heat seep into my bones. Closing my eyes, I imagined better now what Luke looked like as he did the same. Knowing every ripple and sinew as well as I did, I pondered him relaxing and washing.

"Quick as you like," Brother Barnabas called, ever watchful for any overindulgence.

I soaped my body and shorter hair, knowing how much it would soon be appreciated by the man beyond the curtain. Dressing, I gave thanks that my tunic was full, and I thought sufficiently of bad things so as not to let my excitement show.

Luke and I emerged at about the same time.

"Much better. Off you go now. Mind you keep out of mischief until vespers."

Again, I held back my comment. But the temptation to ask what trouble we should find at vespers was strong. Not wanting to anger our novice master lest he change his mind and keep us close, I remained silent.

Not having fully dried, the air was cool against my damp thighs as it drifted upwards when we walked out of doors. I shivered, still unused to the sensation. It was an adjustment in progress, living in this world without braies or hose. To be thus exposed to drafts was…different. Whether it was pleasant or disagreeable was still being decided upon.

In the dormitory, I found myself smashed into the wall with the force of Luke's kiss, our hands soon roaming everywhere.

"I have missed you, and am in great need," Luke told me, his voice hoarse.

"Tell me what you need, my lief." Mouths trailed kisses between comments.

"You. I need to be inside you, one with you, feel your soul as my own."

"Claim me, Luke. Fill my body until there exists only you."

Staggering, we made it to his bed, discarding our tunics and ripping back the blanket. My eyes travelled along the sinews of his body but did not linger, for they focused on his proud pillicock. I licked my lips.

Shaking his head, he told me, "Nay, my sweeting. One taste from you and I shall be undone."

Grabbing the bottle of oil from my wallet, I applied it to him and to my aching hole. How I clenched with need. With a deep kiss, Luke coaxed me to lie upon my back.

Gazing into the icy fire of his eyes, I checked, "You think you can do it lying thus now?"

"With your guidance, I can do anything."

Drawing my legs up, I bared myself to him. "Then slowly enter in."

I aided in lining him up. Despite our urgency, Luke followed my instruction, and took his time, allowing me to adjust to his presence. Surely, he breached my first wall and slid in the rest of the way, my muscles sucking him onward. And oh, he pressed against my deepest part delightfully. My eyes rolled up as my head fell back.

"So good, Paul. Like that. Yes. Give yourself unto me."

My back arched, eager for more.

With great care, Luke drew outwards, but mercifully not entirely. He was naturally gifted, it seemed. And I gave thanks. My hands reached for him, and he returned, with a kiss.

"You are not hurt?" he asked.

"Prythee, continue," I gasped.

He glid out and in, continuing his slow movements until my fingers clutched his buttocks in desperation. "More!"

Seemingly gaining confidence from my urging, he gathered pace, each time grazing where I needed him most.

"Oh, my lief!"

Faster and harder he went until he was little more than a rutting bull. And how I rejoiced. I took myself in hand, desperate to contain the throbbing. No sooner did I do so when my body went rigid and soared into spasms, the vision behind my eyes as white as the copious seed spilling onto my belly.

Pounding, Luke found his own release almost immediately after, filling me to the brim. His cries were stifled by my dry hand. Once finished, I guided him out. Collapsing down onto me, he breathed heavily.

"God bless you, my sweet honey."

"I am already blessed. You are my life's greatest blessing," I murmured.

We held one another, nuzzling as much as our spent bodies were able. Inhaling, I bathed in his musky scent made sweeter by the herbs of earlier. Our breaths drew together in the still, fusty air.

With a chuckle, I told him, "You are an excellent student after all."

He chortled. "You give me a passing mark?"

"With honours."

We almost fell off the bed as we rolled onto our sides to face one another, but he saved us, holding tight. We both giggled.

"We should get dressed," he said.

"Nay, stay a little longer. I would feel you thus until my mind has captured it fully. My arms need to learn to feel you when you are not there," I pleaded, my fingers trailing through his hair.

"They do not already?"

I grinned. "Mayhap they do. But I would remind them."

"Ah, it is good to be certain."

"Indeed."

We nipped at one another's mouths and stared longingly, savouring the precious moment.

"Come, we risk too much," Luke declared at last.

"Aye, you are in the right. But know that I would hold you thus forevermore."

"And you think I would not, mayhap?" His grin was awry.

"I never doubt you."

We did redress but lay back down after ensuring all trace of our activity was removed and had remade the bed. Idly, we talked of everything and nothing, content to be in one another's arms.

Chapter 14 – Neither Do Men Light a Candle

We celebrated the Nativity of the Virgin Mary and partook greatly of the feast. For, all too soon Ember Days would be upon us for The Exaltation of the Holy Cross. As we entered the time between excess and scarcity, I worked in the infirmary as usual.

One day, as I was tidying the back room, my fingers lingered over the box of beeswax candles. It was surprising as they were usually kept locked and stowed away, for our candles were most precious. Brother Giles was allowed them in the infirmary to help aid people's healing.

I should have shut the box immediately and taken it to its rightful place. Yet whispers were in my mind. How appealing the candles' shape; tapered and just the right thickness. In my schooldays, other boys had whispered of rumours of these sacred treasures being used in unholy ways. I had dismissed their tales as schoolboy prattle. But now the idea grew in appeal.

Would Luke ever like to be the one to receive me? And mayhap these candles, slimmer than my own girth could help prepare him for such? Or, if not, I could use them on myself when Luke could not ease my need. My hand hovered over the forbidden items.

I slammed the lid shut, determined not to listen to the devil. I would not steal. Not from the monastery and certainly not from Brother Giles who had shown me nothing but kindness. Yet, why were they left out so? As though he had left them in deliberate invitation.

As if called by my unlawful thoughts, Brother Giles walked in. He stopped and looked pointedly at me. "Oh, did I leave those out? How forgetful I am become in my old age."

"I can return them for you. It is no great matter."

"We burn through them slowly enough so as not to be regularly counted. Hm? I beg pardon. My thoughts were straying. Aye, please do ensure their safe return. I think I should go and rest a while."

I was not taken in for a moment. Brother Giles' faculties were still as sharp as a pin. However, I blushed to think mayhap he had been in a rush to make use of them before my arrival. Would he? At his age?

But there was also a hint in his words that I was not stupid enough to be oblivious to. I seized a candle and placed it in my wallet, filled with anticipation and a little naughtiness. This was what Brother Giles intended, was it not?

I had no excuse for its presence should it be discovered. Mayhap merely to light my way in the dark? In case of urgent chasing away of demons? But nobody had shown any particular interest in my wallet thus far. Biting my lip, I returned the rest to their rightful place, decision made.

My candle lay unused in my wallet for a while. But as Luke's birthday was at the beginning of the month of October, I thought to make a gift of it. Bubbles of excitement ran through me every time I imagined what his reaction may be.

However, we all had to endure abstinence first. The Wednesday, Friday and Saturday of The Exaltation of the Holy Cross were Ember Days; we were forbidden any food before nones. And even then, we were severely limited as to what was permitted—no flesh of warm-blooded animals, and no milk or eggs.

Again, our cooks came to our aid, producing the best they could. One day, we ate Tart in Ymbre Day; a dish especially created for such times. Onions, cheese, herbs, saffron and currants were baked together in pastry to provide some form of edible food.

With so little sustenance, the elder monks were encouraged to rest. Luke and I were excused lessons but not permitted free time. When not in church, we were with our other tutors. In my case, this served a dual purpose for I was to aid Brother Giles with any such persons who felt faint, but also to watch over him. I did so gladly.

One of the people who came into the infirmary was Brother Hector, accompanied by Luke.

"He denies it, but he looked about to fall into a faint. I wished not to take any chances," my lover explained.

"Amidst much grumbling, I daresay. You are brave and wise to act so. I commend you for it," Brother Giles said.

"It is all a fuss and bother over naught," Brother Hector complained.

"May it be so, but I will listen to no grumbling. I would far rather you arrived here healthy than remained unwell slumped in your room."

The monk emitted unhappy noises but said no more whilst Brother Giles assessed him.

"You see how it is? I am hale and hearty."

"Brother Hector, do not force me to remind you that you are no longer a lamb of springtime. You must have a care. I am sure you were at your books too much this day when you should have been resting."

"Is it my fault if the lad still has much to learn, and takes his time about it?"

I bristled at his condemnation but clenched my fists and held still.

Mercifully, Brother Giles replied, "Nay, but he strikes me not as neither a dalcop nor cumberworld. Not all knowledge must be forced upon him at once. You shall both remain here until prayers. I shall be glad of the extra hands, and you, my friend, shall lie upon this cot and meditate upon how to spend your days at a slower rate and with a more compassionate tongue."

"Of all the…"

Brother Giles held up his hand. "Brother Hector, I say this not out of impudence but out of concern."

"And if those words were not thus cloaked in the language of hostility I should be more inclined to listen."

"Enough. I have stated my concerns. How you receive my words is between you and God. I shall not stand in debate. I too should be taking some time in reflection."

Turning to Luke and I, he commanded, "You two, you are able to warm some water without my assistance, I trust? And Paul, you know where the distilled water of the roses may be found. Prythee, ensure all is in preparation." At the end of his speech, Brother Giles laid himself on the next cot along from Brother Hector.

Luke and I disappeared into the back room, where we fell about kissing as soon as the door was closed.

"I should not find joy in illness, but it is good to have an excuse to see you," Luke whispered.

"I am somewhat glad of it myself. And it is a relief to see Brother Hector is recovering already."

He halted his kisses, turning serious. "He has me worried, Paul. Brother Hector is more often plagued with headaches and giddiness."

I held him close. "Brother Giles has noted the same. Still your mind, for our friend is watchful."

"I am glad to hear it."

"Now, my lips are ever so cold. I fear to catch chill."

"That would never do, I had best warm them for you." His mouth was indeed warm upon mine as it swept back over my lips.

However, I had to step back. "Luke, you are excessive in your care. I fear I am now aflame, and we are far from alone."

He shook his head. "Come, let us busy ourselves with these herbs and water. What would you have me do?"

"I would have you do so much. But let us focus on these," I said, indicating some sage leaves.

I provided our remedy to Brother Hector, who seemed to regain colour in his cheeks for lying down. And I also gave some to Brother Giles who remained upon a cot. They both tried to resist but I was determined to bring comfort to them.

With a goodly amount of self-control, Luke and I got through the afternoon with no more than a few stolen kisses. I did make us each some root of liquorice tisane to help. To be so near him and yet be kept so far was vexing.

I clearly remained distracted as there was a tug upon the hood of my cloak as we prepared to leave the quire after compline. Hastily, I drew my hood up, hoping nobody had noticed my lapse. I was still getting used to the proper behaviour of hood lowering and raising. And with other thoughts filling my mind, it was harder still to remember what one must do.

I smiled my thanks to Luke. And kept my head bowed as we passed sub-prior Gervase who regarded us all intently as we filed out in silence.

Happily, we made it to St Matthew's Day without too much incident. And we once more indulged in a feast, all the more enjoyable for the Ember Days beforehand. But a few days after, Luke came to me at night.

"Paul, I must tell you something. I would have you hear it from me," he whispered at my bedside.

Sitting up, I came fully awake. "You have me concerned. Something is amiss?"

My heart thundered as he sat on my bed and took my hand. "More awkward than amiss. Brother Hector has set up a meeting with Harry."

"My brother Harry?"

"It must be. You mentioned his location and it matches our destination."

"You are to travel to him? He comes not here?" My face fell.

"Hence my telling you. I am sorry for it. But he is much engaged at present and cannot come here. I had urged him to do so through Brother Hector under the guise of it being to his benefit. But alas, it is not to be. And it feels wrong to me. But you must write or tell me if there is any message you wish me to impart to him on your behalf."

"When do you go?"

"A week after Michaelmas."

"I shall think upon it and entrust any message to you. But tell me, shall you return the same day?"

He stroked a thumb across my cheek. "It is not so very far distant. We aim to travel there and back again within a day."

"Yet he has not been to see me these many months."

"Paul, take it not to heart. He is effectively lord of the manor now. Your father entrusts him with the land on which he resides."

"It is well Harry learns this way. I am certain my father is watching over him from afar."

"And mayhap there is some awkwardness, if you'll permit my saying? We are sworn to the monastery, giving up all we once had. Your bonds of blood can never truly be broken, but mayhap he feels obligated to give the appearance of such? And family visits here are not generally encouraged."

Closing my eyes, I huffed. "It is surely so."

Luke wrapped me in his arms and kissed my head. "He still loves you, I am sure of it. But mayhap not as much as I do."

Leaning back, I looked at his smirking face. "I think nobody could outdo you in that regard."

He kissed me, long and slow, pouring all his love, affection and tenderness into it. Our foreheads rested against one another as we took a breath after.

"You are my own heart's root. But I must bid you good night," he whispered.

"My thanks. God grant you good night, my lief."

He had done right to tell me of his plans. Surely he was accompanying Brother Hector to ensure his safe keeping as much as to learn from the experience. But it was unsettling that he should visit upon my family without me. Dejection scraped my heart, keeping sleep at bay too long.

A week can last an age. Luke and I were kept busy between services. Brother Barnabas had us copying out a manuscript which was an honour and something I enjoyed. However, it took a great deal of concentration. And in the infirmary, Brother Giles and I were preserving and drying herbs for the winter months ahead.

All of this activity should have made the time sail by on a breeze. However, as Luke and I were unable to spend time alone, it seemed stuck in the silt. But Michaelmas did arrive eventually.

There were no corn dolls made in the monastery, but I was sure the farmers would see to it. Back with my parents, the folk used to spend this time giving thanks for the completed harvest and praying for the next year.

There was a darkness to the end of summer, a sense of foreboding. And yet the joy of a good harvest brought that into balance. For myself, it had previously been the end of frivolous times with my family and a return to school. However, now, there was only the continuation of my monastic life; my upheaval was done, and there was to be no great change from hereon in.

We did feast on goose in the misericord, however. And a greater portion of bread. Listening to the feats of St Michael, including dragon slaying, I was reminded to maintain courage always. Any images of the archangel now were compared to Luke with his mass of blond hair and blue eyes. And he was brave in his own way.

Infuriatingly, the next few days were spent in separation. However, there was one surprise.

"Brom. I had thought you had abandoned our little corner entirely," I greeted as the dark-haired young man emerged in the physic garden where I was working.

He grinned. "Nay, only busy with the harvest. But I do not think you missed me so very much."

"Fie! Tell me not that we are enemies or that my refusal has left a scar upon our friendship, for it would pain me to think so."

"In truth, I am glad to hear you declare it. I did not want my foolishness to be the cause of our ruin. I have not many companions here whom I may talk with."

I nodded. "Then let us remain as brothers."

We shook hands upon it as though a business deal had been struck. The formality was mayhap a reminder to him that he should not ever attempt more. I valued his friendship but would not encourage anything further than that. My heart belonged to another.

With his welcome assistance, I gathered a good supply of herbs for drying and tidied the beds. But looking up, I saw him cross the garden to where a cluster of stinging nettles grew. I frowned as he bent down and picked some leaves.

"Hey, there. What are you about?"

"My apologies. I should have asked. I thought nobody would mind. Not that I thought much at all..."

"Calm yourself, Brom. I mean no rebuke. I was surprised and curious. You were not near any stinging nettles. Indeed, you had to walk over to them. Surely you had not stung yourself, yet here you stand with leaves of dock wound about your hand."

He rolled his eyes. "There speaks a man who has never toiled hard in the fields."

I gaped. And frowned. Then cocked my head. "Prythee, explain, for you venture close to impertinence."

"I beg pardon. I meant no disrespect." Holding out his hand without leaves, he continued, "You see, haymaking and harvesting come not without leaving their mark. And, well, using the tools just now, they hurt me afresh. I only sought comfort. The leaves of the dock soothe, and they were right there."

I squinted at the red, raw hand before me with its fresh blisters. Gently, I took up his other hand and removed the leaves. "Brom! You mean you were working here by my side in this state?"

"I mustn't complain."

"This is too much." Grabbing him by the wrist, I pulled him into the infirmary.

"Brother Giles. We may help this lay brother, may we not? His hands are in a frightful state. Might I apply some ointment?"

"Certainly."

He followed me into his room and looked on as I selected the desired pot, and nodded approval at my selection. "Very good."

Brom sat patiently as I applied the ointment as softly as I could.

"We shall not bind your hands, young Brom," Brother Giles announced, "For it would attract derision from your fellow laymen, I fear. Some people attempt to be too hardy for their own good. But pray, return tomorrow and we shall apply more of this ointment to ease your suffering and help speed along the healing."

Brom stood and embraced the infirmarer. "Many thanks, Brother Giles. You are most kind."

"I merely do what I must. Run along now before you're missed."

Once the grateful young man had left, Brother Giles said, "That was well done, Paul. You have the makings of a fine infirmarer."

I beamed. "Thank you. But prythee, might we look at your compendium. I do not recollect the dock leaf being mentioned. And Brom has reminded me of its varied uses."

"Hmph! It is quite possible that I overlooked the humble plant. It grows where it likes, uncultivated by my hand. Come, let us look now."

We indeed discovered its absence from his pages. "Might I be allowed to write out a page for it, if you please?"

He smiled. "That is a fine idea. If there is not time in your lessons with Brother Barnabas, you must bring page and ink here to do so."

Joy filled me at the prospect. I could be of use, expand knowledge and practise my writing.

It was with great pangs that I bid Luke farewell soon after. We had not managed to unite, but I did pass him a letter to deliver to my brother, conveying my good wishes and news of my contentment.

I worried all the day. It was pure folly.

"Come, there is no need for gloom. He will return this evening," Brother Giles consoled.

"I know. I cannot help but long to have accompanied him. It is a missed opportunity to visit with my brother and his family. I have not yet seen my nephew, but Luke shall. It seems wrong."

"Ah. It feels cruel, perhaps?"

"Not intentionally so. I infer no wrongdoing."

"And yet the hurt remains." He patted my hand. "I am certain I would feel much the same in your position. But take comfort for Luke will surely tell you all and is the best person to do so. And so long as they form a good deal, perhaps your brother may be enticed to visit here in turn, eh?"

"I had not thought of it in those terms. Thank you."

"It can be difficult to see through pain, Paul. It is understandable. But it gladdens me to help open your eyes."

I nudged his shoulder. "You always do. You are like father, brother, friend and wise counsel in one. The Lord is generous in his gift of you."

"Oh, now, you are grown over-sentimental. Set you about that pestle and mortar harder, for you have far too much room for thought."

The pounding of herbs was a lengthy process, and indeed, it did not challenge my brain. So, as I continued, I began to hum and then sing. The songs strayed from religious themes, but Brother Giles indulged me. He was far too kind. For which I was thankful.

"There. Now the essentials are done, how would you like to start your writing project? I saw you brought parchment with you."

I nodded eagerly. "Very much, yes please."

He sat me down at a bench where I began to write what I knew of the dock leaf, and what I had read about in a book in a stolen moment. That is, how the leaf may be used not only to soothe stings from the nettle, but also to soothe cuts, scrapes, insect bites or stings, blisters and sprains. Staunching of blood is also an important use. But made into a compress, it may heal bruises.

The seeds can help treat coughs and colds. The roots for ailments of the skin, boils, rheumatism, constipation and diarrhoea. Nothing was left unsaid of this useful plant. I even drew an image of it.

So caught up was I, that only the bell for vespers stayed my hand. It had been a welcome distraction.

Chapter 15 - Fear Not, Believe Only

I was abed but not asleep when Luke returned. Clutching my blanket, I awaited the weight of his body next to mine. He was wise to wait, checking he had not disturbed the others in the dormitory, but I know not how he managed it. I surely would have rushed immediately to his side in his place. But come to me he did, wrapping an arm around me.

"God give you good night, sweeting," he whispered.

"I am glad you are returned safely. How did you fare?"

"All is well. I will tell you all on the morrow."

"You must be tired."

"Aye, very. Your horse, Solatium, carried me well and made it easier I daresay."

"She is a fine animal, but no longer mine. I have no possessions."

"As you say. But there is much I would tell you after my rest. Fatigue pulls at me. For now, know that all is well."

"God grant you good night, my lief."

"God grant you good night, my honey sweet."

Between our meal and nones, Luke pulled me into the parlour for our promised discussion.

"Prythee, Luke, what news have you of my brother, Harry?" I asked before he could say a word.

He smiled. "Harry is in full health and wishes the same upon you. He looks quite like you, you know. Only he is not so beautiful and has a beard. Has he always? I do not recall you mentioning one."

"Nay, that is new."

"His wife, Sybil, seems to suit him well. She was very kind to me and took me aside when Brother Hector and your brother were much engaged. It was important to her that she show me baby Percival, for so your nephew is named. He is a delight, and just like his father and uncle, I think. Sybil is most perceptive. Her unnerving blue eyes see much. But she conveyed only compassion. She whispered of how I blushed once when you were mentioned. I then told her how eager you were for news of your nephew thus she ensured we were well acquainted so that I might tell you."

My mouth gaped.

"All is well, I assure you. They are a happy family, and only wish you joy. I believe she shares your interest in herbs. Strange for one such as her, I thought, but who am I to be the judge? She intimated that Percival has yet to show any signs of sickness, but she has a store of remedies in case he does. She meant to say how well she will look after your family, I think."

"I am glad she is so willing."

"Your brother has made a fine match."

"As did I," I whispered, earning a smile from Luke.

"Oh, and I should make mention that the farms on your family's lands shall receive our surplus grain and spent malt for their animals on mutually beneficial terms."

"You did well, my lief."

Luke looked about us.

"We are not watched, be still. I would offer you praise and gratitude in words if I am unable to embrace you as I ache to do. I realise the risk of intrusion is too great here and we must not linger."

"I have missed you greatly."

"And I you. But we must have patience. I have hope that we can celebrate your birthday tomorrow."

He beamed. "You remembered."

"I have sought some time for a little revelry befitting us young men."

"You are astonishing."

"Indeed I am."

We did risk a brief embrace then, relying on our ears to hear any approaching footsteps.

Not all of the day could be spent in celebration, so Luke and I went to prime with the brethren. Our prayer times had gradually changed with the light, so winter already seemed upon us. We were to break our fast after this service then to spend a little time together until terce. Brother Barnabas had excused us from morning lessons as even he allowed that Luke should be permitted some merriment.

We sang the psalmody. But Luke's voice faltered. I glanced at him, but he attempted to collect himself and continue. Again, he erred. His hand went to his head, seeming in a daze.

"Forgive me…I have a head…" but he did not finish his mumbled words.

I caught him against me as he fell into a faint. Brother Giles was by our side in an instant. "Prior, prythee send for a leech with all haste. Paul, come, help me carry him to the infirmary."

The prior looked shocked at such an interruption to the office yet offered no resistance. Unease churned inside me.

Brother Barnabas assisted us, but it was an awkward walk through the cloister. The rain fell upon us between there and the infirmary, but it was not enough to revive Luke. He remained insensible throughout. Not even a groan passed his lips, and I began to fear the worst. But surely people did not drop dead so suddenly. Why had Brother Giles sent so soon for a leech?

Quelling any misgivings as much as possible, I helped lay Luke's limp body upon a cot.

"Paul, fetch the smelling salts. Let us begin with those. And some cold water. Brother Barnabas, perhaps you would be so kind as to stoke the fire," Brother Giles instructed whilst patting Luke's cheeks and hands.

I ran to fetch the requested items, desperate to help my beloved yet not wishing to leave his side. Wafting the salts under Luke's nose, he at last groaned. But he was far from himself. I saw and felt his body shiver. Brother Giles was already piling blankets atop him.

"Brother, you know something of this, I think. Tell me, prythee."

His eyes looked at me with unwanted sympathy. "I know nothing but fear a lot. I have heard of a sweating sickness. It seems my prayers that it should not be visited upon us may have gone unanswered. Paul, if this be that…it is most serious. And mayhap you should not be here for it prays on the young, it seems."

"God himself could not remove me except in death. Use me how you must, but here I must remain."

"I understand but prythee steel yourself. Brother Barnabas, do you also remain?"

"I feel I must. Might I pray?"

"Aye, do. We shall need all assistance before the day is through."

"My head…" groaned Luke.

Stroking it, I whispered, "I am here. We will ease your pain."

Brother Giles whisked away, but returned with a bundle of rose, lavender and sage. Holding it to the fire, he brought it smoking to Luke and swept it over him. It seemed to be of no use, as he curled tightly into a ball.

"Paul, you remember my keeping a bottle of four thieves vinegar?"

I nodded.

"Fetch it now."

I did so, and together we rubbed it on Luke's hands, ears and temples. Brother Giles insisted I apply it to myself also for protection from plague.

Brom burst in then. "I heard of a commotion. Might I be of service, Brother Giles?"

He looked aghast as he saw me bent over Luke's prostrate form.

"I thank you, Brom. Yes, fetch a sliced onion from the kitchens, if you would," the infirmarer replied.

"Of course." He ran out of the infirmary as surely as if the devil himself were upon his heels.

"Paul, mop his brow with the cool water. I shall boil up some coriander. Do your best to keep him awake."

There had been much groaning from Luke all the while. I stroked his hair. "Brother Giles says you are to stay awake, Luke. And I think you would not like to miss your birthday surprise, so you had best heed his words."

I dipped a cloth in the bowl of cold water and applied it to his forehead which was burning hot. But no word was spoken from his lips.

"There now, you will be well again. Stay with me, Luke. Is this not better? Feel the cool water and call to your mind the chill of the river."

How he writhed and moaned. I am not sure I had ever witnessed such pain. But there was no time for alarm. Again and again, I applied the cool, damp cloth despite no sign of its bringing any relief.

Brom returned with the onion slices, and so I tied them to the soles of Luke's feet.

Brother Giles came back with his remedy also. "Here we are. Paul, help me raise his head so he may sip. Do you think you can do that, Luke?"

His cry of agony rent my soul as I tried to position him. But still, I would not give sway to alarm. I took the cup from Brother Giles and held it to Luke's lips.

"Drink for me."

At first, he seemed not to hear me. So, I repeated my direction more firmly and in a louder voice than I had thought to muster. He managed to take some herbed hot water in, then clutched onto me. "Honey!"

"Does he call for honey?" Brother Barnabas asked, who had been standing in prayer.

I slightly shook my head at Brother Giles.

"I believe the delirium is taking him. Pay no heed. Ah, here is the leech."

Brother Faramond brought the man in. "Greetings. Let me at him," the stranger said.

Examining my beloved with not so very gentle hands, he declared, "Aye, we must let his blood, of course. You there, young chap, be so good as to hold this bowl."

I did not like his familiarity and resented his rough command, but for Luke I would endure and obey. The leech pushed Luke's sleeve up and took hold of his arm amidst more groaning.

Looking at Brom, he demanded, "You there, hold him about the shoulders to keep him still."

Scowling, Brom also complied. He paled terribly as the leech sliced into Luke's vein. I thought he may vomit, but he was intent on keeping Luke still. It is likely that I did not appear much better, for the sight of this gruff person cutting my beautiful man filled me both with anger and fear. The blood collecting in the bowl in my hands began to quake.

Aaron's Blessing fell from my lips, "*Benedicat tibi Dominus et custodiat te, ostendat Dominus faciem suam tibi et misereatur tui, convertat Dominus vultum suum ad te et det tibi pacem.*" (The LORD bless you and keep you; The LORD make His face shine upon you, And be gracious to you; The LORD lift up His countenance upon you, And give you peace.) [Numbers 6:24-26].

The two monks repeated it when I did. And the blood continued to pour.

As the leech finished and bound him, Luke quietened. And all went still within me as if frozen by ice. I looked towards Brother Giles for guidance.

But it was the leech who spoke. "We have done all we can for now. Let him rest." He took the filled bowl from my hands, surely to empty and clean it but I noticed not what he did.

My eyes were fixed upon Luke, my breath held as surely as my grip upon his unharmed arm. It was Brom who rubbed my back.

"He is strong. He will fight this," he said.

I could form no reply. All words were caught in my throat. The smiles were nowhere to be seen upon his pale lips, the light was shuttered from his eyes as they closed against the world, not even a hint of rose was visible upon his cheek.

With a terrible wail, sweat began to pour profusely from every part of Luke.

It was Brother Giles who chanted the *Agnus Dei,* and that more than any other thing filled my eyes with despair.

"Agnus Dei,
quitollis peccata mundi: miserere nobis.
Agnus Dei,
quitollis peccata mundi: miserere nobis.
Agnus Dei,
quitollis peccata mundi: dona nobis pacem."

(Lamb of God, who takes away the sin of the world, Have mercy on us. Lamb of God, who takes away the sins of the world, Have mercy on us. Lamb of God, who takes away the sins of the world, Grant us peace.)

"Oh, dear God," I murmured, tears threatening to set loose.

But I would not cry. I refused to give in. Whilst there was breath in my lungs and blood in my veins I would believe in the Lord and his grace, that he would heal Luke and not take him from me. Not yet. Not this way.

I set about wiping all the sweat from him with the cool cloth. Brom, bless his soul, fetched new water for me without being asked. Brother Barnabas raised his voice in prayer. And Brother Giles joined him—I was almost undone. But I had a job to do.

The leech stepped forwards as if to take more blood.

"No! You shall torment him no more. See how he has worsened with your interference. Let him be," I yelled.

Brother Giles stepped between us. "The boy is distressed. Pray forgive his outburst. But I would also ask that we let Luke alone for now."

"But he will surely worsen. You see how his fluids are turned to poison. They must be purged."

"I also see how verily he rids himself of them through profuse sweating. Let us try to bear his way, for mayhap it is for the best."

"Should he—"

"Luke's recovery is in God's hands. And we pray to Him for His favour."

"Then I can be of no further assistance here." The leech stormed out.

Giles shrugged. "Let us turn to other methods, then. Wine is cold and dry. Do you think you could get some hypocras into him, Paul? Surely Hippocrates shall come to our aid."

"I can but try."

Luke was lost to me, roaming in his own delirium. But with the help of Brom and Brother Giles, I got a little of the spiced wine into Luke's mouth which he swallowed. But it was precious little. Most ended up trickling down his pale cheeks and neck.

Needing activity, I returned to dousing the flames of his brow with my damp cloth. "Do not leave me. Come back to me, Luke," I whispered.

"Brom, prythee, add some leaves of the pennyroyal mint and rosemary to the next bowl," I requested.

"You think to cool him more than heat?" Brother Giles checked.

"Brother, if he grows any hotter he may burst into flame. Cooling seems sensible now. I would not let the devil take him."

"But should he not be aided in his purge of heat. Does he not boil away the demons?"

"Did you not do likewise with the coriander? Mint may warm the insides whilst cooling the outer, but I am not sure we can get any into him this moment. But it is useful after bloodletting. And is it not diuretic? With the addition of rosemary to protect from both spiritual and bodily harm."

"Mmmm....hmm...you may have the right of it, I suppose. Let us try. If he shows signs of worsening, we will alter our approach, yes?"

"Thank you."

"I shall boil some mint in case he can be made to drink any."

When Brom brought the herbed water, I swept it over Luke who seemed worsening. "You shall not leave me here alone. You are to come back to me, my lief. Fight this evil. Prythee, fight with all the power which yet remains in you. And when that fails, take any and all of mine. For all I am I give to you."

A tear escaped my eye, but with vehemence I did brush it away.

We all played our part, doing all we could for the ailing Luke. I had to spoon water into his mouth, but surely a trickle got into him.

"Brother Giles, the Lord would not take Luke on his birthday, would he? It cannot be so."

He rubbed my shoulder, for I was still knelt on the floor. "I would hope not."

I knew when it was midday, for Brother Barnabas tried to place a bowl of pottage into my hand. "Try to keep up your strength."

But I shook my head. "Nay, I cannot."

It was not so very long after, I think after nones, when all the brethren came into the infirmary. And truly I did quake at their looks of pity. Disaster seemed ever nearer but still I would not accept defeat.

Whilst everyone stood at prayer, I continued to whisper pleas into Luke's ear whilst wiping his body clean. "Come back to me."

As if the demon cast a shadow on our sorry scene, the sun began to dip in the sky. The threat enlarged in my mind.

"A candle, someone, prythee," I commanded, anger pushing aside fear.

Brother Giles placed a lighted one in my hand. Holding it aloft, I recited the Our Father prayer which the others joined in.

Whether it was frenzy or the power of God which filled me, I cannot tell, but I called out, "Archangel Michael, prince of the Heavens, I beseech you to come to our aid. Here lies a devout follower of Christ, besieged by demons. Lend us your sword and smite the demon away from he who would be a monk. Leave us not in despair. Amen."

Everyone else fell silent.

Holding the candle close to Luke's face, three times I bellowed, "I command thee in the name of Jesus Christ to come out of him, foul demon."

Luke writhed and moaned, but a change seemed to come about him. It could have been pure fancy, but it appeared as if his sweat diminished. We all began to chant prayers louder, chasing the retreating demon away.

The others went to vespers, but I could not be moved. Only Brother Giles begged leave to remain to keep watch over us both. I had spent the entire day in prayer, I needed not to go into the church to do so. Luke was in greater need.

Luke gasped, taking a deep breath. Every muscle in my body went rigid as I looked intently to see what would come next. His eyes fluttered open a little, squinting. His hand fell to his forehead.

"You are in pain still?"

"Meurgh."

"If I give you some willow bark, do you think you could chew?"

"Meurgh." I took that as agreement.

Brother Giles went to fetch some. I placed it in Luke's mouth, watching carefully to see that he chewed but did not swallow. He only managed a few bites before spitting it out into my cupped hand.

"Mayhap you have a thirst?"

He licked his dry lips.

There was herbed warm water waiting which I then held to his mouth. How my heart leaped for joy as he sipped. But before long, Luke was clutching himself.

"Piss!"

I quickly grabbed the pot set aside for such use. His limbs were still weak, so Brother Giles helped lean him whilst I directed his stream. And so much urine I ne'er had seen. It was a wonder the stinking pot did not overflow. He collapsed back down with a groan.

"Now you are awake, I shall get some caudle made," Brother Giles announced.

As he departed, I asked, "Brom, will you help me move him to this next cot along? These sheets are soaked through."

He nodded and moved to Luke's feet. Our charge tried to form protest but was unable to form sensible words, so we ignored him. Surely dry bedding was favourable, and he was in no condition to move himself.

Sitting, I clutched him to my breast. "My lief, my lief, you are returned to me. Praise be to God. Thank you Heavenly Father." Tears finally broke their barrier and I wept like a babe.

Brom cleared his throat. "I think mayhap he still needs rest."

"Oh!" Realising I still held him, I promptly lowered Luke to rest.

"Oh!" I realised Brom had witnessed my outburst.

"You think I would betray your confidence? Nay. This? It is far more than I would ever have dared hope for. Fun was my only aim. Truly, I am happy for you. However, it may be that the monks will find their own knowledge after this day."

"Was I truly so forthright?"

"You were very earnest in your devotion to his care."

"Which is only fitting for an infirmarer," Brother Giles added, returning.

"Truly, it can be thus explained away?"

"Enough to assuage any naysayers, I think. Besides, it is only to be expected that you two should form a close friendship, given your age and position. Paul, I am very proud of you this day. Your resilience is nothing short of extraordinary."

I wiped at my face. "Prythee, do not make me sob anew."

He grasped my shoulder. "You cry all the tears you need. You are amongst friends. And your relief must be second only to my own."

Looking up, I saw his eyes were swollen and reddened. I gave him a faint smile before leaning my head against his hip.

He rubbed my back. "There, there. The danger seems past. Let us turn our attention to Luke's continuous healing now. Truly, he seems weakened by his experience."

"I think anyone would be."

"Indeed, it seemed quite the ordeal." He bent down to Luke's level. "But you are improving now, are you not?"

"Meurgh."

Poor Luke, he was still terribly drained. But he was awake and no longer sweating. I took a bowl of caudle from the lay brother who brought it in.

"Four bowls?" I asked Brother Giles.

He smiled. "None of us have taken sustenance. And I did not wish to put the kitchen to additional labour, so we must all eat the same."

"Luke, can you manage it?" I asked, holding some to his mouth.

Gingerly, he partook a little. He sank back down onto his pillow. I took the opportunity to gulp down some of my own. No sooner had I done so when Luke pointed to his mouth. Smiling, I helped him take some more of the thick, warm, sweet drink.

"Thanks," he said, his voice hoarse.

With his head back on the pillow, I stroked down his hair and along his temple. "You make sure you return to full health now."

"I…came back…to you." He grasped for my hand, so I reached out and squeezed.

I could have wept. He had heard my pleas and obeyed. Pulling our joined hands up, I placed a kiss upon them. Luke's eyelids fluttered closed, and we let him sleep.

Brother Barnabas returned, but after eating, he remained quiet as we all watched on.

"You will not make me go to the dormitory?" I asked Brother Giles when the bell rang for compline.

"Paul, should I be so foolish as to thus instruct you, it is my belief that a whole drift of boar could not drag you there. Nay, you will remain here." He looked pointedly at the novice master.

"Thank you. Again."

"There is a cot for your use here." Under his breath, he added, "Not that you shall make use of it."

Brom returned to his own dormitory, Brother Barnabas to ours, and Brother Giles retired to his bed in the back room. "You know where to find me should the need arise."

"God grant you good night, Brother."

"Aye. And you."

Nestling down next to Luke, I wrapped my arm around him. He stirred.

"Is it acceptable to you that I am here?" I checked.

He clung onto my arm. "Prythee, don't move."

"Happy birthday."

He groaned.

"Not to worry. I shall be certain to celebrate all the more when you are returned to full health." I kissed the back of his head.

A quiet moan of approval came from my lief.

I lay there, smoothing his hair until he fell asleep in my arms.

Despite his rapid decline into illness, the recovery did not follow in kind. And although I had been indulged whilst Luke lay in mortal peril, I had to return to my regular way of life the very next day.

Brother Giles awoke me for prime, vowing to keep watch over Luke. I made sure to offer plentiful prayers of thanks at every opportunity. Indeed, the horror of that day did not fully descend until I was knelt in prayer. How very close I had been to losing my beloved did not bear thinking of.

In the carrells, Brother Barnabas grew impatient with my inattention, so accompanied me to the infirmary to check that Luke had not sickened again.

"There, you see. He is as well as may be expected. Brother Giles has some experience in healing the sick, as you are well aware, and is taking good care of him. Are you now satisfied?"

I looked at the ground. "Yes. Pray, forgive me. Brother Giles, I meant no affront."

He ruffled my hair. "I should think not. But the worry over friends does tend to remove good sense. Be not despondent, Paul. He is over the worst."

Luke smiled lazily from his sickbed as I was marched back to my studies.

On our walk, Brother Barnabas told me, "We sent word to enquire after your family."

"Oh, dear Lord, I had not thought to ask. Mercy be. Are they well?"

"They are all well."

"Thank you, Lord."

"And they are on their guard for the least sign of illness. But I am confident no harm shall befall them."

"How can you be so sure?"

He shrugged. "I cannot say. But I have faith."

"Then I shall too. But will pray that it is so."

As I lay in bed that night, sorrowfully did I feel alone. There was no Luke beyond the curtain. The horrors of that emptiness haunted my dreams. I awoke in a sweat, and momentarily feared the illness had been visited upon me. But I soon cooled in the chill night air of the dormitory. Yet the fear did not relinquish its hold.

I thanked God over and again for Luke's recuperation. It was selfish, but I couldn't help it. He was my beloved, and we had spent so little time together. I hungered for more and was glad of the prospect.

It dawned on me also how much his presence formed my decision to remain. Without him, would life here hold any appeal? For certain, it was peaceable but to be kept so silent was not something which I desired. Luke offered me a chance to speak my mind, and I him. We needed one another in so many ways. Yes, my body craved his touch, but we went beyond that alone. My mind was pleased by his. It was as if my very soul required his presence.

Chapter 16 – Breath Like Apples

What had been feared, that Prior Ambrose should have me brought before him to answer for my wanton desires, never came to pass. Brother Giles suggested that although the prior may have suspicions, he would not wish to cause embarrassment by having those confirmed. As he did to the visitations of the ladies, he closed his ears and eyes to the extent of my relationship with Luke. Mayhap he reasoned it was brotherly, spiritual friendship which we shared. Either way, it was an unspoken acceptance of which I was thankful.

I was also fortunate that my alliance with Brother Giles meant I must spend time in the infirmary. There was no place I would rather have been in those few days. My monkish friend attended upon the others in the infirmary whilst I sat with Luke, feeding him fortifying food and drink. Softly, I regaled him with stories to stir his mind and sang quietly to soothe him.

In whispers, I spoke words such as, "I am so very glad you came back to me, Luke," and at contrary times, "Do not ever bring such fear to my door again."

His answer to both ardour and admonishment was, "I love you too, sweeting."

Slowly, Luke's complexion lost its deathly pallor, and a blush of rose rested once more upon his cheeks and full lips. The light sparkled once more within his blue eyes. And so, he returned to life. In an odd sort of way, it had been a blessing to be able to spend so much time at his side, even if I wished never to have it repeated thus.

I noticed that Brother Barnabas was less severe upon Luke, at least in the weeks succeeding his ailment. And Luke told me how even Brother Hector had become less sharp with him. In my relief I risked much, grabbing him aside for kisses and embracing him at even the slightest opportunity.

It was some three weeks hence that the next feast day was celebrated, that being for Saints Simon and Jude. *Together*, they were Apostles of Christ and missionaries of evangelization. *Together*, they were martyred. And I wondered if they were together in the same way as Luke and myself. If so, surely Christ himself accepted the love which forms between two men.

It was still in the early hours that we broke our fast, and the time we should spend reading before terce was given to us to finally celebrate Luke's birthday. Brother Barnabas was most lenient and understanding of our desire to be on our own to do so. He seemed now to acknowledge and respect our friendship, if not openly. But then he was never fully expressive of anything.

How well it suited my purpose, for our necessities of nature had been attended to after matins. My lief would be as ready as he ever would be for his gift.

Rain hammered upon the roof as we stood alone in the dormitory. I took charge of our kiss, pinning Luke to the wall with my body. My pillicock was already jousting at him.

"Luke?"

"You are in doubt that I am myself?"

I rolled my eyes. "I am making an attempt to be serious. Luke, I would ask you something."

"Then you had better be out with it."

I nodded, gathering my courage for doubt had crept in that mayhap he would not like my plan. "Should you like to know how it feels?"

He squinted. "How what feels?"

"Would you...mayhap like to receive me...into you?"

He grinned and I could breathe again. "I think I might like to at least try."

"I have an idea to help. For it would certainly be too much an intrusion if we came about it at once."

He cocked his head. "Now you have me curious. What would you do?"

Leading him to my bed, I sat us down and reached into my wallet to pull out the candle I had kept for so long. I wiggled my eyebrows, holding it up and inhaling the sweet, earthy, honey scent.

"That? You would...use that...in me?" he asked with a gulp.

"Mmmm...Only if you agree. It is slenderer than me, and so smooth that with a little oil it should slip in gently."

He gulped. "I will not ask where such thoughts came from."

"From rumours of naughty churchmen."

He laughed. "I said I would not ask. But, oh my, do you think they really did such a thing?"

"Regard the candle's appearance. Does it not beg for the deed in itself?"

"Only to the bawdy-minded."

"Do we befit that description?"

"It would seem we do." He licked his lips and shifted where he sat.

"You do trust me, do you not?"

"With my life."

I kissed him with the full force of my passion. So much so that I was lying atop him and grinding my hips afore I was aware of my actions.

"Paul, should we not disrobe?" Luke muttered.

Swiftly, we removed our clothing. Luke's pillicock stood proud and rosy.

"You do like the idea," I noted.

"I love everything that is you."

We kissed where we stood, our naked bodies meeting.

"Lay you back down and draw up your knees," I quietly commanded.

He did so, his breathing becoming shallow.

"Relax, my lief. Fear not. I wish you only pleasure. Loosen your nerves."

Bending down, I kissed him until he whimpered. Kneeling at his feet I applied oil to my fingers and ran them around his hole. He tensed a little but melted as my touch continued. With my other hand, I slowly stroked his shaft. Another whimper escaped him.

Leaning down, I licked his columnar part and sucked at his tip.

Once he was in a suitable daze, I pushed my finger into him. Slowly, slowly, I worked it further inside. His eyes shot open but he said nothing.

"Ease, my lief. It shall soon feel better than anything of this world."

I stroked his length again, encouraging him to take his pleasure. Once more, I pushed my finger onwards, his muscles sucking upon it, and I knew the location had been found as he groaned appreciatively. I stroked in and out slowly until his moans increased.

Bravely, he took another finger inside and emitted wondrous mm's as I worked them back and forth. And he began to move along with my actions. Indeed, he looked beautifully forlorn as I withdrew.

"Be still, my lief. Something better is coming."

Gently, I introduced the oiled candle to his entrance.

"Oh," he cried.

Thus prepared, it took not long for him to start working himself along its length, his movements matching the rhythm I set.

His moans and whimpers increased. Witnessing his need, I took hold of his pillicock again and stroked him vigorously until he burst forth with a cry of, "Oh, Paul!"

Carefully, I removed the candle and wrapped it for cleaning, wiping my fingers free of oil at the same time. Lovingly, I gazed upon Luke's glorious form as he revelled in ecstasy.

His blond locks were delightfully dishevelled and sweat trailed along his smooth skin. His shapely arms moved as if in a dance up above his head as he stretched. I could not resist trailing kisses up his bare stomach, chest, neck...then he leant his head so I could meet his lips.

"Thank you," he whispered.

"Happy birthday."

"A very happy birthday, if not a little late."

"But worth the wait?"

His arms pulled me up along him and he covered my face with kisses. "Worth the wait. And now you truly are my honey sweet."

"You took that so well that I think next time you could accept me."

I felt a stirring beneath me in response.

"Luke! You grow greedy."

"You make me greedy. I hunger for all you offer."

"And I you."

"Truly, a match made in Heaven."

Wrapping my arms about him more tightly, I clung on. "It would seem so. Thank you God for the gift of Luke."

"And thank you, Lord, for the gift of candles."

I gasped. "Luke!"

"I should not give thanks for them, mayhap?"

I thought about it. “Thank you Lord, for the gift of candles.”

“Hmmm. But tell me, is there nothing I can do for you in return?”

“Nay, it was your birthday gift. I took pleasure enough in the giving.”

Using a little of the water in the pitcher and my secret linen, I cleaned us before redressing.

As we filed out of sext, Brother Maynard whispered to Luke, “Happy late birthday.” With a wink, he walked past.

At first, I worried he had witnessed our activity. It was only once desserts were served that I realised why he looked so mischievous, for we ate apple fritters. Whether he alluded to our silly time all together there, or he inferred he knew more of what Luke and I got up to in the orchard, I did not know. But I smiled over to him in any case, for it was a kind gesture on his part, if not one filled with mirth.

Two days later, the church bells rang out all across the land, for King Henry was officially crowned seventh of his name. There were surely great celebrations throughout the kingdom. We held a special service for him, but we lacked frivolity.

I had grown accustomed to the subdued nature of my life. However, there were, of course, still times I longed for dancing and merriment. There had been so few moments spent in wild abandon in my life, enough only so as to whet my appetite. Upon entering the monastery, I had given up all expectation of amusement. But that seemed not to translate into surrendering all hope or want.

However, November arrived and an air of something akin to jollity descended upon us, despite our now short days. We had a grand feast on All Saints' Day, after a special Mass for the martyrs. White lilies filled the church with their perfume where they sat alongside red roses.

The apples whose blossoms and shade Luke and I had enjoyed so much previously, now contributed to the cider we imbibed. Our region of Kent was blessed with fine orchards, many of which our priory and mother cathedral owned. Most of the cider was sold. But on occasions such as All Saints' Day, we partook plentifully.

We even had a game of snap-apple; an apple was attached to the end of a piece of wood and suspended from the ceiling of the calefactory after supper. However, a lit candle was on the other end. As it spun around, we each took a turn at attempting to bite at the apple.

Cheers echoed all around as I won a bite. Luke's eyes reflected the heat of the candle glow as I swiped away the juice running down my chin.

"Would that it were some other prize more rewarding than an apple," he whispered close to my ear, sending tingles throughout me.

"My lief, you seem under some misguided notion that it was an apple in my mind that I sought."

He laughed. "That would explain your keen aim."

Not all participants got the apple, and some received hot wax in their face. However, as no serious injury was caused, even that was a source of hilarity. Especially when Luke came away with drips down his cheek.

Walking back to me, he held up a hand. "Prythee, Paul, do not say what I see is upon your tongue. I need not the confirmation of what you would liken dripping candle wax to."

Grinning, I carefully peeled off the cooled wax from his face. "Then I shall venture no comment."

How sorely I wished to kiss that cheek. But I was not yet so far in my cups as to forget myself entirely. Instead, I brushed my fingers against his, hidden between us. And his smile shone upon me.

A great bonfire was lit afterwards, and we all gathered around whilst Prior Ambrose spoke his words of reverence. But then more cider was drunk, and there were not enough nuts to combat its effect.

"We shall avoid Purgatory, shall we not?" I asked Luke, staring into the flames.

Squeezing my hand, he replied, "If we cannot then who can? Besides, even should we fall, the monks shall light these fires and our souls shall find their way to Heaven."

My head fell upon his shoulder, and briefly he held me to him before gently nudging me. "Have a care, sweeting."

I looked up at him and smiled. "Mmm...your breath smells of cider. Aye, oh, apple of my eye, core of my heart. Thee I do obey."

"Luke, did I not task you with taking him into your care?" Brother Giles admonished, striding over.

Scowling, I defended, "I am no winebibber, and require no nursemaid, sir." And hiccupped.

They both chuckled, but it was Luke who ruffled my hair and placated, "Of course, you don't. However, it would seem you do require a minder of cups. But then I was drinking freely myself and had not noticed how loose of limb you'd become. My apologies."

Propped up between them, I was walked around, beyond the throng of merry monks.

"I am in no worse condition than any of them," I slurred, nodding towards the others.

"Aye, if you say as much, I believe you," Luke replied whilst bodily urging me to continue walking.

The cool air and exercise took the numbness from me. My senses began to return. And the bell rang for compline, echoing through my skull.

It was mayhap ill-advised to drink so heartily; more than one monk walked unsteadily. Remaining somewhat fuzzled myself, I giggled at the sight. And nobody was able to censure me for all about also sought to contain their laughter.

There was an odd sort of solemnity to the Mass for All Souls the next morning. Sore heads surely furrowed all the more in their devotion. Squinting against the candlelight shining all too brightly from my hand, I sang out as clear as my abilities would allow.

Looking pointedly at Luke then the candle, I tittered. He, however, stepped on my foot, turning me serious. With great urgency did I pray for all the souls, saving as many from purgation as possible.

Our lessons that morning were spent quietly reading. At least, Brother Barnabas instructed as much. However, my unfocused eyes stared blearily at the page.

My stomach railed against the eel served at dinner. However, there was a small ray of hope. No soulers were expected to visit us, yet the cooks made soul cakes to put out along with nuts and apples for the visiting souls of those who once lived here. And there were also some for the living to delight in, and which seemed to quell the riotous waves in my stomach. Also, I was certain that the almoner included some of the cakes in the offerings for the poor that day, which warmed my heart.

"Oh my, you do look queasy," Brother Giles told me as I crept into the infirmary, "Do you come to aid me or to seek my aid?"

"Might it be both?"

"Come, sit you down here. Eat some bread and drink a little myrtle tea. You are not the first to do so this day. But I do wonder at not having seen you before. Why did Brother Barnabas not send you?"

"Pray, do not seek to condemn him." Pausing, I rubbed my middle. "I was not so bad before the eel."

"Ah. But that should help. Why do you think it is cooked today?"

Wincing, I replied, "I would rather not think upon it, if you please."

Tentatively, I bit into the bread and slowly chewed. And washed it down with sips of myrtle. Bit by bit, the rolling torment ebbed away.

"Many thanks, Brother. And my apologies for not being of better use this day."

"Pah! Treating you is good practice. And I am nothing but glad to see the positive effects upon you."

The air grew more chill and we were provided with drawers to keep ourselves warmer under our thicker, fur-lined, winter robes. Having not quite gotten used to the feeling of freedom there, the undergarments were a welcome addition to my attire. And I was glad to have use of the corridors to keep out of the persistent rain, although the fresh fragrance was joyful.

My eyes widened as Luke and I walked into the carrells. On the desks lay a bounty of paints.

"Today, I thought we would try you both at painting," Brother Barnabas announced, rubbing his hands together. "Luke, you have some colours mixed so you may fill in the outlined picture, working from the copy in the book. Paul, I have something a little different for you. Brother Giles showed me your entry for dock leaves in his compendium. We were both impressed by your neat writing and fine representation of the plant. He would like you to add more entries in that style. And so, here you are to practice. You each have some parchment cut-offs, but please treat them with the care and respect owing to them."

"Thank you, Brother," Luke and I chorused.

It was surprising to see Luke so eager, given he had struggled so with writing before. However, he had continued to improve in that regard. And mayhap drawing held more appeal. Whatever the cause, it was good to see him happy.

The rain out of doors grew heavier, tapping more loudly on the glass windows. The darkening sky shadowed our room, so we worked in candlelight. Having drawn the outline of a head of meadowsweet, I mixed a green pigment to colour its stem and leaves.

I couldn't stop smiling, both because of the task itself and the memories stirred by the plant. Even the master of novices had a faint smile upon his lips as he watched on.

To my shame, I was amazed when viewing Luke's beautiful artwork. How can he be so masterful with the quill when drawing and less so when writing? My pondering must have shown upon my face.

Luke shrugged. "Shapes and colours make more sense to me."

"But writing is also a series of shapes."

"More uniform ones. But yes, appreciating that has helped me, it seems."

"You are both coming along nicely," Brother Barnabas praised. "But do hush and concentrate on the task in hand."

Pride bloomed sinfully within me as warm as a summer's day at his words. And I was sure to make confession of it at the next opportunity.

On the eleventh day of November, we held Mass for St Martin of Tours (Martinmas); the Roman soldier who reluctantly became a bishop. Dances and games would be enjoyed outside of our walls. Inside them, we dined on Martlemas beef, having eaten goose for All Saints.

Luke tipped his head to one side as I drank a cup of Saint Martin's wine, made from the first grapes of the harvest. I needed not the pointed look, remembering to restrict myself to only this one.

This was the end. Harvests were all gathered, blessed and stored. Livestock had been slaughtered for winter provisions. Days grew steadily darker and colder. Winter was here. Fasting for Advent would begin tomorrow, three days each week until Christmas. I sighed.

Nudging my shoulder and kicking his head upwards, Luke smiled, willing me to not be glum. But alas, for once, I could not comply with his wishes. This time of year always brought sadness in its cold, dark hands.

Glancing around, he returned his gaze to me and blew on his forefinger. That almost made me laugh in the quiet refectory. Fortunately, I managed to reduce it to a grin, for he had made the sign of a candle. Oh, sweet mercy, what have we done? The pure, innocent light is now made impure. And yet I did not truly feel guilt. For it was such a fine deed. May the Lord forgive me for my lack of remorse.

After nones, Luke and I followed Brother Giles to the infirmary.

"May I be of assistance? Are you unwell?" he queried as we entered.

"Might I please take the key to the herbarium?"

He rolled his eyes. "If you must, but bring it not into disarray, and have a care."

I embraced him, my understanding friend. It was raining heavily, and the dormitory may be sought by more than just we two before vespers.

"What on ever shall you do when you no longer have the leisure time of a novice, hm? No, I do not truly ask. Be off with you."

Wet soil filled the herb garden with its musty scent, but it was mercifully empty of people as we passed. I unlocked the door to the herbarium, entered and locked it from the inside. And blew on my forefinger.

Luke's eyes blazed. "I would ask that you replace the candle with yourself this day, my sweet."

"Ask and you shall receive. However, I would caution that we begin with the candle, so you are better prepared to take me. It gladdens me to find you so bold and eager, however."

"It has been two weeks. I am beyond eagerness to experience your touch."

"And my pillicock?"

He tittered. "Is that what you call it now? It is better than pintel, I suppose."

"You seemed to take against that word."

"Aye, but not what it represents."

"So, you are indeed eager for it?"

In response, he leaned his head down and kissed me. Our mouths mashed together in a frenzy. So long I had waited for this, and now I was unrestrained. Driven wild by desire, my mouth was desperate for his, tasting the rich wine therein. My hands wandered about his person seeking more of him.

Breaking free to draw breath, Luke held me close. His heartbeat sounded out like a drum as I bent my head to his chest. There remained material between us. Quickly, I stepped back and removed my clothing, giving my tunic a shake to free it of the water droplets which had fallen upon it. I laid it out along a bench so it may dry a little. Luke copied my actions.

I was entranced by his fingers deftly untying his drawers. Slowing his movements, he lowered the garment down his thighs. I bit my lip.

"Your turn," he murmured, stepping close and ridding me of my drawers.

Fire raged through me, burning away all else except the desire to be inside this beautiful man. My pillicock throbbed at the thought and grew harder. But I had to be patient a while longer for I would not hurt him in my haste. Forcing my hands to still their shaking, I took hold of the candle from my wallet and anointed it with oil.

"Bend you over this workbench, my lief," I instructed hoarsely, laying some moss and strips of linen next to him.

Such a wondrous sight I beheld as he bent himself forwards. His pert, pale buttocks were full in my face as I knelt behind him. I could not resist planting a few kisses across those orbs and even bit down a little in a nibble which made him squirm but not complain.

My tongue travelled down the crevice between those cheeks until it found his hole. I lapped willingly, tasting his glorious musk. My greed was beyond control, and I sank my tongue into his tight entrance. He did wriggle more then, but it was accompanied by such a delightful groan that it only served to urge me on. In and out, I thrust my tongue until Luke's moans almost became cries.

Thus prepared, I added a little oil to my spittle. And slowly introduced the candle.

"Oh, Paul," Luke cried.

Once his body had accepted my offering, I began to drag it in and out slowly. Luke gripped the edge of the workbench until his knuckles whitened.

"Prythee!"

Taking pity on him, realising he was beyond words, I removed the candle. He whimpered.

"Have no worry, my lief. I shall give you what you most desire," I whispered.

Applying oil to my pulsing pillicock, I aimed it at his opening. His tight muscle resisted me.

"Breathe deep, my lief. Permit me admittance. I know you want this as much as I do."

Stroking his back whilst he obeyed, I waited for him to relax. His body sagged slightly, and so I pushed myself forwards a little. There was still some resistance but with perseverance, I was able to overcome. Gradually, I drove in further.

"Augh!" Luke cried.

"It does not hurt too greatly?"

"Nay. Prythee, do not stop now."

Up his channel I travelled, until the marvellous point where his body then pulled me in of its own accord.

"Oh!"

"'Tis a cry of pleasure?" I checked.

"Oh, aye, aye."

Holding still, I waited for Luke to adjust to me. And when that moment came, I pulled back a little, easing my way slowly. His backside drew towards me, however.

"You grow greedy, my lief."

He thrust himself back more assertively, making me chuckle. I slid back in. He wiggled, almost as if dancing. My happy love. With more force and speed, I withdrew then dashed onwards.

"Aye, more, prythee, Paul. More."

Taking up the bunch of moss I had laid down, I reached around and held it over the head of his weeping tip with one hand.

"Oh!"

His body tensed under me. With gathering speed, I thrust into him, our sweating bodies smacking together in a lascivious symphony. His cries became more frenzied even as he attempted to muffle them.

My rutting was relentless. Lust overtook me and I was lost as my body stirred to its own rhythm. Luke moved in harmony with my every movement.

A great chorus of groans built between us. Until he burst forth with a cry, dragging me into that other realm along with him. Greatly I did gush into him, shuddering until I feared to fall.

I drifted in brilliant white bliss, feeling the presence of Holy angels. It was as though I could hear their song. Beauty and peace beyond comprehension enfolded me in its warm embrace. Gently, I was held in love.

Gliding back to Earth, I held onto Luke's shoulders, clinging on tightly. A tear had wound its way down my cheek. "Extraordinary!"

"Incredible."

We remained joined as we gulped for air, gradually calming our spirits. Crumpling up the moss, I placed it on the workbench. Carefully, I removed my presence from him and wiped us with the linen strips. And placed a kiss upon his shoulder. "There now."

"You fill me with astonishment, my sweeting," he said, turning to face me and wrapping his arms about my middle.

His mouth nuzzled my neck. And I bathed in his gratitude. "As you do me."

We wrapped ourselves up in one another, still grounding our senses.

"Would you like to repeat that deed?" I asked.

"Mayhap some other day, sweeting."

I laughed. "I did not mean now."

"Oh. Aye, I would like that to be done again. But, if I must own it, I think I prefer it the other way about."

I sighed. "I am glad to hear it for it is in accordance with my own sentiment."

His eyes shimmered as he smiled. "Good."

My lips drew over his in a lingering kiss. "Good."

Chapter 17 - Fox and Geese

After supper, the older monks daily withdrew to the comfort of the calefactory with its communal fire. There were some days that we all did, more so when it was particularly cold. Luke and I preferred to go to the dormitory whenever possible, where we could be blissfully alone, if not a little cold.

Of course, the monks we shared the room with were likely to also come and go unless otherwise distracted. So, we did not often risk getting naked. But our reading did frequently fall into kissing. And mayhap occasional touching. We had to be ever mindful to listen for footsteps, however.

Mostly, we would simply sit and talk. It mattered not what was said, I could lie me down and listen to Luke's dulcet tones forevermore. We covered many topics, usually serious. Rarely, absurdity would win out.

"I find there is something to be thankful for in winter after all," I announced.

"Hm? You do surprise me, oh sorrowful one. Pray, tell me of this marvel which alters your regard of the season." Luke's mischievous smile danced upon his lips.

"I mean, of course, the pleasures of partridge."

Shrewdly, he regarded me. "Do you speak of partridge or...*partridge*?"

"What other meaning would you derive from it?"

His hands descended upon me, tickling all over. "Wretch! You know full well what other meaning the partridge holds. Should I quote the Aberdeen bestiary to you? '*It is a cunning and unclean bird. For one male mounts another and in their reckless lust they forget their sex.*'"

I was laughing too much to form a response.

Moving all of a sudden, he was atop me. "Or mayhap I should lay you out and pound the definition into you?"

"I would choose the latter. Methinks you should thrust hardly your meaning. But alas, now is not the opportune moment to thus instruct me."

He cast his gaze and hands Heavenward. "Why must you begin what cannot be finished?"

"I was but thinking aloud."

"Oh, vexing wastrel. You are fortunate that I love you sufficiently to forgive such false enticement." His eyes showed that love of which he spoke as his head lowered to impart a soft, lingering kiss.

It was tempting to make good his offer. All I need do was to open my mouth and permit entrance to his devouring tongue, and all sense would be lost. But, with a mixture of fortune and regret, we had become well-versed in resisting temptation. And so, Luke left my body cold with his departure, and we sat upon our respective beds to read.

"I'm so hungry," I complained when I had tried and failed to read the same passage several times over.

"It is your own fault for daydreaming of partridge. Fortify yourself with the gospel instead. Here, let me read of St John's Gospel to you."

I listened but had to entreat, "Nay, speak not of wine, prythee, Luke. I am sorry for my ill-timed speech. I beg forgiveness."

He laughed. "Very well." The rustling of pages was all I could hear until he decided upon a passage. "*Now there is at Jerusalem by the sheep market a pool, which is called in the Hebrew tongue Bethesda, having five porches.*" [John 5:2]

"No. It shall not do, varlet. For the thought of pools and water brings our first union to mind and ignites a different hunger. I thought I was forgiven. I cry mercy."

Luke put down his book and sat next to my still prostrate form, rubbing my stomach before leaning down to kiss me quickly. "My poor sweeting, how he does suffer this day."

"I do."

"Shall I sing to you? Would that chase away your pouts?"

"I would not risk so much."

"I shall not sing the psalmody. If caught, the sin is less. And I was but bringing succor to one in despair."

Without awaiting my response, he began to softly sing a beautiful melody which did indeed act as balm to my soul. I lay quietly as he lulled me into peacefulness.

On the twenty-second day of November, we raised our voices in veneration of St.Cecilia, the patron of musicians. But my cheeks burned as I heard tell of how she remained a virgin even in marriage. Whilst appearing to listen to the reading, my mind wandered.

"And I heard a voice from Heaven, as the voice of many waters, and as the voice of a great thunder: and I heard the voice of harpers harping with their harps:

And they sung as it were a new song before the throne, and before the four beasts, and the elders: and no man could learn that song but the hundred and forty and four thousand, which were redeemed from the earth.

These are they which were not defiled with women; for they are virgins. These are they which follow the Lamb whithersoever he goeth. These were redeemed from among men, being the firstfruits unto God and to the Lamb.

And in their mouth was found no guile: for they are without fault before the throne of God." [Revelations 14: 2-5].

I have not lain with a woman, so might I not claim the same state of virginity?

It seemed as though St Cecilia spoke to my heart, that this verse of song and harp should arrive to me then. Surely, I was a lamb of God, an obedient follower. My love for Him and Luke was each of the purest kind; I was filled with light from both. And mayhap the love which flowed through Luke to me was a gift from Heaven, and thus must glorify Him. I considered myself then both blameless and blessed.

With greater clarity and zeal did I sing the next psalm. Humbly, did I give thanks.

Two days beforehand, the first candle had been lit, nestled within its circle of evergreen foliage of the Advent Wreath. Readings from The Book of Isaiah had begun, prophesying the birth of Christ.

The day prior to St Cecilia's had been one of fasting. And so, it was with great relief with which we ate more heartily that day.

On the twenty-third day of November, Luke and I were given leave from lessons and work in order to celebrate my birthday. This was aided by it being another fast day, and therefore more rest was allowed. During the hour normally dedicated to reading after prime, we returned to the dormitory.

"I pray thee, a happy birthday. May God's blessings be upon you," Luke chimed before leaning me against the wall and kissing my mouth soundly.

Growing heated, I whispered, "We should have a care."

"Nay, fret not. I am sure we are given our privacy this day."

"How are you so certain?"

He shrugged. "Observation. So, prythee, how would you have me cherish you? We may not be permitted personal belongings, but of myself I may give freely. I need only direction in what manner I should bestow my gift upon your body. Might you like the candles used upon you, for instance?"

"I may make any request?"

"Name it and it shall be done."

"Hmmm..." I kissed him whilst pondering. "Methinks your mouth upon my parts would be a fine gift."

Luke beamed. "Nothing would bring me greater pleasure. But wait. Does this not count as breaking fast?"

"Whilst I surely declare not my offerings as either meat or milk, you know as well as I that we are not supposed to fornicate during fasting."

"Hm, and for you to ejaculate into my mouth is the greatest offence of its kind." His smirk suggested he did not consider it so.

"But it is my birthday."

"Which should be greatly celebrated. And surely our fast days will not be in vain."

"Aye, one could almost argue that we should make them worth their while."

"Hmmm...I shall not swallow what you squirt," Luke knelt where we stood and disappeared beneath the skirts of my tunic.

"A fine compromise."

There was a tugging about my drawers. My breaths drew deep and culminated in a gasp as the linen was pulled down my legs. The wall against my back was cold but the breath about my nether was warm; the variance made my head swim. Wasting no time, Luke's warm, wet mouth descended upon me entirely, making me groan aloud and clutch the wall.

I whimpered as he drew back and I popped out of his mouth. His hand gripped me, and his tongue teased my tip in tingling circles. My hips moved forwards in my need for more. But then all contact was withdrawn, making me whine.

"Rejoicing in hope; patient in tribulation; continuing instant in prayer," [Romans 12:12] he reminded me, his voice muffled beneath my clothing

"Do not mock, prythee. Nor make me desperate."

He kissed my pillicock, and seemingly ran his nose along it. "I do not mock this. But I would take the time to honour you fully. You should savour your gift, my sweeting." He ran his tongue along my columnar part once.

Through gritted teeth, I said, "It would seem you are the one savouring."

"Mmmm…you are rather a delicacy." His mouth swallowed me in and out again.

I could not bear it. My hand lowered upon the bulge in my tunic, pressing his head closer to me.

"Very well. I must do as you wish, I suppose," Luke conceded with a chortle before lowering his mouth but not fully, for he laid a hand upon me also.

His groans of enjoyment quivered down my length and made other areas tighten, stoking my internal fires. I was soon yelping oohs and ahs as quietly as possible. My fingers tightened against the wall. The hand which had been upon Luke's head travelled then through my own hair, gripping tightly at the top.

Luke's free hand held my hip as I began to buck. It merely encouraged me to thrust more. Oh, his mouth, his hands, his tongue, his hot breaths…greedily, he did gorge until I was all sensation.

I melted in a fiery pool as he continued to suck and pull. Back and forth. The warmth of his mouth combined with my own growing heat. Steadfastly, his mouth remained upon me as I surged harder and deeper into it, no longer in control of my actions. My legs trembled greatly, but Luke's hand held me in place.

Teeth. Oh my, his teeth grazed as he next withdrew. The threat of sharpness was replaced with softness upon his descent. "Ahh!"

A great suction pulled upon me. Then eased. Then returned. "Oh!"

My hand went back to Luke's head to encourage more of that. His 'mm' of amusement struck like lightning, travelling to my very core. As he continued to dip and suck, my body went rigid, and I knew transportation was nigh.

With a few more movements, I launched into his mouth, spilling my seed and sharing my soul. I splintered into the realm of light and heard the Heavenly choir. As I fell back down, I realised my knees had buckled a little. But Luke was making his way up my body to support me.

"Come, you should lay down," he urged, guiding me.

"Oomph!" I muttered as my back hit the bed.

Luke straddled me, smoothing my hair. "Glad tidings."

I grinned, reaching up to stroke his cheek. "Many thanks."

"I shall keep watch should you wish to sleep."

"But what about you?"

"It is of no matter."

"But I mind it ever so much."

He placed a kiss against my eyelids. "You need rest for you took much enjoyment as was my want."

There was no argument to be had. Luke's fingers rubbing my brow drew me into slumber. When I awoke, he was reading upon his bed. I smiled at him.

"Now, that may be my greatest gift."

"What?"

"To see you being studious whilst I take my rest."

He chuckled. "It is quite the reversal, is it not?"

I walked over to him and lay his book aside so I might kiss him. We sat contentedly in an embrace. Together, we read and talked until the bell rang for terce.

Between offices, we idled the morning away in easy conversation and reading. I blushed as all the brethren wished me a joyous birthday in passing.

Our dessert that day was apple muse; a sort of pottage made of apples, bread, almond milk, honey and spices of sandalwood and saffron. It was a warming, sweet, hearty treat. And there was even some elderberry syrup to lend a sweet yet tart, purple adornment. And I limited myself to one cup of wine.

As the others seemed eager to make my day special, after supper, we all went into the calefactory. I was enticed to play a game of halatafl; Brother Faramond played the fox piece whilst I was the thirteen geese. However, he was not so cunning as to capture all my pieces on the cross-shaped board.

"You let me win," I accused.

"Not at all. It may have escaped your notice, but we all hereabouts are full aware of your intellect, young man. And I would not thus insult you. Nay, you won under your own merit."

My mouth gaped. "Truly?"

He chuckled. "Aye. But make me admit it no more for it shall injure my pride to do so."

Those who had gathered round to watch were applauding. And I knew not where to look. A hand rubbed my back, and I needed no glance to know it was my beloved.

"That must make it my turn," Brother Maynard declared, exchanging places with Brother Faramond.

"Ah, the man who supplies great delights. It would be wrong to go against you."

"And yet here we sit," he said, rubbing his hands together before resetting the board. "As the challenger, I say you get to play the fox this time."

My eyes narrowed. "As you wish."

"Oh, now, surely I have erred. For you even take on the appearance of that sly beast."

"It was your choice. It is made." I grinned.

"I suspect you have met your match," Sub-Prior Gervase called upon his approach.

Patting my shoulder, he added, "Do not hold back, Paul. This man is monstrous hard to play against. But I have confidence in your ability."

"I see how it is," Brother Maynard said, looking pointedly at the larger crowd on my side. His words lacked any malice, however.

"It is ever the way of champions," I told him, shrugging.

He laughed. "Champion now, is it? I do not believe I would go so far as to call myself that. I am not entirely unbeaten. Am I, Sub-Prior?"

"Maybe not. But my wins are far overshadowed by yours."

As I took his final goose, a great cheer went up around me—it was actually quite alarming. But again, that hand found my back through the chaos. And I managed a smile.

I remained not victorious. For Sub-Prior Gervase showed how excellent his skill was and surrounded my fox in the next game.

"It was well played," he told me.

"Aye. I look forward to our next match."

But the bell rang for compline, and so any further games had to wait for another day.

"Have you noticed that we remain undisturbed?" I asked Luke a few days later, as we were in the dormitory alone after supper.

"Aye. I had not wanted to say as much lest it should bring interruption upon us."

"Is it by design or chance, do you think?"

He shrugged. "Does it matter?"

"It matters a great deal. Brother Maynard is young and stout. Surely he does not need the warmth of the calefactory so greatly."

"And yet, if it is done with consideration, we have not been brought before the prior. And nobody has made mention. He has not so much as indicated any notion of knowledge."

"And Brother Barnabas?"

His hand brushed my cheek. "You worry yourself without cause. If either suspected they would check on us more or report us if they intended harm. They do not. If they remain ignorant, then all the better. Or mayhap they have their own distractions elsewhere that we are not aware of."

"I had not thought of that. But should we not gather in the calefactory?"

"And waste this precious time? Do you grow tired of my company already?"

"Nay, impossible."

"It is natural for the young not to want to spend their free time with their elders. They make allowance that Brother Barnabas keeps a close watch upon us, and so a little freedom is desired."

"Before I arrived…did you…" My question was interrupted by his kisses.

"I preferred my solitude. But silence now. It is not a day of fasting, and I would take my pleasure."

His mouth kept me from asking more than his instruction did. Those full, soft lips pulled me into a world where there dwelled only we two. Blue eyes dazzled me as we drew breath, holding me captive as surely as his weight descending upon me.

Traces of sweet herbiness from the ale at supper titillated my tongue as it swept along his. Earthy yet floral flavours mixed with his unique ones—a heady mixture indeed. Inebriating in its own way. And my thirst increased.

Hungrily, I took all he offered, our mouths working wider, our bodies writhing together.

Reaching into my wallet, Luke took out the items he knew to be there. But when he wrapped a strip of linen about my end I frowned.

"To contain your spillage," he whispered.

"Hmph!" But I allowed it as there was some sense to his method.

Sweeping our tunics up but not off , he rid us of our drawers. Liberally, he applied oil to himself and then me. His finger slid inside. "Ahh!"

My knees had drawn up of their own will. Wasting no time, Luke pushed inside me, causing gasps of delight mixed with a pinch of intrusion. Carefully, he withdrew and sank back in.

My fingers dug into his creamy skin. "More!"

He surged forwards the next time, throwing my head back with both force and ecstasy. "Again!"

Oh, sweet stinging joy. Like a rampant bull, he rutted again and again. I was made a quivering wreck as he jousted his lance mightily into me as though I were his quintain: his target, his object of desire.

"Strike forth," I cried.

Pleasure like I had never known surged through me as Luke struck my happy place with brutal force over and over again. The bed battered the wall behind us.

"More, prythee."

I gripped onto the edge of the mattress behind me with one hand, as I held my wrapped self in the other. At last, I was consumed. That familiar tightening proceeded the expulsion as my soul was catapulted into oblivion.

Luke roared as he spilled inside me with a final thrust, sweat beading his brow.

"Oh, my," I yelped.

"You are not hurt?"

I shook my head.

"Paul, I know not what came over me. I am sorry. It was beyond eagerness. And it made me forget myself."

Biting my lip, I replied, "It was most enjoyable. Although, I think we grew a little raucous."

Quickly he pulled away and tidied us up. "Oh, my. What did we do?"

I stood and held him in my arms. "I believe we let loose our full passion."

He chuckled. "Aye, but it was careless."

"I hear no tread upon the stair. Happily, we are far enough removed from the others that I am hopeful they did not overhear. And I would not have you sorry for such an incredible deed."

He wiped a sleeve across his brow. "And it was one way to keep warm, at least."

I laughed. "Oh, we copulate to protect against the cold now?"

"If I may use that as an excuse to do so more, then aye."

"You need no such excuse."

His hold tightened. "Apparently, not."

Back on my bed, Luke held me in his arms whilst we whispered words of nonsense until the bell called us to compline. Which I walked to and endured with some awkwardness. But despite my soreness, I could not be anything but grateful for the thorough attentions Luke had bestowed.

The next day, the second candle of Advent was lit. The day after that I spent devoutly in quiet prayer, penance and reflection, observing the fast.

Chapter 18 - Where There Is Darkness, Light

The thirtieth day of November heralded St Andrew, brother to St Peter (formerly known as Simon); fisherman, apostle and martyr. He died on a *crux decussata,* the sideways cross, not believing himself worthy of dying on the same type of cross as Christ. He and St Peter did not travel as brothers, choosing instead to go their separate ways. Brotherly disagreement, or other interests?

It was an odd festivity, for it was a feast day yet in coincided with an Advent fast day. So, we abstained from flouting the rules—we didn't eat meat. We ate a fine dish of vegetables instead. And we may have enjoyed a sweet treat afterwards.

The hours of the summer seemed now reversed. Instead of spending time alone on saint's days, after supper, Luke and I went to the calefactory to join the others in the celebrations.

It was probably in order to avoid the build-up of too much competitiveness that the halatafl board was not brought out. It was disappointing not to be able to challenge Sub-Prior Gervase to a re-match.

However, it pleased me greatly to watch Luke as he played a game of tables with the almoner, Brother Cuthbert. Both were surely well-versed in using counters in their daily lives. And it was fascinating to watch them push their discs along the arrowed board.

Chance was relied on by the rolling of the dice. The skill lay in how the pieces were then moved. And I glowed with pride at seeing Luke's stratagem. When he won I had to content myself with a congratulatory slap of his shoulder whilst secretly longing to hold and kiss him.

And when even the severe Brother Hector congratulated his student, I had to school my features to avoid a smirk. It was a victory indeed. I wondered if it pained him to acknowledge that my beloved was not as foolish as he would make him out to be. Hopefully so. The churlish old goat.

Any ill-feeling was swept away as the next game began. Luke remaining in place to be challenged. No money was exchanged, of course. We played for honour only in the monastery. And such honour did my lief receive when he won the next game also. A round of clamorous applause rang out. And again, my frustration arose at not being able to congratulate him properly. But his sparkling gaze found mine, and all was said without action or words.

Besides, when alone the very next day, I made sure to offer my congratulations in their fullest terms.

We were careful not to repeat the boisterous behaviour of before. Mayhap we grew complacent in our fervour, but we did not lose all sense. We joined together as often as we could. The more we were granted, the more we yearned.

"Luke, I begin to fear for our souls," I told him the day after the feast of St Nicholas, lying abed in a state of satisfaction.

"How so, my sweeting?" he asked before kissing me and brushing his fingers through my hair.

"I begin to resent the saint's days."

"Oh, fie! You cannot be in earnest."

"As pleasant as it may be to spend time playing games, I would much rather be here."

"Ah, but that is only the evening of which you speak. You do not resent the veneration of the saints themselves."

My lips pressed together. "Hm. You have the right of it. Of course, it remains a source of joy that we may celebrate the saints as befits them. But then there is the matter of fasting, today being such an observance, and yet here we lay."

He smiled. And kissed my forehead. "There are times, my honey sweet, when I would wish your mind to be not so lively."

I bent my head down, but he brought it back up with a gentle finger. His kiss upon my lips was tender and lingering. "But most of the time, I am grateful for your intellect for it protects us both."

"It does no such thing."

He hissed. "I say it does. And I would remind you not to call me a liar."

I bit my lip. As soon as my teeth relinquished their hold, he sucked upon it. "Many times over have you thought of reasons for us to be alone. Your quick wit has even saved us from uncomfortable questioning on occasion. Add to this that you have helped bring me along in my own studies where once I struggled. And that has surely kept me also by your side."

Awkwardly, I smiled.

"I mean only to thank you, Paul."

"But it is I who would thank you. For you have raised me out of dullness. You have brought a light and joy into my life I had not known to be lacking."

"Then we have saved one another."

"And are happy."

"And we are happy."

We embraced more tightly.

Some part of my concern must have been recognised by Luke, as from then on, we were more careful to observe the days of fasting by our private abstinence. We sat and discussed religious matters or read during those periods instead, albeit holding or touching in some small way.

St Lucy's Day brought three ember ones in addition to our fasting for Advent. We were much fatigued by the lack of sustenance, and also seemed leeched of warmth. And so, we spent the evenings quietly reading in the calefactory. Everybody about seemed subdued.

We had bathed prior to this period, of course, but noticed not whether the brethren had gone to enjoy the company of women. I suppose they did. Luke and I had eyes only for each other. But through our time of penance, we ensured to atone for our sins. All of them.

It was all a great cycle; sin, repent, pray. Such is life.

The time of rejoicing was truly begun, however. For St Lucy had brought the light—the shortest day, the winter solstice was over. And amidst candlelight, the prayer had been said:

"Saint Lucy, you did not hide your light under a basket, but let it shine for the whole world, for all the centuries to see. We may not suffer torture in our lives the way you did, but we are still called to let the light of our Christianity illumine our daily lives. Please help us to have the courage to bring our Christianity into our work, our recreation, our relationships, our conversation - every corner of our day. Amen."

The worst of the darkness was over, and so a week later, we celebrated St Thomas The Apostle. There had been much cleaning throughout the day, and delicious smells had wafted from the bakehouse. We were treated to breads and pastries to our heart's content at supper in a balance to the day.

The fourth Advent candle had been lit; the end was nigh.

One more fast day was endured, and then Christmas arrived in all its glory. On the twenty-fourth day of December, we all made confession and completed penance. We also bathed. Nobody strayed from the rules. We were fully cleansed in readiness to celebrate the birth of Christ. Not one of us would pollute ourselves.

At midnight, wrapped in our cloaks and wearing warmer shoes, we descended the night stairs into the holly and ivy decorated church to hold Midnight Mass. Additional candles had been lit, and leaned a glow to the otherwise dark confines. As was Christ, the Light of the World, born into the darkness of human sin.

There was shuffling and coughing beyond the rood screen. We were mostly concealed by the partition, but it was apparent that the congregation of lay brothers was present. Christmas Masses were of solemn importance to all.

Prior Ambrose, in a voice as crisp and clear as the night, sang out, "*Et dicet in die illa ecce Deus noster iste expectavimus eum et salvabit nos iste Dominus sustinuimus eum exultabimus et laetabimur in salutari eius.*" (And it shall be said in that day, Lo, this is our God; we have waited for him, and he will save us: this is the Lord; we have waited for him, we will be glad and rejoice in his salvation.) [Isaiah 25:9]

And we all of us chanted *Laetentur caeli* of Psalm 96, filled with hope and joy as we sang to the Lord.

I listened with awe to the readings of God's loving mercy, of the genealogy of the Lord (including great saints and broken sinners), and the coming of the saviour. The miraculous conception never ceased to inspire warmth within my breast. How the Blessed Virgin Mary brought forth our salvation.

How excited I grew at the declaration, "*And Moses and Aaron said unto all the children of Israel, At even, then ye shall know that the Lord hath brought you out from the land of Egypt:*

And in the morning, then ye shall see the glory of the Lord; for that he heareth your murmurings against the Lord: and what are we, that ye murmur against us?" [Exodus 16:6-7].

The Lord was within me, and us all. Seven times daily I praised Him, but even more so in that office.

We departed, quiet as mice. Elsewhere, laity congregations would surely enjoy the ensuing liturgical drama of *Officium Pastorum*; an enactment of The Nativity according to St Luke. In my youth, whilst at home with my family, I had enjoyed the spectacle of shepherds, angels and the manger. I had even been permitted to take part sometimes. My '*Gloria in excelsis*' and '*Iam vere scimus*' were always sung with great zeal. All far too frivolous for my monkish self, however.

We returned to an empty church after attending our bodily functions. Lauds was celebrated with renewed vigour. The hours after were spent in quiet contemplation and prayer.

As daylight approached, we held Mass at Dawn, the Solemnity of the Nativity the Lord. And the lay brothers returned. Making our processional, we sang *Puer natus in Bethlehem* (A child is born in Bethlehem) with much reverence. Its many 'alleluias' hailed the adoration of Christ as he was brought into the world, visited by the ox, ass and the magi.

Prior Ambrose then proclaimed:

"The people that walked in darkness have seen a great light: they that dwell in the land of the shadow of death, upon them hath the light shined.

Thou hast multiplied the nation, and not increased the joy: they joy before thee according to the joy in harvest, and as men rejoice when they divide the spoil.

For thou hast broken the yoke of his burden, and the staff of his shoulder, the rod of his oppressor, as in the day of Midian.

For every battle of the warrior is with confused noise, and garments rolled in blood; but this shall be with burning and fuel of fire.

For unto us a child is born, unto us a son is given: and the government shall be upon his shoulder: and his name shall be called Wonderful, Counsellor, The mighty God, The everlasting Father, The Prince of Peace." [Isaiah 9:2-6]

We chanted back Psalm 92. And indeed, it was good to give thanks and sing praises to His name.

Readings were read, psalms and alleluias sung, and communion taken. And the first rays of light streamed through the great window in a cascade of colours.

A third Mass was later held, that of The Day. In which, we celebrated the divinity of Jesus.

"And the Word was made flesh, and dwelt among us, (and we beheld his glory, the glory as of the only begotten of the Father,) full of grace and truth." [John 1:14]

So that by the end of the three additional Masses, we had celebrated Christ in his genealogy, light and glory, and divinity.

A special sermon was said during our chapter meeting. And our usual offices were still held around all of this. It had already been a full, long day when we entered the misericord. But what a feast lay before us, including a Grete Pye. I cannot in all certainty say, but I believe the meats within were beef, duck and hen. Whatever they were, they were delicious and satisfying.

The open arse fruits from the cloister had been baked into a tart. And there were even yellow and red bryndons; the yellow cakes sitting in a red wine sauce of fruit and nuts. Spiced wine washed all of this down nicely.

"I am replete," I exclaimed, rubbing my belly as Luke and I waddled through the cloister afterwards.

"Aye, mayhap I over-indulged, but it was all too delicious. And one should not be wasteful."

"Indeed, we should not." I smirked, bumping his shoulder with mine.

We successfully made it through nones but retired to the dormitory for a nap afterwards. And we were not alone.

Everybody seemed to be made lazy yet joyous as we gathered in the calefactory that evening. It was then that we were all bestowed with our gifts of new robes.

Of course, that was not the end of Christmas. It was only the beginning. Two additional Masses were held on St Stephen's Day, the Feast of St John the Evangelist, the Feast of the Holy Innocents and the Feast St Thomas of Canterbury – that is each day from the twenty-sixth to the twenty-ninth of December. The thirty-first day of December held only one extra Mass, for St Sylvester.

But then the first of January arrived. Prior Ambrose gifted us each a new knife. And we celebrated two Masses for The Feast of the Circumcision of Christ, and the Octave of Christmas. His first blood was spilled, and there began our redemption.

"And when eight days were accomplished for the circumcising of the child, his name was called Jesus, which was so named of the angel before he was conceived in the womb." [Luke 2:21].

It was almost a relief when we observed the two Masses of Epiphany on the sixth day of January. Prior Ambrose also said a sermon in Chapter. The magi had brought their gifts of gold, frankincense and myrrh, and celebrated for eight days (the Octave of Epiphany).

Clapping his hands together, standing in the infirmary, Brother Giles smiled. "Well, Paul. We shall soon see an end of all this gout, constipation and flatulence, eh?"

"There has been a great quantity of sufferers."

"Ah, as is always the case during Christmastide. All the merriment and feasting lends itself to such. You will note how I ensured we had a good supply of remedies."

"You are wise."

"I am old and have born witness to such ailments many a year. But it is better than starving over winter. We must take comfort and give thanks for being well fed hereabouts."

Smiling, I rubbed my belly. "I am indeed thankful."

Chapter 19 – Through The Eye of a Needle

January crept along with fingers of ice. The water in our dormitory wash basin was frozen most mornings, and we had to break the surface if we were to have a chance of getting cleaned.

One day, it even grew so cold that the water froze in the pipes to the lavatorium. Lay brothers had to fetch buckets of heated water from the kitchen so we could wash our hands before eating. Brother Ulric, our refectorian, was full of blushes despite our assurances that we did not blame him.

The cold also meant that Luke and I spent most evenings in the calefactory. Any grain of warmth was welcomed in those dark, cold, bitter nights. We often shared a bed as we slept, huddling close for warmth. Brother Barnabas said not a word.

I had yet another reason to be thankful for my role in the infirmary, as there was always a fire there. Although, I then felt the cold more keenly when leaving its cosy confines. But I was kept busy, as people came with coughs and colds.

It was here where Brother Faramond discovered me, his face flushed. "Paul, make haste, you have a visitor in the outer parlour. I have sent word for the prior to attend as well. Have you some restorative? Mayhap my small supply of wine is sufficient—"

Brother Giles interrupted his rambling. "Brother, calm yourself. Who is this visitor who inspires such frenzy?"

"Why, Sybil is come, your brother's wife, Paul."

My stomach lurched. "Sybil? But where is Harry? What is the meaning of this?"

"Your brother is gravely ill and she seeks your intervention."

"Me?"

Brother Giles placed a kindly hand upon my shoulder. "Come, Paul. We will go together and discover what the nature of this illness is. Mayhap we can supply a remedy, eh?"

Struck dumb, I merely nodded. My feet only moved when Giles' hand pushed against my back.

"Oh, Paul, you are here," Sybil shrieked, rising to her feet and throwing herself into my arms.

"But of course. Where else would I be? Pray, sit. Have you partaken of any wine? May we get you something else? Slowly and calmly, we will hear what you have to say."

Whisps of brown hair had escaped her hennin, her cheeks were ruddy, and there were yet unshed tears in her blue eyes. All of this I observed yet made no mention. Prior Ambrose looked upon the scene in bewildered silence.

"You look so like him. Might I call you brother?" Sybil asked.

"Aye."

"Oh, brother…Harry…" she took a breath. "He has a fever. At first, it was his tummy which hurt. But my…apothecary's remedy seemed to have no effect. Then there was," she lowered her voice to a whisper, "blood in his stool."

Brother Giles leaned forwards. "And has the apothecary been again?"

"Aye, and bled him, decrying the *bloody flux*. But his fever worsens. Paul, I fear for his life. Then where will we all be? I have tried...every remedy recommended," her face fell into her hands as she began to weep.

I rubbed her arm, not knowing what to say and looked to Brother Giles.

"Indeed, it sounds like dysentery. My dear, how long has he been suffering?"

"Four days. He grows weaker and shrinks before my eyes," Sybil replied through her tears.

"I beg one more question. I know it is distressing, but we must know. Which herbs have been tried?"

"Peppermint and honey in vinegar, sir."

"This is all?"

"The apothecary said the bloodletting should have been sufficient to balance his humours. And I have prayed. Oh, how I have prayed."

"Very well. Prior Ambrose, does Paul have your permission to attend to his brother as requested?"

"Err, yes, if needs must."

"I fear they do. Would you be so kind as to ready a horse, Brother Faramond?"

"Two," Prior Ambrose insisted.

"Two?"

"Paul cannot travel alone. It is most improper. Can we find that Brom fellow? He has surely learned something of some use whilst working so often near the infirmary? And looks handy in case of brigands. He will do nicely."

Giles bowed. "I shall seek him out on the way to prepare something for Paul to take with him."

I was ushered out of the parlour and was aware of the prior leaving shortly after as we strode across to the infirmary.

Brother Giles was muttering oaths under his breath against foolish apothecaries the entire way.

"Brom, praise be. Come inside, we have an errand for you."

He explained to Brom as we went into the back room. And proceeded to gather bottles and jars. Syrup of damask rose, yarrow and plantain made up one bottle. And in another was a drink with salt and honey.

"Paul, fetch an egg from the kitchen on your way back, and when ready, crack only the egg white into a cup and mix it with some of this," he said, holding up the bottle with the salty concoction.

I nodded.

"He will need this first. The yarrow is to be mixed with wine. You may also bathe his head with a vinegar solution."

Again, I nodded. "Might I take some pennyroyal mint for that same purpose?"

"I understand why it is that which you favour. Of course, you may."

"Thank you."

"Good. Keep your head, mind. You know what to do. I would go myself, but you were requested and will surely be quicker in any case. God speed, my young friend. Brom, take care of him on the road."

"It will be my honour."

"Now go. May God be with you both."

We rode hard. It did not take long for me to gain a long lead. Solatium seemed eager to meet my demands, keeping her strides long and swift, responding to my every flurry of reins and nudge of heel. There was a small voice warning me of the dangers of this, but I ignored it—my urgency was master of all. The sooner I got to my brother the more likely his survival, if it were not already too late. But no, I could not entertain that notion. I would reach him in time and God would prevail.

Brom did his best to keep up. Sybil lingered behind with her servant at her side; at least she had the presence of mind to bring a man with her. Questions of why she did not send him alone as messenger would keep. She had ridden this journey already and was no doubt weary.

With every hoof beat, I offered a prayer that I be not too late. That Harry would overcome. I could not think what would happen to Sybil and little Percival if he did not. And from her emotional state and the way her hand kept returning to her belly, there may be another babe soon. Oh, calamity for them all without Harry. My heels struck my horse's side.

Our steeds tired, so I stopped at an inn to exchange horses for Brom and myself, with a promise to collect them on my return. Solatium remained precious to me, and I would not sacrifice her to this journey. Not to mention I had no desire to incur Prior Ambrose's wrath by losing such a fine mare. She belonged to the monastery now.

I was unrelenting in my fast pace. Sweat poured from both myself and the borrowed horse who snorted often. But at length, we arrived at the house. A servant came outside and looked about.

"Sybil will arrive in due course. My hurry was too great to wait for her. Would you be so good as to show Brom where to get a large bowl of hot water when he arrives, he is not far behind. And I shall need a cup and some wine."

"You are Paul?"

"Yes, of course I am he. Show me to Harry this instant." My manners were lost to concern, and the servant flinched at my tone, so I added, "If you please."

"Very good, sir."

I ran to my brother's side. How frail he looked, lying upon his bed. Memories of Luke lying likewise fought to surface in my mind, but as these only increased my panic, I quashed them.

Brightly, I greeted, "Harry. Good to see you. Now, we shall soon have you on the mend. I will caution you that I am unaccustomed to grumbling of late, so will hear none. You shall drink what you are given and that will be an end to it."

Harry groaned, clutching his middle. The servant who had been at his side got up and took away a foul-smelling pot. And soon returned with it emptied. Brom arrived with the items I'd requested.

"Many thanks," I said.

Quickly, I broke an egg white into the cup, leaving the yolk in a separate dish. "Brom, mayhap the cook would like to make a caudle with this?"

He silently took it from me and disappeared from sight. I added some of the mixture Brother Giles had given me. And helped Harry sit up a little.

"This shan't be the most pleasant drink you've ever had, but I daresay it won't be the worst either. Drink it up now," I instructed, holding the cup to his lips.

His cheeks blew large.

"Uh, huh. Drink it down."

A forced gulp was gained with a grimace.

"Well done. Rest now."

I added some vinegar and pennyroyal to the bowl of hot water, and mopped Harry's brow. He was suspiciously silent. But he was awake and not delirious. There was hope.

Not long after, I assisted him as he refilled his chamber pot. Which dear Brom took away and brought back fresh. The household servants seemed to take our presence as a means to keep away, not that I could blame them.

Sybil stood at the bedchamber door.

"He is being cared for, sister. Do not partake of this miasma more than needs be. I shall tell you of any change."

"I am glad you are here," she said quietly before leaving.

I mixed the other tincture next and got him to drink that. Brom took over the application of the cloth to Harry's forehead whilst I chanted Psalm 56 three times. Then the 'Our Father' nine times. And, at last, he fell into restless slumber.

This is what I could give that no other could. My initial vows brought me closer to God. And I prayed he would listen now, just as he had with Luke.

I may have renounced my family and belongings upon entering the monastery. But I was still a man and could not entirely sever my heart and blood. The bonds remained unbroken.

Harry was a good man and did not deserve this. I would not believe that he had sinned so greatly as to bring God's punishment upon himself. There had to be some error. I added my own prayers for recovery.

When he awoke, I got Harry to drink more of the salty mixture. I wasn't sure how often to administer it but thought it best to replace what he may have lost in his last movement. He also managed to partake some of the caudle which was brought in. I made sure to thank the servant who did so. I know he should have been fasting, but caudle was surely beneficial. How I longed for Brother Giles' guidance. I was all confusion.

Prior Ambrose had not made any conditions upon my visit, so I stayed with my brother all night and the next day. Whatever fluids he lost I tried to replenish. There was no need for further bloodletting – there was plenty present in his pot.

There was little change, and I began to further doubt my actions. Should I make Harry fast completely? But he was so gaunt and weak. Surely, he required some sustenance. And it was all in liquid form. But mayhap it was his bile which was imbalanced, and he required drying out? Why was it me who was sent? Brother Giles would know precisely what must be done.

"Do you have any suggestions?" I asked Brom in desperation whilst Harry slept.

"I'm sure you know best."

"But look at him."

"I think he is using the pot a little less?"

"Possibly."

"When in doubt, pray," he said, shrugging.

"Indeed. Will you join me?"

Bless him, he was not so well versed but chanted along as best he was able as I recited the Psalm again.

Kneeling by my brother's side, I took his hand in mine. "Fight, Harry. If not for me, for your wife and Percival. For your unborn child, come back to them. If ever you have wronged, if it be in my power, I forgive you. Prythee, do not leave."

Overcome, I walked out of doors and knelt in the golden hues of the setting sun. Raising my hands, I implored, "God, won't you spare this good man, this humble servant, my honourable brother? I beseech Thee."

I waited with bated breath for a sign of being heard. But none came. All about was silent. And I wept.

"Oh, Lord, won't you hear my prayer? I am lost in shadow. Won't you guide my hand? For I know not what to do. Have I erred? Is this not what was planned for me? Tell me not now that I have been suffering under misapprehension. Is this punishment? I am here at your bidding alone, your servant in all things. Speak and it shall be done. But tell me, what I must do.

"*For thou art my rock and my fortress; therefore for thy name's sake lead me, and guide me.*" [Psalm 31:3]

Again, I waited. But this time, as I sat in the fading light, calm enveloped me, allowing my breaths to be drawn with their usual regularity. Wiping away the mud from my tunic as best I could, and generally righting my appearance, I returned to my post to continue the work I'd been given.

With a steadier hand, I administered the medicines. With a firmer voice, I offered my prayers. With love in my heart, I kept vigil.

During the night, with blessed relief, the fever stopped. Brom hurried to inform Sybil, who came in immediately.

"Harry!" she cried, collapsing at his side.

As weak as he was, he turned his head and smiled at her. His look was filled with such love that my breath caught in my throat. Luke often gazed upon me with the same countenance. And once again, I marvelled at how blessed I was.

The next morning, Sybil begged my attention. I left Brom to look after Harry as I went with her.

"I cannot ever thank you enough."

"My brother's return to full health shall be all the thanks I require. But I offer caution, for it may take some time for him to be fully restored."

"I understand you are much skilled with herbs, as I have seen. You surely have knowledge I do not."

She held up a hand as I opened my mouth. "Do not dismiss what I have to say, prythee. For I have in my possession some knowledge which mayhap you do not. I do not presume to state this as fact. But it occurs to me that a meeting of minds is a wondrous thing. So, I entrust to you what my mother did to me."

She slid a large pile of papers to me. "My family...we were wise women. But on this occasion, I knew not enough. I would not risk that happening again. Would you write down the information that you judge may be most useful to you, and return this with some which is lacking from mine? I ask only a fair exchange. For Harry's sake."

"I...errr—"

"To protect our family, Paul, might we not help one another?"

"Well—"

"I swear to God that the information will be seen only by myself and any daughter who may come into this world. It has been our way, and the secret has never been spoken of until this moment. Mothers have taught daughters for generations to read and write for this purpose."

"But you are not a wise woman?"

"There is an apothecary here who would not take kindly to my interference, so it is kept secret. But there have been those before me who lived openly, dispensing remedies."

"But not for dysentery?"

"You mock me. But of course, I had tried those which had previously been effective before darkening your door."

"Forgive me. You had told Brother Giles—"

"I told him what he needed to hear. And I spoke no lie. But the herbs of which I spoke were from here, not that useless apothecary."

"I see."

"Prythee, Brother. Do not spurn me. I know we can help one another. I know it."

"Far be it for me to dismiss an opportunity to learn. I shall look over these papers."

"Thank you."

"I may take them with me?"

"So long as you return them."

"On that, I give you my word."

She embraced me then, a thankful sister to an unworthy brother, for I held great doubt that there was anything new for Brother Giles' compendium. Still, I took it, if only to avoid causing further offense. I could at least add a page on the dysentery remedies which had saved her husband.

Chapter 20 – Fine As Frost on The Ground

The journey home was colder than the one there. In my haste, I had whipped up warmth to combat the chill. Now, it seeped into my every bone as we made slower progress. The ice glistening in puddles shone with the perils I'd risked. But I would do so again. Harry was out of danger, and that is all that mattered.

Brom and I retrieved our horses from the inn. He held the silence I craved. My mind was pondering much. From the intensity of my family bonds which were not supposed to remain— did this mean I was not truly ready to become a monk? To the tied pages which lay hidden in my wallet—could some country woman know what the most learned in the land did not? And had I acted as I should? Was this my true calling?

Surrounding all of this lay my desire to get home. The last days had been an ordeal, and all I wanted was for Luke to hold me until I felt whole once more, until all doubts disappeared.

We returned in time for vespers, but Brother Giles came to greet us at the stables. Someone must have informed him of our arrival.

"Brother Giles, greetings. Is there anything amiss?"

"Mercy, no. I am having baths drawn for both of you and wished you to go to the bath house immediately."

"Me also?" Brom asked, aghast.

"Certainly. You have both been breathing the dark miasma of a sick room. And I would not have you breathe it back out amongst the brethren. The perfumed steam should dampen down and chase away any foulness. May you be cleansed of any lurking demons which would threaten us all. Paul, your brother is well, I trust, else you would have other words upon your lips, I think?"

"Aye, he is out of danger at least. Oh, Brother Giles, how lost I was without you."

"Nonsense. Your brother is recovering. It seems you did precisely the right thing."

"I was so unsure."

He tapped his nose. "There are times when we all question our actions. We cannot possibly know everything. Then we must draw upon the knowledge we do have and act in a way which reason suggests is most sound. It is why I created my compendium, for nor can I remember everything at all times, and it is good to have notes to refer to."

He urged us into the hot water which contained yarrow and vinegar. It seemed over cautious. I was not unwell, so surely this was not necessary. But I would not gainsay the wisdom of Brother Giles. Besides, after the bitter cold, the warmth was more than welcome.

The monk remained with us. I suppose he did not trust Brom alone with me in a state of undress. But he missed vespers for two people who were not sick, which gave me concern.

We soaked until the water ran cold. And as I was getting dressed, a mass of blond locks poked around the door. With a rush which brought in cold air, my lief flung himself at my person, almost knocking me off my feet. Kisses were pecked all over our faces as we clung on to one another.

"You are home. You are home safe," Luke murmured.

"Aye. How I missed you."

"And I—"

A cough sounded behind me, and we leaped apart. "Apologies, Brother," we chimed.

Brother Giles chuckled. "I am glad we are in safe company but let us not get carried away. Paul, I have a special supper awaiting in the infirmary. I thought mayhap you would like Luke to join us?"

"We are not going to the refectory?"

"It is a fish day. I could not have you wandering back half starved. Whether the news was good or ill, I felt privacy was required. Our work is never easy, Paul. Some days seem to be challenges sent by God to test our fortitude. We must ensure we ourselves are at our best so we may endure all and are better able to serve others."

"You are too kind. But Luke?"

He smiled. "Is to join us. The prior agreed you should have a friend nearby lest...well, least said."

Brom bowed but was stopped from leaving by Brother Giles' hand upon his arm. ""You too, you sweet fopdoodle."

Brom's jaw worked silently, his eyes wide as he cast his gaze between us all.

"Do not look so astonished. You both must own that you undertook a perilous task. One which demanded a great deal from you. Do not think me ungrateful. Come."

To say the four of us made a merry party would be to undermine the serious nature of our gathering. However, it was a glimpse of a normal life which was entirely unmonkish. A taste of what could have been if circumstances had been different. Friends dining together, talking sociably. The conversation was not entirely frivolous, however.

"Paul, I feel I must beg your forgiveness."

My knife dropped with a clatter at the admission from Brother Giles.

"You should never have been asked to attend your brother. It was too cruel. I should have insisted on going in your stead. In not doing so, I failed you and am most sorry for it."

"No. No. You said yourself, you felt unequal to the speed which was necessary."

Brom sniggered. "I am not so sure Paul was up to it. You should have seen him. I thought his horse would fall at any moment. But ice melted under Solatium's hooves, I swear it. Else she had grown wings."

Luke turned his concerned gaze to me. "I am glad she kept you safe." Under the table, he held my hand.

Brother Giles, ever the voice of reason, tsked and added, "Praise be to God for bearing you safely there and back again."

"We thank you, Heavenly Father," the three of us chorused.

At the end of our meal, Brother Giles sent Brom and Luke to clean the plates. Once alone, he turned to me. "Paul, in this, God has been gracious but also a little cruel."

I started.

"Allow me to explain. Twice now you have stared at death in the dimming eyes of a loved one. Twice now you have succeeded where few others would. You have a God-given talent. But even He will not save everyone. Where there is life also is there death. And it pains me to remind you that sooner or later, death will win. For we are all called by God in our time."

I gasped.

"It is the way of things. We are none of us immortal. I have seen the fervour with which you perform your duties, and it is to be commended. But I would have you prepared, Paul. To lose…" His voice faltered.

I took his hands in mine. "Brother Giles. My friend. My teacher. I thank you for the reminder which I see has caused you pain. It is an important lesson, and the one I am least eager to learn. But if I can bear it with half the strength you do, I shall be most blessed."

He wiped at his eyes. "I am a sentimental old fool."

"You are no such thing, as well you know."

The boys returned and we prayed. Luke and I gave our thanks and readied to depart alone. Indeed, we had gone a few yards before I realised I'd forgotten my wallet. Turning on my heel, I dashed back inside. There was a scuffling.

"I beg pardon. I left my wallet," I explained, swiftly retrieving the item and hurrying away.

Luke was waiting at the door, and I hurried him away.

"Is everything all right?" he enquired.

"Fine."

Not until we were alone in the dormitory did I dare confide, "I think Brom and Giles had been…embracing?"

He shrugged. "Possibly. I am sure Brother Giles missed his helper."

"And one is thus affectionate with every lay brother and servant?"

"Oh, I see. But he's so old. It is not likely. Surely, he is friend and father to Brom as he is you."

"I suppose."

"Do not look for more than is there."

"Mayhap I want too greatly for my friend to have comfort. Brother Giles remains grief-stricken. I do not think his heart can bear it."

"Well, I am certain he finds solace in his own way."

"Indeed. It is not for me to question where and how. But Lord bless Brom. He was of great service to me these past days."

Luke raised his eyebrows. "Not too great, I trust."

"Beast!" I cried, playfully slapping his arm.

"Grr," he roared, pushing me back onto the bed.

He lay atop me, grinding and making more animalistic noises. I laughed yet was curiously aroused.

His eyes narrowed and glimmered as he drew near and devoured me with kisses. Removing our drawers and robes with fumbling fingers, we lay naked. It did not take many strokes of Luke's hand to bring us off together.

"I truly missed you," he murmured.

"And I you."

It had been an odd few days, and my nerves were fraught. But between Luke's caresses and our daily routine, tranquillity was restored. The offices brought their own serenity as my soul sought God. How stark the contrast; the dangers outside these walls seemed to amplify the serenity within. And I gave thanks.

In my quiet moments, I began to read the pages given to me by Sybil. Determination to find anything which may better prepare me drove me into a frantic search. For I would never again feel so lost as I did that desperate night. Knowledge must be obtained. My studious nature would at last be the making of me, and not a hindrance.

I had not told Brother Giles of the pages' existence. But upon gleaming some discernment, it was necessary for me to compare it with his compendium which meant seeking his permission.

"Fascinating," Brother Giles remarked as I finally shared some insights, "That by simply making use of what was to hand, these women have come by some useful discoveries. Yes, I can see now how this would cool the blood, balancing the sanguine. Yes. But then, this to calm the melancholic black bile. They may not term it in such phrasing. Whether they realised it or not, there is sound reasoning behind some of this. I shall inspect it all and inform you which should be written up. You did a splendid job last time."

"Thank you, Brother."

"I see how you hesitate. Speak. What else would you ask?"

"You do not mind my obtaining this?"

"Paul, God delivers what He sees fit in many ways. It is not for us to question how. We must always remain grateful for learning."

"And...would that learning be granted both ways?"

"Your brother's wife asks for an exchange?"

"It seems only fair."

"In equal quantities. For sometimes, a little knowledge is a dangerous thing. And I would not have her cause harm or seek advancement. I shall advise you also of what you should write for her."

"Thank you, Brother. She has sworn to use it for her family alone."

"I'm not sure what the prior will make of all this."

"Must he know?"

"Paul! Still your tongue."

"But she holds this secret close. I should not even have told you."

"Why so?"

"The apothecary seems to think any other influence an affront."

"Hmm…some people are too full of their own importance. This puts me in a very difficult position. I should not keep secrets from the prior."

"I understand."

"But then, perhaps he only needs to know I have come into possession of some knowledge which should be recorded, and not the source? I can hardly ask for several sheets of parchment without any explanation at all. Leave it with me. I shall be discreet."

"You have my gratitude, Brother. Truly, I know not what I should do without your wisdom."

He patted me on the shoulder. "You would find a different way."

On the 18th day of January in the year of our Lord 1486, bells rang out in a full peal across the land. King Henry VII of the House of Lancaster married Elizabeth of York. It had been whispered that he'd applied for Papal dispensation to wed her. The House of Tudor now supplanted all the ugliness of what went before. Now the red rose and the white combined to herald peace. May God grant it so.

Indeed, it was quite a time of feasting for soon after, we celebrated the Saints Fabian and Sebastian, then Saint Agnes, and finally Saint Vincent of Saragossa. So many martyrs. So many gave their lives in the name of our Lord in order that we may all worship. Persecution of the innocent. Why must there be so much hatred?

My sad ponderings made me all the more thankful that the remainder of January passed quietly, if not coldly. The hoar frost often lay so thick it seemed like snow; grass, trees and bushes grew white spikes. And our feet certainly stung with bitterness as we trudged about the monastery and shivered our way through the offices. We spent as much time huddled around the precious few fires as we could. But, when my fingers could move sufficiently, I began work on Sybil's book.

Chapter 21 – You See My Heart, You Know My Desires

February creaked in. I had always enjoyed the celebration of Candlemas, or the Feast of the Purification of the Blessed Virgin Mary. And this year was no exception.

Prior Ambrose, dressed in a stole and cope of purple, recited five orations and anointed the years' supply of candles, blessing them. We then sung the Canticle of Simeon, *Simeon, Nunc Dimittis,* including the antiphon, *Lumen ad revelationem gentium et gloriam plebis tuae Israel* (A light to the revelation of the Gentiles and the glory of thy people Israel). Warmth spread throughout me, knowing this came from the Gospel of Luke.

The saint's namesake stood next to me with shoulders shuddering as he held back a fit of giggles. By means of looking straight at the altar and focusing on the ritual, I maintained a more dignified composure. And nudged the fopdoodle, who cleared his throat and stood still once more.

Candles were then lit, and we carried them in a procession whilst chanting, "*Adorna thalamum tuum, Sion*" (Adorn the bridal chamber, O Zion). In so doing, we honoured the entry of Christ, who is the light of the world, into the Temple of Jerusalem.

We proceeded into the cemetery and returned to the church door where Prior Ambrose stood with an image of the Holy Child. We all entered, intoning the Canticle of Zachary.

Finally, we sang *Gaude Maria Virgo,* in honour of the Blessed Virgin Mary.

We did not sacrifice a lamb per se, but we did dine on a dish of it in the misericord.

When we were next alone, I did rebuke Luke for almost luring me into foolishness during a solemn occasion.

"It is not as though I could help it," Luke defended, grinning.

"Please do try harder. Unless, of course, you would have us both turned out."

"They wouldn't dare lose such a skilled healer."

"Luke, pray, do not elevate me above my position. I did what any other infirmarer would."

"And yet have brought two people back from the brink of death."

"Luke, I urge caution."

His smile grew wicked. "But I would give thanks."

"You already have."

"But should I use my mouth or a candle this day?"

"You are determined to ignore me."

"You would deny me?"

Rolling my eyes, I assented, "That I cannot do, as well you know."

Readying myself, I offered up silent prayers that God would forgive the abuse of a sacred candle.

"It is a blessed act, surely."

"Do try to be less blasphemous."

Lurching across the bed, he snuck a kiss. "You make me feel blessed. And God looks kindly upon us. Else I would not be here to say such fiendish words."

I kissed him back. "Let us not try His patience."

"Very well. I beg pardon. Do you forgive me?"

Only after kissing him more soundly, did I reply, "Always."

He disappeared behind me and licked around my hole, making me groan with pleasure. "Your own skill increases."

His moan of acknowledgment sent tremors throughout me. Inwards, his tongue plunged, and I stifled a grunt.

There was an infuriating pause as he oiled a finger, which followed the same path as his thorough tongue lashing had. And as he beckoned, that place within me was reached.

"Oh, sweet mercy," I whispered through clenched teeth.

The desecrated candle soon replaced his finger, and blood thundered in my ears. My hips rocked back, eager for more as Luke took his time drawing the candle in and out.

"It is not enough. Luke, I want you," I pleaded.

Wasting no time, making no argument, Luke complied. With great mastery, he plunged in and out of me, making me clench around him most wantonly. So eager was I that my hips drew nearer him.

Oh, wondrous bliss. His thrusts were as powerful as they were exquisite. As his hand reached around to my pillicock, I clutched onto the bed covers, burying my moans into them, as I was sent to Heaven.

With a stifled cry, Luke too was given release. And collapsed atop me. "Tell me again how this is not a blessing."

"I cannot recall any sound argument." Turning, I found myself in his arms, and we covered one another in kisses.

Delicate white and green snowdrops peeped their heads through a blanket of snow. It was too great a temptation. After prime and breakfast, Luke and I rushed out of doors in the eerie morning light.

Breathing deep, the air felt crisper and oddly less cold than of late. Silence seemed to echo around the grounds; all trace of sound was loud in its absence. Leaning my head back, I opened my mouth, ready to catch falling snowflakes upon my tongue. No sooner had I succeeded when there fell a thump on my back, closely followed by a cold dampness.

"Did you just throw a snowball at me?" I cried.

"It is possible that is what happened," Luke replied, his eyes sparkling as he smirked.

Whoomph! Another hit me. "That was not you."

"Nay."

Looking about, I sought the culprit. Laughter alerted me to where my attacker lurked, just around the corner of the lavatorium. Bending down, I scooped up snow in my hands and ran forwards. Luke threw a snowball as Brom tried to make a run for it. His fell short, but mine struck the lay brother in the face, making him shriek.

"Good aim," someone called across, applauding.

I was momentarily stunned, realising it was the normally serious sacrist, Brother Godfrey.

Taking advantage of my lapse, Brom hurled another snowball which caught my arm.

"Try this then," Brother Godfrey called, aiming at Brom.

"Hey!" he whined, shaking snow from his hair.

"Don't start what you are not prepared to finish, young man."

"Is that so?" he queried, giving as good as he got.

Laughter peeled behind me, as a snowball hurtled towards Luke from Brother Ulric, who had come out of the refectory. "It cannot be left at three to one."

"Aye, that would be most grievous," I agreed, defending my lover with a steady aim.

"My children," Prior Ambrose admonished as he approached. But from behind his back, he too produced a white orb, which was thrown at Brother Ulric.

Sub-prior Gervase seemed a little too gleeful as he caught his superior in the face. Shouts, hollers and laughter rang out all around as the other brethren entered the fray. We packed the snow less and threw gentler near the elder brothers, although they were enjoying themselves mayhap more than any of us. We were all of us boys again in the purity of the snow.

Even the servants had joined us at play by the time we finished in a mass of heaving, panting, damp bodies.

"Come along, everybody to the calefactory before you all take ill," Prior Ambrose announced. "And I mean everybody. Just this once."

Two of the kitchen staff joined us a while later, bringing a goodly supply of warmed hypocras. We all sipped eagerly as our fingers and toes burned with returning feeling. We stomped on the spot and huddled around the fire. But not one person seemed sorry for our frivolity, no matter the consequences.

The day after was far more subdued as we celebrated St Agatha. Yet another beautiful young lady reported to the authorities by a spurned would-be suitor.

"*Jesus Christ, Lord of all, you see my heart, you know my desires. Possess all that I am. I am your sheep: make me worthy to overcome the devil,*" she prayed with tears in her eyes as she faced a judge. Despite almighty sufferings, she never renounced her faith.

With sorrow in my heart, I partook of the feast in her name.

The Shriving Bell rang out on the fourteenth day of February for Shrove Tuesday. We all bathed and made confession, and our confessor shrived us and apportioned penance. Much of the day was spent in quiet contemplation of such, and thus Luke and I had no lessons with Father Barnabas.

All within the employ of the priory were fed with pancakes. And many also enjoyed a feast of beef, cheese and ale. I enjoyed it as heartily as possible, knowing the trials of Lent would begin the next day.

In this same spirit, there was even a game of Tug of War played – the brethren versus the workers. It was no great surprise that the workers were the victors, but we cheered them loudly all-the-same. They did so much to support our community, and in our small way, we acknowledged that.

After additional Mass and supper, the monks retired to the calefactory. All were gathered around games of tables. Only once we were certain of their entire preoccupation did Luke and I slink away.

We, of course, found refuge in the dormitory. It was still bitterly cold, but Lent was nigh and we had vowed to abstain from all sin for the duration.

"I would celebrate St Valentine this day, my honey sweet," Luke murmured. *"For this was on seynt Valentynes day, Whan every foul cometh there to chese his make."*

"Would you call me a bird?" I asked, feigning offence.

Holding me closer in his arms, he whispered, "Nay, I would name you my mate."

Our kiss was full of tenderness and wonder, and I melted into his embrace. My breath was stolen away, and I had to stand a while to steady myself.

Rubbing my back, Luke checked, "You are well?"

"My lief, I am in full health and full emotion. I was but momentarily overcome." I stood upright once more.

Stroking my cheek he confirmed, "I meant it."

"I know and thank you for such lofty sentiment. You must know I return the same regard."

"I do."

"But mayhap I should choose not to quote from Chaucer's *Parliament of Fowles* the now, but from the bible. For I feel the truth of '*This is my commandment, That ye love one another, as I have loved you. Greater love hath no man than this, that a man lay down his life for his friends.*'" [John 15:12-13]

"I am not certain even Christ himself could love you as I do."

"Mayhap, it is merely not in the same fashion?"

We chuckled. "I should think not. Nay, I think it safer to remain with Chaucer. '*Saynt Valentyne, that are ful hy on-lofte, Thus syngen smale foules for thy sake: Now welcome, somer…*"

I completed, "*Now welcome, somer, with thy sonne softe, That hast this wintres wedres overshake.*"

Luke broke into song, and I joined in the harmony as we two sang out *Dit de l'alérion*, a love song of four birds.

"You even sing of birds?" I asked with a grin once we were finished.

"Aye. My little sparrow who came back to me."

"When did I leave?"

"You…went to your brother."

"Because he was sick, believed dying."

He shrugged and cast his eyes down. "You had opportunity to escape."

"Oh, Luke, tell me not now that you doubted my return? For a month you have held this sorrow and unfairness within? Why?"

With a waft, he sat upon his bed and raked his hands through his hair. "I am sorry for it."

Walking across, my hands traced the path of his. "And so you ought to be. I cannot believe the thought so much as crossed your mind."

"It fills me with shame, prythee do not seek to create more."

I knelt down in front of him, catching his gaze and thumbing his cheek. "I would not. It was merely surprise which took hold. My lief, there was no doubt in my mind. It had not even occurred to me as a possibility. This is my home. With you."

"I did not intend to ever tell you."

"But you did."

"Quite by accident. I knew myself as a fool as soon as you returned. But you were gone so long, and I could not help but worry. You could live outside these walls."

I kissed his cheek. "I am sorry to have inspired such fear. But why would I choose to live out there when there is so much in here? Pray, do not doubt me again. Let this day of confession serve its purpose. Shrive such doubts."

"I had thought them to be dismissed already."

I sighed. "Not in fullness, it would seem, else the words would not have been upon your tongue. Luke, I will never leave you. In every sense, you are my life. Do you hear me?"

"I am sorry," he whispered, pulling me to him.

We held onto one another in the dark quiet of the dormitory. After several deep breaths, I dared to move my head enough to nuzzle his neck. "I love you."

"I love you too. To distraction."

Slowly, we unfolded from our embrace. Tentatively, we kissed. Finding the answers he had sought, Luke took more, plunging his tongue into my mouth. I gladly gave him all he required.

Raising his robes, I took ahold of his stiffness. His hips jutted so he slid within my grasp. Luke's eyes shone with need, and so I knelt at his feet and took him into my mouth. He gasped.

Sucking him in more, I moaned in pleasure. And was answered with a groan and a push of his hips. His fingers travelled through my hair, to the back of my head and urged me onwards. Relaxing my jaw, I obeyed. But as our movements quickened, he suddenly pulled out.

"Paul. I would enter you another way."

Looking up, I saw his urgency and nodded. Despite the chill, I removed my tunic and drawers, and he copied. Applying oil, I laid me down upon my back. Reverently, he lay atop and slid inside me. I was determined to allow him to set the pace, but how I longed for it to be faster. My need seemed to exceed his.

Seating himself fully, Luke looked at me. Either my desire showed, or I agreed to his for he began thrusting powerfully. My hands clutched his flesh as I rutted back mindlessly. What began as sweet devotion dissolved into frenzy.

Wildly, he bucked. My legs kicked out. Together, we grunted and gasped. I gripped on tightly to the bedding to steady us. But to no avail. We only grew more frantic.

Sweat trickled, turning instantly cold on our warm bodies. Tingles shivered through me. My muscles clenched tighter, and my joy increased. I felt it build then, the fire within which would propel me to Heaven. I was so close.

Seeming to act on instinct, Luke risked reaching with one hand, unbalancing himself but righting me. With only a few strokes, I was there—the white behind my eyes shining in divinity. I floated in that special place, basking in love.

Luke's cries brought me back to myself as he filled me. Opening my eyes, I saw his ascent. Such bliss smoothed his features after the initial release. I beheld true beauty which was too much, I had to reclose my eyes and breathe it in.

His kiss upon my nose made me look at him. We smiled at one another. We were complete. And blessed. No words were spoken as he cleaned us and sank next to me. We clung onto one another and shared gentle kisses.

Shivering, we both reluctantly dressed. But embraced as soon as we had done so.

"Oh, my fairest of fair," I whispered.

"Oh, my honey sweet."

Chapter 22 – Rejoice

And so began Lent. In the morning service of Ash Wednesday, Prior Ambrose took up ashes and formed a cross of them upon the forehead of each of us. "*For dust you are, and to dust you shall return.*" [Genesis 3:19] – it was a symbol of our repentance.

All of the crosses and saints were now veiled in the church. Forty days of fasting and abstinence loomed large and doleful. One meal of bread, herbs and water was to be eaten after sunset that day, being a Black Fast.

Luke was the weekly server, so I didn't even get to sit next to him at mealtimes. Although, mayhap, the less temptation the better.

The cooks at the monastery were very generous and creative during Lent, providing well-sauced fish in a variety of ways. For instance, they turned *Viaunde Cypre,* which was a stiffened dish usually made of ground pork, almond milk and spices, into one of ground crab meat and pomegranates.

It was a good deal better than my school days. I shuddered at the recollection of the miserable, dry, sparse dishes forced upon us there. The fayre at the priory had continually exceeded my expectations.

Reflecting on Luke's confession, I found that I was indeed content. There was a roof over my head, most of the monks were companiable, my work was interesting, the days were not overly arduous, there was food in my belly and Luke by my side. What more could I want or need? My body and soul were well tended.

Acceptance filled me with warmth. I had already pledged as a postulant and novice, and it was possible I would soon be asked if I was ready to take my vows. And I was. Without realising, the decision had already been made. So long as the brethren were in my favour.

After nones, I went to the infirmary and was tidying when my thoughts were interrupted.

"Paul, you seem distracted," Brother Giles said.

"Hm? I beg your pardon?"

"Precisely my point. Pray, tell me what is troubling you."

"It is not a concern so much as a thought. Luke has been here much longer than I have. Yet he still has not taken his simple vows..."

"We each perform our duties in our own way. Some take longer than others."

"I appreciate that. I do. But he will be accepted, will he not?"

He chuckled. "Ah, I see. Do not trouble yourself. I do not believe he was ever in any great danger. He is a good lad who simply needed to fully embrace our ways. In this, I think you have been a good influence. He seems far less restless of late. Before your arrival, it was as if he could not sit still and was ever in tumult. There was a battle being waged within himself, I think."

"And now?"

"Oh, now, I would say his heart and mind are in full agreement. His duty was always clear. The will of his parents was plain and strong. But now he has found his own reason to perform that duty wholeheartedly."

"Oh." I looked at the floor.

"I do not say this to embarrass you, Paul. As he has had a beneficial influence upon you, you have done likewise for him. You are good for one another. And that is for the betterment of us all. For when we find peace, we are better able to let in God."

"Thank you, Brother Giles. Your wisdom, once again, has also brought me peace of mind."

"What else am I here for?"

"To worship God?"

He lightly clipped my ear. "The influence, however, is not all good. Mind your tongue, you knave."

I rubbed my ear, more from shock than pain. "My apologies."

"Accepted. Now, apply yourself. And prythee, set those jars in their correct order."

To my astonishment, I indeed found that I had been placing items in entirely the wrong location and set about righting my wrong.

The following week saw my turn to be server. But the three Ember Days were observed in full austerity; they were the hardest of the year as any prospect of a feast was far off. And there was nothing but fish for weeks to come yet.

It occurred to me, inconveniently during morning meditation, how far from The Rule our meals strayed usually. Our Order was supposed to live on a Lenten diet, so we should hardly notice the change. We abided by that yet celebrated a good number of saints days and fully enjoyed the feasts. And how I lamented those meals.

Clearly, I was hungry. Bowing my head, I returned my thoughts to devotion and prayer. Until my stomach rumbled. And mine was not the only one.

Silently, I prayed, *"And the Lord shall guide thee continually, and satisfy thy soul in drought, and make fat thy bones, and thou shalt be like a watered garden, and like a spring of water whose waters fail not."* [Isaiah 58:11]

I huffed in frustration; still, my thoughts turned to my empty belly.

I tried again. *"Lead me in Thy truth and teach me, for Thou art the God of my salvation; on Thee do I wait all the day."* [Psalms 25:5]

Better!

Much of that third Ember Day was experienced in a stupor. And after sext, a couple of the older monks had visited Brother Giles for some caudle.

I was with him all day, trying to work quietly. But by vespers, even I was succumbing to the strain.

"Oh, sweet mercy, Paul. Here, sit. You have overexerted yourself."

"Apologies, Brother."

"Nonsense. Just have a care." He spooned some caudle to my lips.

"I shouldn't."

He raised an eyebrow at me, and I saw argument was useless, so took the offering. And the rest of the small bowl he held out. "Thank you."

"Very well. It is without censure that I have a supply ready on fast days. I would have you remember that. And that you must take of it also when in need. For if you fail in your wits, who else is there to look after the brethren?" He partook of a spoonful himself.

Brother Giles spoke of a time without him, and my heart sank. He had been speaking that way more of late. It was surely to prepare me and said with good intent. And it was not my place to tell how deeply his words injured me. So, I silently prayed that God would give him long life.

February gave way to March, the days grew a little brighter, and our tempers less frayed. The snows had long since melted and the air was less biting. But not so much that the calefactory was not a blessed relief.

Having snuck away from the warm room, Luke and I were under the covers of my bed, cuddling whilst fully clothed.

"I miss you," he whispered.

"And I you. But we promised."

"I know. But it feels as though I'll burst if I do not gain release."

"Luke, no. God has been good to us. It is still Lent. No pollution of any kind, even or especially not the self-kind. You would not anger God, would you?"

He pouted. "Nay, I would not."

"Mayhap being so close is not wise?" I could not pretend to not also be suffering for he surely felt how stiff I was; our robes were not thick enough to disguise that. I tried to back away.

Luke grabbed me tighter. "But I'm cold."

"You're being churlish. Would you return to the calefactory?"

"I like it here."

"Then you will stop in your attempts to pursue that which you know to be impossible?"

"If you insist."

I pecked his full lips. "I do. You know it is right."

He snorted.

"Let us turn our thoughts to other matters. Brother Hector eating, mayhap?"

He chuckled then. "That may dissuade me."

"Cold, rainy days."

He pretended to shiver.

"Rats crawling across your bed."

"No. Stop, I beg. You go too far."

"Well, let us read instead. *Bede's Commentary on the Proverbs, Super Parabolas Solomnis,* shall set us onto more wholesome thoughts. You hold the book and turn the pages, I'll hold the candle and read aloud."

We changed position so that he was sitting between my legs with his back to me; we were still close but far less likely to fall into kissing. And I was very mindful of not doing damage with the candle. Thus, our souls were prepared.

This had become our favoured way of reading together. Luke had told me how my voice soothed him, and that he seemed to learn more when I spoke the words. And it brought me joy to do so.

Much of March passed in this gentle manner. Eat fish, pray, lie snug.

On the twelfth day, we honoured St Gregory, but without the feast. He held a special place in all our hearts as not only "the Father of Christian Worship", but also the patron saint of musicians, singers, students, and teachers. There was a deepened reverence to our services in his name.

Palm Sunday began Holy Week with an elaborate service, telling of Christ's entry to Jerusalem. We each received branches of yew and catkined hazel to represent palms, and those selected also carried out relics as we processed into the churchyard.

Prior Ambrose conducted the ceremony before leading us to the west door which he struck with the foot of the cross—Christ demanded entrance. We filed in behind. And the veil which had been covering the large wooden crucifix which hung aloft, was now raised whilst we sung the antiphon, *Ave Rex Noster* (Hail our King). And the gospel was read.

On Maundy Thursday, we held a solemn service then stripped the altar and washed it with water and wine before placing branches upon it.

Afterwards, we held the *Mandatum*; the poor came to the almonry, where we washed their hands and feet, and gave them food including barley bread, as well as money.

Then all the brethren queued for hair and beard cuts in the cloister.

Finding a quiet corner once the deed was done, I ran my fingers through Luke's hair. "It grows ever shorter."

"Yours likewise."

We both looked glum. Surely, our tonsures were not very far away. These shortened styles seemed significant. And disheartening. I loved playing with Luke's golden locks. They were like an unruly crown adorning his beautiful head. I squinted.

"You are imagining a tonsure, you fiend," he said.

"I am. Or trying to. I cannot quite picture it."

"Shall it suit, do you think? Or will I become hideous?"

I sniggered. "You could never be ugly in my eyes."

"Then let us not worry. Besides, there is a while yet before we must face such monstrous style."

We risked a brief embrace, one which could be easily explained by brotherly consolation if discovered.

After vespers, Prior Ambrose washed, dried and kissed the feet of all the brethren.

The next day, we celebrated The Annunciation (Good Friday) with another hard fast. It was the day Jesus died in our name. A day of sorrow and penance.

In a Tenebrae service, Prior Ambrose read the Passion narrative from the Gospel of St John. A cross stood atop the missal which was now unveiled. A hearse of lit candles shone next to it. One by one, each candle was put out after each verse.

Unashamedly, I wept through Christ's mockery and beatings, his condemnation, the placing of the crown of thorns and the carrying of his cross. How greatly He suffered for us. Despite all of the pain and suffering, naked and hanging from the cross, He forgave those who crucified Him.

"Father, forgive them; for they know not what they do." [Luke 23:34]

And as the sun darkened, and the veil of the temple was rent, I all but sobbed.

"Father, into thy hands I commend my spirit: and having said thus, he gave up the ghost." [Luke 23:46]

Prior Ambrose continued to read. *"And he bought fine linen, and took him down, and wrapped him in the linen, and laid him in a sepulchre which was hewn out of a rock, and rolled a stone unto the door of the sepulchre. And Mary Magdalene and Mary the mother of Joses beheld where he was laid."* [Mark 15:46-47]

The last candle was blown out.

The loud closing of a book echoed through the dark church—Christ's tomb was closed. A lit candle emerged and was placed atop the hearse—Christ was our light. Barefoot, we knelt in darkness and crept on our hands and knees to venerate the cross and kiss it.

As we did so, Prior Ambrose intoned, *"Have mercy upon me, O God, according to thy loving kindness: according unto the multitude of thy tender mercies blot out my transgressions. Wash me thoroughly from mine iniquity, and cleanse me from my sin."* [Psalm 51:1-2]

We then sung The Reproaches.

At the close, Prior Ambrose carefully wrapped then carried the cross to the sepulchre. And we took Communion. A watch was kept all night over the candlelit 'Christ'.

Filing out of the church, more than one of us wiped our eyes.

During service on Holy Saturday, all the candles in the church were lit, put out and then relit.

†††

At dawn on Easter Sunday, we sung at the church door before Prior Ambrose led our joyful procession to the sepulchre. Incense and herbs were lit and wafted as we walked.

The prior jubilantly raised the cross from the sepulchre, the bells rang out, and we chanted *Christus resurgens* (Christ is risen) as loudly as our voices would allow. We followed as the cross was carried around the church.

The other figures of Christ and the saints were now also unveiled for the first time since Ash Wednesday. The sepulchre was empty and would remain so, lit by candles for the week.

We were all of us filled with joyous spirit, celebrating the Resurrection of Christ. We were all of us saved and renewed. We quite forgot ourselves, embracing one another, kissing cheeks. When Luke entered my embrace, I was sorely tempted to run off with him.

It was necessary for me to turn away and think of loathsome things a moment. But all about were so exuberant, mayhap they would not have noticed.

The entire morning felt jubilant as we performed the offices and duties expected of us. But it was with even greater fervour that we went to dine. We were as silent as our high spirits would allow as we finally entered the misericord.

What lay before us made my eyes widen and stomach grumble loudly. Luke grinned at me. A glistening roasted lamb was laid out upon the table. The meaty fragrance vehemently greeted my nose. There was a great clatter as we all hastened to take our place.

The carver made an elaborate show of slicing into the juicy meat. Eager hands took their portion, and delighted murmurings filled the air as the ginger sauce was passed around. The lamb of God came to our aid again.

A delighted, "mmm..!" escaped me as I took my first bite. Oh, sweet mercy. Dark, rich delight. After naught but fish for forty days, it was as though I was tasting meat for the first time. And it was marvellous.

Even the day's reading rang around us with mirth.

Once the worst of my hunger had abated, I observed the colourful eggs decorating our table and the greenery hung about. We even had a dish of eggs to eat. These too I had missed, and now ate with delight.

Mead washed down all of these treats, adding more sweetness to the meal. And when I thought I could stand no more, simnel loaves were presented.

It is a curious thing; monks filled with glee yet unable to fully express it. It came not out of their mouths, for silence was still expected whilst we ate. Yet it was ever present in their smiles and eyes. Bliss in its purest form spilled out, through and amongst us.

Brother Giles beckoned me after our meal, and I went with him to the infirmary so we may both issue remedies for indigestion, which we both partook of ourselves.

"So much rich food after so much abstinence is a violent blow to our stomachs," he told me.

I think every person of the community visited us that afternoon, including the lay brothers and servants. And yet we had plentiful supplies, thanks to Brother Giles' foresight.

With queasiness quelled, we went to the calefactory after supper where we played halatafl a while amongst much laughter.

Unable to resist any longer, I pulled Luke's arm and led him away to the dormitory. Where we rejoiced in one another. It was one of the happiest days of my life.

Chapter 23 - For Ye Were Strangers

It took some time to settle back into normality. For we had been solemn and repentant so long that it almost felt wrong to not be forever bowed down under its weight. The joy of Easter Sunday was but a day and it soon settled.

But a balance was reached nonetheless; not too sorrowful and not too jubilant. A quiet, respectful happiness which drifted us along on its ripples of peace.

Even Luke and I found ourselves enjoying our pleasures in moderation. The periods of restraint served to increase our joy when we gave sway to it.

Contentment was achieved and maintained by the Feast of St George on the twenty-third day of April. It had been almost a month since the end of Easter, and our dish of meat was a welcome reminder that such luxuries could be enjoyed.

But two days after, my family paid a visit; my father, mother and brother, Harry, were all present in the outer parlour.

"Harry, it is good to see you looking so well," I greeted with a warm embrace, having first welcomed our parents.

Slapping my shoulder, he replied, "Aye, and with all due gratitude to you, brother."

"Ah, but I was merely God's hands doing His work."

"But you were indeed the one who was there when all others failed. And for that, I am ever in your debt."

"You are no such thing. To see you well is the only reward I require."

Turning to our parents, he said, "You see how it is? Paul is a monk already. I say again that our presence is unnecessary."

I laughed. "And yet most welcome."

Taking our seats, my father, ever serious, spoke. "Paul, you two may treat this visit with derision, but it is upon your prior's request that we are here."

Bowing my head, I turned solemn. "My apologies, Father. I meant no injury. It is good to see you all, and mayhap I was over-excited."

"It is understandable," my mother interjected.

"Son, you have been within these walls a year."

I bowed my head in acknowledgement but needed not the reminder. Prior Ambrose had already spoken with me ahead of this meeting, as we exchanged views on my progress.

"There is time yet before you must take your vows, but your prior thought it best to meet with you now. You have reached an important milestone in your career here."

I took a comforting sip of wine, grateful that Brother Faramond had supplied such.

My father continued, "I am led to understand you have behaved admirably within this community, as well as coming to the aid of your own brother."

Again, I bowed my head. Both from modesty and alarm at such praise from the stern man before me. Words were stuck in my throat.

Placing a heavy hand upon my shoulder, he caught my attention and looked me direct in the eyes. "Paul, we are proud of you."

"Thank you," I whispered, dipping my gaze, fighting back tears.

"But I would remind you that there is still a choice before you."

Clearing my throat, I roused my courage. "Sir, I mean not to gainsay you. But I am of the belief that there is little choice to be made. Your intentions were always made clear. My childhood was spent preparing me for this life. And since my arrival, I have vowed as both a postulant and novice. Every step has led me here."

"But you have done so much. Surely, enough to appease your father's vow. Would you not to choose to have a family?" my mother asked, her voice breaking.

I took her hands in mine. "Mother, dearest, I love you with great fondness and thank you for your care. But I do have a family here. We are brethren. And I am of service. I am needed by God. And there can surely be no greater calling."

A tear trickled down her pale cheek which I wiped away. "Pray, do not feel sorrow. For I am doing God's work. It is the greatest good possible. Prythee, let these only be tears of joy." My own voice began to tremble, so I stopped any attempt of further explanation.

My father's lips thinned, but he nodded. "Good."

One solitary word. No one needed more. I had spoken and he had given his approval. We all sipped our wine.

"But pray, tell me, how do you find married life?" I asked Harry, breaking the silence.

"It suits me well. Sybil sends her regards, and regrets not being here herself. But there is Percival to take care of, and she is grown large. Travelling has lost its appeal as her time draws near."

"I pray for her safe delivery."

"Thank you. From you, that seems to carry more weight. Who would have thought it? My little rascal brother, a holy man." He chuckled, as did I.

"I was never so very boisterous."

"Ah, that may be so. Still, I had not expected you to wear a habit so well. But I am glad to see you happy."

"And I you."

Our conversation grew less and less serious. We spoke idly of many inconsequential things. And our spirits were lifted. It was a comfort to be amongst my own family, yet an unfamiliarity had emerged.

They spoke of an entirely different world from the one I now inhabited. Theirs was lively and raucous, filled with matters of estates. Mine was quiet, filled with duty and prayer. The Work of God rejoiced in the offices, the communal brotherhood sought through manual labours and the growth of mind and spirit brought about by reading – the *Opus Dei, opus manuum and lectio divina.*

I had always struggled to imagine myself as a husband with a family. It was never likely to be my life. But now it felt utterly impossible. I had already journeyed down my road and was glad to do so.

Our parting was far less desperate than that of the year previous. But tears were shed as my mother held me close. Even Harry's eyes were not dry. A sorrow sunk in my heart, but it was of a different nature. My family was less a part of me somehow. They were becoming my past. And that felt sad. But my brethren were indeed my new family, as I had proclaimed them to be. And that brought me comfort.

Luke sought me out at the earliest opportunity, and silently enclosed me within his arms.

"It is not likely I shall ever see them again," I sobbed into his shoulder.

I had lied to myself, thinking whatever I needed to get through our meeting. Now, in safety, I gave sway to the pain which cut through me like a knife. And it sliced deep. My family had been so very good to me. I loved them. To be forever parted seemed too high a price to pay. Yes, my brethren were now my family. But the one just leaving carried a piece of my heart with them.

Luke held on tightly as I wept, never saying a word. For there were none to be found.

Once I gathered my wits, it occurred to me to ask, "But Luke, do your family not come?"

"Nay, I expect them not."

"But surely you are being considered? I feel it must be so."

He shrugged. "It may be so."

"Then why do they not come?"

He jostled me in his arms. "Have I not explained how my family are, sweeting? Hm? They did not even accompany me here. My father sent his steward with me, where I was deposited with as much ceremony as a sack of grain. I have neither seen nor heard from my family in several years. I am given to understand they maintain correspondence with the prior to ensure I have not fled and am living up to expectation. Nothing more. I should be more surprised if they did arrive."

"And I am sorry for it."

Stroking my cheek, he said, "Do not be, for I am not. And, seeing how it pains you to say farewell to yours, I may even now be a little grateful."

"I suppose that is some small blessing. If I had but truly understood, I would have had you share in mine."

"Nay, my love. I would not borrow a familial love from which I must immediately be torn asunder."

"Ah, it was a foolish notion."

"Nay again. 'Twas sweet sentiment of the like which makes me so very fond of you. It was merely not thought through."

"Most unlike me not to think fully before I speak."

"Ha. A rare occasion, but one which brings its own hope. Come, let us turn our thoughts to happier things. What do you think we shall have for dinner tomorrow?"

I chuckled. "You and your stomach."

"I am more concerned with yours, for you are happier when it is full."

"Not as happy as when we two are like this." I lay a sweet kiss upon his lips.

On the first day of May, a new candidate for postulancy entered the monastery as a guest. News of his arrival had been announced to us beforehand, and yet surprise gripped my limbs upon seeing him. I was accompanying Brother Giles to make his assessment, for one day I too would have to inspect incomers for lice.

There stood before me an average young man with brown hair and pale green eyes which seemed to shine with an inner intelligence. His mouth, however, was set in a grim, thin line.

It was strange, viewing the proceedings. What had felt an intrusive humiliation when endured now seemed a methodical, impersonal matter when conducted.

"All is well. We each undergo this upon arrival. I would assure you that no harm is intended," I told the young man when he flinched. "I am Paul, a novice here under Brother Giles, the infirmarer now lifting your arm."

He gave a slight nod but barely glanced at me. "I had not thought any different. The brother's hands are merely cold."

Everyone was staring at me. Clearly, I had spoken out of turn, and it was deemed unacceptable by all. I held my tongue. Brother Giles blew on his hands and rubbed them together.

I would make allowances for this stranger. It may yet prove to be that he was nervous. Surely, I would not have liked anyone to judge me upon my first moments here. Yet, he seemed disdainous. It was present in how high he held his chin and looked down his nose, and in the manner of his stride as he had walked in. Yes, I found him alarming.

We left him in the care of Brother Faramond.

"Edmund seems a little superior," I said quietly to Brother Giles as we walked to the infirmary.

Of course, he chuckled. "And how amiable do you think you were upon your arrival?"

"I have been trying to tell myself the same thing. We should not form any conclusions. But, Brother, there is something unsettling about the boy."

"Whether you like him or not is beside the point, Paul. He is here. Prior Ambrose has deemed him worthy of the attempt. Like you, he will have to undergo much to become accepted. But I would remind you that acceptance does not mean fondness. I daresay there are brethren here we would not choose to befriend outside of these walls. And yet, we must live alongside them peaceably."

It took me a moment to catch my breath. Such an admission from my counsellor was astonishing. I turned the idea over in my head. "You share my misgivings?"

He patted my shoulder. "Mayhap I do. But then again, it is always a worry when someone new arrives. We must get used to them as they must get used to us. But that is the very purpose of postulancy, I suppose, to ensure we can all live with one another."

"I suppose it is. I'm very glad you do not find me too irksome." I grinned.

He ruffled my hair. "You are far from that, my friend."

Warmth swelled my heart, stopping any further words in my throat.

"It is a pity. You shall have to be more vigilant. You and Luke must more closely guard your secret, for we know not how Edmund would react. But, as his companions, you must also try to befriend him. *And if a stranger sojourn with thee in your land, ye shall not vex him. But the stranger that dwelleth with you shall be unto you as one born among you, and thou shalt love him as thyself; for ye were strangers in the land of Egypt: I am the Lord your God."* [Leviticus 19:33-34].

My spirits fell at the reminder. Luke and I had already foreseen a need to be careful. It was like Lent all over again.

Chapter 24 – He That Is Slow to Anger Appeaseth Strife

As much as Luke and I wished to make the most of our final private moments of affection, we were, regrettably, in the middle of Rogationtide. And so, instead, we proceeded to Mass and listened to the readings of James and Luke, being reminded that He never turns away empty-handed those who call upon Him in penitence and trust.

"If a son shall ask bread of any of you that is a father, will he give him a stone? or if he ask a fish, will he for a fish give him a serpent? Or if he shall ask an egg, will he offer him a scorpion? If ye then, being evil, know how to give good gifts unto your children: how much more shall your Heavenly Father give the Holy Spirit to them that ask him?" [Luke 11:11-13]

My head hung low in prayer. Edmund was come to us and I had no right to shun him. In thought, I had sinned. But in deed, I would improve. I felt a hand upon mine at my side. Moving as little as possible, I looked at Luke who smiled his encouragement upon me.

Since the end of Easter, our hours had changed to the summer timings. Therefore, there was a long wait before Luke pulled me into the parlour.

"Prythee, tell me what furrows your wondrous, dark brow," he whispered.

"I have already failed Edmund."

He laughed quietly. "That is quite an accomplishment. Come, he has not set foot inside as of yet. The offense cannot be so very great."

"I was inclined to dislike him."

His grin remained. "Paul, only you could worry over so slight a matter. Nobody can like everybody. We shall give him a chance. What say you?"

I nodded feebly. "Aye. But I shall remind you of this conversation when first you two meet."

With my promise pledged aloud, we hurried to our morning lesson. And later, I made my confession so I may do penance.

A few days later, Edmund was ushered into the chapter house where he bathed our feet. I looked pointedly at Brother Giles, for there was an absence of herbs in the water. He looked all innocence. But I knew him well. Certainly, he shared my misgivings.

However, watching the postulant kiss gouty feet did soften me towards him. It was not a pleasant task; he flinched and grimaced every time. I congratulated myself that my own disgust had surely been better concealed.

Alone, he sat on the other side of the rood screen as we attended High Mass. Then, accompanied by Brother Barnabas, he was shown the longer route to the carrells to join in our lesson.

Luke and I smiled at our new companion as he approached his desk. He scowled in return. I raised a brow at Luke who merely shrugged.

He did seem competent in his understanding as he answered Brother Barnabas' questions well. As far as we were aware, he had not been brought in with any particular duty in mind. He was destined to become a choir monk until such time as need arose. The roles of sacrist or almoner seemed most likely. Either would suit his superior attitude well.

At my desk, I bent my head and prayed for forgiveness, for I was being uncharitable again. I must not think myself better than he. For was not that the very issue I took with Edmund himself? However, I refrained from laying prostrate at his feet. It was a stray thought which I had not given voice to, and he was not yet so much as a novice.

Why did this person inspire such meanness of spirit within me?

It was a relief when he was sent to dinner.

"I am come to make a count of your…err…gardening tools," Luke announced as he swept into the infirmary.

Brother Giles chortled and pulled out the key to the herbarium. "Very well."

Poor Luke, how his face fell.

The chortle became a laugh. "As I thought. You may tell Brother Hector that I have not lost or broken anything, and my numbers remain unchanged. Now, you had best say what is really upon your mind."

"Why can he not be more like you, Brother?"

"Oh, he is older and in more pain, I daresay. We may be forgiven our sour disposition after a certain age."

"Of course. Forgive me, I did not mean—"

"But that is surely not what you came to say?"

His brow crumpled in confusion. "Oh. I beg pardon. I came to beg your indulgence, for I fear our friend is thinking too hard again, and I would speak with him whilst certain ears are not near."

Brother Giles looked Heavenward. "And you doubted my ability to offer guidance?"

"No, no. Not at all."

"Ah, then it is, in fact, yourself who now is also troubled."

Luke looked at the ground, silent as stone.

"Luke, I shall tell you what I told Paul. That it is to be expected to feel troubled when there is a new arrival. You remember, do you not, your misgivings when Paul came to us?"

I surely looked as shocked as I felt.

"Methinks that was for an entirely different reason. But how—"

"I have eyes which see well enough."

"Aye, sometimes I forget how very attentive you are."

"Still, I would urge calm."

"This from the man who came not to Edmund's aid?" I asked before clapping my hands over my mouth.

"Calm, Paul, being the very opposite of that outburst."

"My apologies."

"I am under no obligation to ease anybody's postulancy."

My mouth opened, but I held back the question which danced upon my tongue.

Brother Giles smiled. "But I may choose to if the person shows promise. Now, mind that for you, I bent The Rule by assisting. **Not** that I infer any slight upon Edmund by letting things be."

I bowed my head.

"He did give us an awful glare as we smiled our welcome, though," Luke muttered.

Again, Brother Giles looked up to God. "It is as if you two have become schoolboys. Is this all that has passed between you? Upon this, you have taken against him?"

"That may be putting it a little strongly. He has shown naught but displeasure. But it is more that I am attempting to think of how we may reach out to him and gain his friendship," I tried.

"And yet Luke saw fit to come here to speak ill of him."

Luke laid himself upon the floor. "Brother, I seek forgiveness."

"Rise, Luke. I shall spare you rebuke or stripes. And you too, Paul. I see how you would have spoken to one another and sought rationality. But it should not be required. Now, you shall both amend your thoughts, and only wish Edmund well. He has enough to concern himself with without you two acting against him."

"Oh, I would never – " I started.

"Ah, ah! This is my final word upon the matter. Do not try my patience. Luke, return to Brother Hector and let's hear no more about these misgivings. Edmund shall come in friendship of his own accord or go in peace."

Luke bowed and went to turn away.

"One moment. Before you go, you had best join Paul in some liquorice tisane."

My wise friend had already been brewing some of the root, and soon poured two cups out for us. Challenging times loomed ahead.

That night, sniffing broke through the silence of the dormitory. Edmund was in the cot the other side of me, and so I crept behind his curtain and crouched at his side.

"Fret not. We are here in friendship. Please know you may talk freely with us. Luke and I will listen. For we too have recently undergone your trials. All you need do is seek one of us out in a quiet place."

Not waiting for a response, I crept back to my own cot but almost leapt back off when a hand grabbed mine.

"That was well done," Luke whispered.

With a silent kiss upon the hand he held, Luke crept away. How I longed to hold him and be held. But this small comfort would have to suffice.

The next day, as we approached the carrells, Edmund caught up to me.

"You may keep your mockery of sympathy to yourself," he sneered, bumping my shoulder as he passed.

"But I was in earnest," I called to his retreating back.

My ear was caught in a pincer of finger and thumb as I was dragged inside.

"Paul, I expect you to set a better example for our postulant," Brother Barnabas reprimanded.

"My apologies, Brother." I quivered, for surely he would make an example of me and bring out the switch. I had been too loud.

"But nor am I blind. I saw how you were provoked."

"If you please, Brother Barnabas, it was not intentional. A misunderstanding only. Prythee, we shall be more mindful. It shall not happen again. We shall be quiet."

His dark scowl was turned upon me. "As you should know, I am not in the habit of leniency. My task is to ensure you are worthy of your place here. There must be no rule breaking. That being said, we all deserve one chance. Edmund, we expect better. You shall not incite unruly behaviour. Indeed, you shall make yourself amiable. Do I make myself understood?"

"Y…y….yes, sir, Brother Barnabas, sir."

"You may dispense with the sir."

"Aye…Brother Barnabas. Thank you…Brother Barnabas."

When Brother Barnabas turned his back, I waved to get Edmund's attention. Closing my forefinger and thumb together, I drew my hands apart—peace. His brow furrowed at my action, but it seemed born more of confusion than derision.

Shaking my joined hands up and down, I gestured 'friend'. The furrow deepened, but Brother Barnabas turned back to us, and so ended my second attempt.

I had quite forgotten how difficult it was to express oneself during postulancy. Edmund was closely watched at every moment. And I was not supposed to be talking to him. Small gestures or a whisper here and there were all I managed. I prayed they were enough to convey that he was safe and need not fear me. In the very least, his open hostility lessened.

But the Wednesday after Whitsunday was an Ember Day, and we were excused lessons. The day was mild, and so I beckoned to Edmund to follow us after High Mass. We led him out of doors, to the cemetery garden.

Quite certain that Brother Barnabas would not be too far away from his charge, I kept my voice low.

"Edmund—"

But he interrupted, his fists up. "Two against one seems a little unfair, but so be it. You shall not find me lacking."

I stood astonished.

"What on ever are you about?" Luke asked, placing himself between us. "Put your fists down this instant. Must I remind you this is a house of God?"

"You do not mean to fight?"

"Indeed not. Prythee, how have we inspired such quarrellous notions?" I enquired.

He slowly lowered his hands, glancing between us. "But..."

"Edmund, I would assure you I was sincere. We mean only friendship. Having so recently undergone the trials of postulancy ourselves, would you have us so unfeeling as to not understand with the utmost sympathy the pains you now endure?" I asked.

"I..."

Luke laid a hand upon his arm. "Come, why do we not sit? Methinks it best you explain your misgivings so we may overcome them."

Edmund cast a wary gaze upon us, frowning before sitting as we had done before him. "You are in earnest?"

Luke answered, "Aye. And we may understand more than you know. If your schooldays have given rise to such expectations of violence, then Paul here may sympathise. If, however, it stems from bellicose older brothers, then I am the one with most experience."

Green eyes peeked up at him. "Mayhap it was both," he whispered.

"Then I am sorry for it. But know that those days are gone. Look about you. Most of the brethren are too old for such folly, if nothing else. And what would be gained by it?"

Edmund shrugged.

I ventured, "The brethren would certainly be unimpressed by such raucous behaviour. And it is them you should aim to please. For they will all hold you in judgement. If you prove yourself devout, pious and agreeable, the priory doors shall open and welcome you in. For, until final vows, nothing is certain."

He picked at the grass. "What you say seems sound."

"I would not persuade you with words alone. Cast your gaze about you as you make your way around, and mayhap you shall see for yourself."

"Perchance, I will."

I added, *"But the fruit of the Spirit is love, joy, peace, forbearance, kindness, goodness, faithfulness, gentleness and self-control. Against such things there is no law."* [Galatians 5:22-23]

"I thank you for your kind words. I should be on my way," he said, standing and brushing himself down.

"Grace go with you."

"And with you."

Once he had left us alone, Luke let out a chuckle. "You know, you sound more like Brother Giles each day?"

I shoved at him. "And that would be a bad thing, would it?"

He held me then. "Not at all. I love your sage wisdom."

"You do not long for my body alone?" I teased.

"Nay. But that is a great temptation, it must be said." With that he kissed me.

We remained quietly conversing in one another's embrace until the bell rang for sext.

Chapter 25 - Do Not Disappoint Me in My Hope

Whitsun Week passed and made way for Corpus Christi. And Edmund grew in confidence. No longer did he wear a constant frown or look afeared at every sound. On occasion, a smile passed his lips.

And so, once his month was up, he took the vows of postulancy and was clothed accordingly. Without any one aim, he spent time with each of the brethren. Brother Giles and I had welcomed him into the infirmary. He showed no great talent there, but it mattered not. He was eager to please and we became better acquainted.

"You do not like Edmund best?" Luke asked in one rare moment alone together.

"Oh, fie! Why would you waste our precious time with such idiocy?"

"You have spoken much of him of late."

I kissed him. "You need have no fear. I wish him well. And it is interesting to see his progress. But that is all. Surely, you know by now that it is you and you alone that I love. And it is a love which shall last until the sun ceases to shine and the stars fall from the Heavens. Even then, mayhap it shall endure."

His eyes glinted with wicked mirth. "And God."

I slapped his arm. "Well, of course, also God. But I love him in a very different way."

"Show me."

Ensuring we were indeed alone, I knelt and took cover underneath his tunic and took him into my mouth until he was relieved of all doubt.

"Are you now satisfied?" I asked, standing.

He smiled at me with heavy-lidded eyes, wrapping me in his arms. "Indeed. Entirely satisfied."

The summer drifted by on gilded wings. Luke and I enjoyed one another rarely. Although we had befriended Edmund, he did somewhat get in the way. But that was not his fault, and we couldn't hold it against him.

He continued diligently, if somewhat subdued. He was reprimanded several times, especially for self-pollution. I felt sorry that he had no close companion. But I dared not supply him with strips of linen for he had no reason for having such if he should be caught with them about his person. And my own secret would then be discovered. But he must have found his own way, for the reprimands ceased.

Time seemed marked only by the saint's days which supplied any variance to the quietude of our daily lives.

At the beginning of August, after Lammas had been celebrated, I was called to see the prior.

"Paul, it pleases me to see how well you have progressed in so short a time. I understand you have even eased Edmund's introduction to our life."

"I thank you, Prior Ambrose. I hope I have been of service."

"In any number of great ways. We believe you to be a worthy vessel of God and acceptable to the Order. And so, I would invite you to take your simple vows, if you feel you are ready and willing to do so. You will be admitted into our community here at Darenth Priory. Should you accept and continue well, your solemn vows shall be taken in four years. Only then will you be a full member of the Chapter with a say and vote in matters of the community."

I sat frozen in astonishment. Although it was not entirely unexpected, the moment caught me unawares. I had feared a discussion of a more serious nature on my way to the prior's room. Yet there I sat with a reward before me.

The prior then read to me The Rule. "You understand, do you not, that you must keep all the rules, and obey all orders given you? You may not ever leave the monastery without my express permission, nor cast off the yoke of The Rule. No longer shall you receive letters from home, for this priory is now your only own home. You shall have no possessions."

I already had surrendered my possessions and accepted the loss of my family. With deep breaths and a great deal of thought, I had prepared as best I could. "I am ready, and gratefully accept the great honour which you offer."

Luke was waiting to go in as I came out of the prior's room. I smiled so he would know there was nothing to fear within.

"Paul, I have finally been accepted," he cried, finding me waiting in the cloister for him.

"My hearty congratulations, Luke."

"Might I offer you the same?"

"You may," I replied, beaming wider.

We embraced, not caring who may see. Surely, this was appropriate given our good news. The jumping up and down like children may have been deemed excessive, however. But our joy would not be contained. Acceptance. It meant so very much. God and our peers had welcomed us fully. We were voted in, viewed as worthy, good enough for this fine home.

We ran to the infirmary.

"Brother Giles, Brother Giles, we are both to take vows," we chorused, rushing to him.

He chuckled. "And you think I was unaware of this, mayhap? That perchance, I was not there for the voting?"

Luke's face surely echoed the look upon mine. I felt foolish.

"But I offer you my congratulations even so. You have both worked very hard and deserve your place." Brother Giles embraced us both. "You may wish to find Brother Barnabas and thank him, however. He was one of the loudest voices in your favour. Presuming you have not done so already."

My cheeks grew warmer. "Nay, we came straight here."

"And I am flattered. But do not forget the others who have aided your progress."

"Indeed. Thank you, Brother Giles."

With one more embrace, we left in search of the master of novices. He was somewhat more reserved in his jubilation but there was rejoicing even with the usually stern Brother Barnabas. And we gave him many thanks.

"I am proud of you both, if it be not too great a sin. But I cannot help it. Especially you, Luke."

"Me?" he asked, his eyebrows rising high.

"Aye, indeed. For you have had the harder road to travel. Your journey was long and arduous, yet you remained steadfastly on the path. You have come very far indeed from the wild boy who arrived full of boldness."

"With your guidance, I have shed my semblance of boastfulness and defiance. You have helped me gain the confidence to show my true self, the one who is worthy of your attention."

He placed a hand upon his shoulder. "I may have guided and even nudged you, but the work was undertaken by yourself. Besides, I think Paul here aided you more than I." He clapped my shoulder as he spoke my name.

"It was mostly Luke," I said, not knowing where to look.

"Indeed, your own diligence is not to be overlooked, Luke. Truly, you are both fine young men and shall be even finer monks. Mind, there is still much work ahead of you."

Luke and I giggled nervously, but it was I who replied, "Aye, which we look forward to with eagerness."

The quiet chuckle from Brother Barnabas was somewhat alarming in its rarity. "And you, Paul, have been raised from being overly studious whilst maintaining a keen interest in book learning. Yes, you will both do very well here. Carry on the good work."

We left him to find Brother Hector.

"So, you are come with a glad heart, boy?" he said, as stern as ever.

Imagine our surprise when he smiled. "As well you might. You have done well. I daresay, when the time comes, the kitchener and goods shall be in safe hands. I am glad you came to us, Luke. I bid you glad welcome."

"I err…errr…thank you, Brother."

We bowed out of his presence and broke into laughter once well away from the old man. "On my life, did you ever think to hear such words from his mouth?" Luke asked.

"Indeed, I did not. Who knew he had them in him? Oh, Luke, mayhap he was merely stern to put you to the test after all? Oh, what a disservice we may have done him."

"Nay, Brother Barnabas is stern for our benefit. It cannot be as you say, he seemed to take too much pleasure in his harsh manner. But then…"

"Whatever the cause for the change, he is proud of you, Luke. As am I."

The sun was shining, and we had time yet, so made our way to our favourite place. With so much joy in our hearts, we had to let it out. And once again, we danced around the apple trees in the orchard, singing and cheering. Only the bell for sext brought an end to our merriment.

We smiled our way through the office. And there were many pats on our arms and shoulders as we passed the brethren. Smiles were exchanged aplenty.

And at dinner, there was apple and blackberry pie courtesy of a grinning Brother Maynard.

It was a day of celebration, and we were excused from our afternoon duties, but Edmund was not. And so, we escaped to the dormitory to rejoice in the fullest way possible.

On the twenty-sixth day of the year 1486, Luke and I, together, took our simple vows. It did mean we endured another visit from the Bishop of Rochester, but we knew now what was expected and it seemed more of an honour than an encroachment.

We had been bathed and even anointed with oils. Our faces were freshly shaven, and our hair close cut. We were not to receive our tonsure yet. The vows we were about to profess were deemed temporary, although there would be no option to discontinue our profession at the end of this period. They were made for four years.

Processing into the church, my nose filled with the scent of incense. With great solemnity, we entered the oratory. And I trembled.

After the readings and psalms, Luke and I both gave ourselves completely to God, who is loved above all, handing our entire lives into His service.

We professed the vows of Obedience, Stability and *Conversatio Morum*.

In obedience, I became like Christ, obedient to the will of the Father, to Prior Ambrose and our brethren, in the spirit of love and faith. I would listen to the voice of God manifested in the Scriptures and in holy teachings. To put the good of others before myself, for the love of Christ.

In stability, I bound myself in body and spirit to Darenth Priory. The Lord was to be my rock, I would depend upon his stability. By striving to know Him better, I would come to know myself more. United as a community, we would become unshakeable in our faith.

In *Conversatio Morum,* I pledged fidelity to the monastic life, to observe all the traditions. My heart wavered at the commitment to chastity but made it in full knowledge that others had done so before me and bent that rule. I still belonged to God and promised myself unto Him. The commitments to individual poverty and simplicity came easier, having lived this way a little already. My life would be devoted to learning, being holy and earning my dwelling place in the presence of God.

The petition I had made as a novice lay upon the altar, and now I signed it a second time, and intoned, "*Suscipe me Domine secundum eloquium tuum et vivam, et non confundas me in expectatione mea.*" (Uphold me, Lord, according to your word, and do not disappoint me in my hope.) [Psalm 119:116]. This was sung three times, repeated by the whole community, with the addition of, "*Glory be to the Father,*" at the end.

Luke did likewise. We then both lay prostrate at the feet of each of the brethren, asking for their prayers.

We ceremonially handed back the hooded cloak of our novitiate. And were presented with the cincture; the cord to tie around our waist as a symbol of self-discipline and readiness for the monastic life. And a pointed black hood (the cowl) was placed over our head and shoulders. In effect, we now wore the full habit of the order of St Benedict. Pride warmed my entire body.

Regarding Luke, I admired how well he looked, especially with the sparkle in his eyes and the smile he wore.

Once we were outside of the church and able to stand aside alone, I whispered, "I applied the anointing oil inside of me too. It contains oil of clove which I understand eases muscles."

His eyes half closed as lust clouded his visage and he drew in a strained breath. And I knew he would avail himself at the earliest opportunity. The excitement of the day had reached such a level as to make me quiver.

Chapter 26 - The Lord Keep You

Our days were amended according to our new status. No longer did we sit in the carrells with Brother Barnabas and Edmund each morning, but instead we went to the scriptorium to either copy out pages or to study texts. There was much light in the room so was best suited for the task. Although, we did often take a book to the dormitory to read.

For now, we immersed ourselves in theological and philosophical studies. The writings of Aristotle, Cicero, Plato and Socrates were now available to us.

Plato intrigued me with his theories in *The Republic;* how ethics, political philosophy, moral psychology, epistemology, and metaphysics are all connected and work together. However, his 'Platonic Love' theory held less weight with me, for he would have us never express love physically. Do we not as monks pray, chant and weep at the word of God? There can be no greater connection to Him, surely.

Aristotle brought me sound reasoning. Having studied under Plato, he rejected a lot of his ideas and enhanced understanding through observation. And yet he also acknowledged that above empirical knowledge there must be an unchanging being at its source—and this, to my mind, must be God.

But, of course, Galen held my keenest interest. As another observer, he gave much to medicine such as the four humours which must be kept in balance: phlegm, blood, yellow bile, and black bile. He also taught us to treat every patient as an individual.

It was not only to Greece that our attentions turned. The wonders of Arabic, Persian and Turkish texts slowly opened up before our eyes also. *The Canon of Medicine* by Muslim Persian physician-philosopher Avicenna was a marvellous font of medical knowledge, combining thoughts from its homeland with those of the Greeks, Indians and Chinese. Oh, how much did I revel in those wise words.

It was temptation in itself to become lost in such heady tomes. However, my Luke was ever present and kept me planted in the mortal realm of men. Another reason to be thankful for the gift that was his presence in my life. With him, my mind was enlightened, my body kept safe, and my soul saved.

In the afternoons, Luke and I still went our separate ways to the cellarer and infirmarer respectively. Brother Giles was always delighted to discuss my newfound knowledge with me.

But one September day, I was out of doors, tending the physic garden when a familiar face approached.

"Brom! How good it is to see you. I had quite given up hope of your return. Where have you been hiding?"

He rolled his eyes, but his grin gave him away. "Must we go through this every year? You know full well I have been in the fields making hay and harvesting."

"You must not mind my knavery, my friend. I must find pleasing distraction where I can."

Patting my arm, he consoled, "My friend, how very dull your life must be. Also, I fear you have been listening too much to Luke."

We both chuckled and embraced. "Truly it is good to see you."

"Brother Paul, as now you must be named, I must offer my congratulations."

I waved him off. "Enough. Tell me what news of you."

His smile was broad. "I may have found a Luke of my own."

"Truly? Wondrous news. Pray, tell me all," I urged, pulling at weeds so no passersby who may happen upon us should be alarmed at our idle chatter and listen too intently.

Brom sighed. "Oh, his name is Ralph. He is a little older than myself."

"By how many years?" The question escaped before it could be stopped.

"Not so very many. Eight if I must be exact. But he has lived such a life. Paul, how you would weep to hear him speak of it. For he was a tenant farmer, lured into marriage by force of his peers. It was expected of him, and he saw no way out but to agree against his will. I shall not burden you with how, but he dutifully managed to fill her with child. And what do you think? The poor innocent died whilst giving birth, and their babe died along with her. The burden of guilt weighs so heavily upon him that I fear it may yet bring him down."

My mouth had steadily dropped further as he recounted this tale. "Brom, this is most shocking. Such tragedy. The poor fellow. But...why do you tell me all this?"

"Ah, you see, I would have you speak with him, if you are agreeable to it."

"How can I refuse when you look so imploringly? But if he wishes to make confession, it is not I who can give him absolution and he would be better off speaking with another."

"But you see, it is not absolution he needs. Paul, you have a far better way with words. And with your book learning, you must be able to draw on some words of solace. Make him see he is not the guilty party in all this, I implore you."

"You are certain I am the best party to speak with?"

"I know no better. You understand me best of any person, so Ralph too by extension."

"Very well. But you must give me time to consider. I would speak sagely and take care not to cause more harm if he is brought so very low."

"May we say three days hence? Might I send him here in my stead?"

"Aye, if it can be managed."

As agreed, three days later, I placed myself in the physic garden, having first obtained the key to the herbarium. Brother Giles had grinned as he handed it to me, surely suspecting a tryst with Luke—to my shame, I corrected not his supposition.

A man of shorter stature than Brom but with similar black hair approached. "You are Brother Paul?"

Bowing my head, I answered, "I am. You must be Ralph."

He nodded.

"Come, let us seek a quieter place."

His kind brown eyes sought explanation, but his tongue held silent, and he followed me into the herbarium. There, we sat upon stools amidst the earthy perfume of herbs. I tried to put from my mind the image of Luke bending over the bench. I needed my full wits about me.

"You know of my sins, and still you agreed to meet with me. You are all kindness, Brother."

"And here we start at the beginning. For you would have it that you have sinned. Tell me, without hope of absolution I would remind you, what sins have you committed?"

"I killed her," he cried out, sinking his face into his hands.

"Ralph, I would urge you to calm yourself. Did you strike your wife? Did you take your knife to her throat? Were you in any way violent towards her?"

"No. No, of course not," he said, shaking his head vigorously.

"Then, I would ascertain that you did not kill her. You are no murderer."

"I should never have married her. I am punished for deception."

"Deception is not a mortal sin and could not possibly merit such punishment. If deception there truly be."

His face appeared from behind his hands as his brown eyes shimmered in my direction.

I continued, "Nay, I would not attach any sin in the matter. For was there lust, gluttony, avarice, sloth, anger, envy or pride involved?"

He shook his head.

"Then we deal not with grave matter."

"Nay."

"Indeed, I might surmise there was a great deal less lust involved than would usually occur in the marital bed. You did your duty as a husband in body alone. And that in good conscience."

His mouth gaped. "You could say that."

"As to the marriage itself, think you the first or even the last to marry out of necessity?"

"Nay, I am not so vain as to believe it so."

"And does every such marriage end in this manner?"

"I think not."

"Therefore, it is unlikely that you are the cause of your wife's demise in the slightest. After all, it is a terrible truth, yet a truth all the same, that a great many women die whilst trying to bring new life into this world. And seemingly without reason but by God's will."

"But—"

"And must being taken to our eternal rest be a curse and not a reward? I know that when I am taken I shall rejoice in His presence."

"When you put it in those terms…"

"What would your life have been like otherwise?"

He sat pondering. "Miserable, methinks. She seemed as wretched as I in our situation."

"And did all of this lead you to our door?"

"But had I made my way here sooner it should not have happened."

"Sometimes, unpleasantness must happen to bring us to ourselves and to God. It seems He has guided your footsteps here in His own timing which may seem perplexing to us but is surely part of His greater plan. If you had been capable of arriving sooner you would have. In this we must trust."

"Aye, you make sense. Truly, you believe it a reward and not punishment?"

"I do. For her, and it may yet prove to be for you too. For in pledging the remainder of your days in the service of God, is there not one who makes life more bearable?"

His eyes widened. "You would speak of Brom?"

I smiled. "I made no mention of names, but if his is the one which arrives in your mind then so be it. Mayhap I cannot condone such an alliance, but nor can I speak out against it with any great zeal."

"But that sin of lust of which you spoke..."

"Aye, if lustful thoughts are inspired then that is your cross to bear. Given that your residence relies upon complete devotion to God, might I suggest you confess a different sin aloud but carry out the penance with the truth in your heart and spirit? Offer up only silent prayers of forgiveness to God."

"That would be permitted?"

I tapped the side of my nose. "I daresay encouraged. For we must not confess lascivious details for fear of inciting the same in others. And you would not be the only person within these walls to carry out private penance this way."

He leaped at me then and gathered me within his strong arms, raising me onto my feet. "Thank you, Brother, thank you."

Whether embarrassment or eagerness carried him forth I know not, but it was certainly done with great haste.

"Benedicat tibi Dominus et custodiat te," I said at his retreating form (The Lord bless thee, and keep thee.) [Numeri 6:24-26].

When I was next with Luke, I held him a little tighter and longer, all the more thankful that our path was less sorrowful than Ralph's. There could be no doubt that we were ever destined to live thus.

As if in reminder of the fragility of life, sorrow befell our community on the 16th day of September in the year of 1486.

Luke had left me early as he was performing his last day of server duty, and I was left alone to study until mealtime. Oh, what a terrible day, when we all gathered in the refectory only to notice a gap where one of us should be.

The brows of Prior Ambrose raised high as he pointed first at the gap then Brother Giles and then the door. Raising my hand, I got the prior's nod and hastened after the retreating infirmarer.

"Brother, I am troubled. It is not like any of us to not be where we ought to be," I muttered.

"Nay. I share your concern. But I fear to make too much haste, for what may be awaiting us is not to be got at quickly."

"You fear the worst?"

"His headaches have been increasing in regularity and severity of late, despite my attempts of aid."

He would say no more. We walked with urgency towards the cellarer's range despite his doubts. Such a sight met our eyes as I wished never to see. Lying prostrate on the floor was Brother Hector, still as stone.

"Oh, mercy!" I cried, sinking to the floor at his side.

His glazed eyes saw naught, his chest drew no breath and his flesh was cold. I looked across at Brother Giles on the other side who was also checking for any signs of life.

"We are too late. Oh, my friend, what have you done? You see where your obstinate selfdom has led? Oh, Paul, he has received not the Last Rites." With this, sobs burst from Brother Giles.

"A bad death is a terrible thing," I murmured. "I shall fetch the prior."

My friend nodded. I was torn between wanting to console him and doing all within our power for the soul of Brother Hector which was in great peril. There could be no greater urgency than the latter, and so I forced my feet into action and ran back to the refectory, caring not for decorum.

Once at the door, I scarce knew what to do. I stood agape. Prior Ambrose looked askance. Shaking my head, I beckoned him. Making the sign of the cross, the prior came. And all the brethren followed. For my look must have conveyed all.

As we approached, we heard Brother Giles intoning through broken sobs, *"O Lord, open thou my lips; and my mouth shall shew forth thy praise. For thou desirest not sacrifice; else would I give it: thou delightest not in burnt offering. The sacrifices of God are a broken spirit: a broken and a contrite heart, O God, thou wilt not despise."* [Psalm 51:15-17]

Prior Ambrose knelt beside Brother Giles and laid a hand upon his head. "My son, ease yourself. He is not in so great a danger as you fear. Are our entire lives not given unto Him? Do we not spend our days in praise? It was but this morning when Brother Hector last made confession. He will be with God. Come, let us prepare him properly now."

The prior gave absolution as if Brother Hector had made his last confession then and there. As a group, we conveyed his body to the church where he was placed upon sackcloth and a cross of ashes. Carefully, we washed Brother Hector's body, cleansing him of any last remnants of sin whilst chanting psalms. Redressing him in his monk's habit, we positioned his hands as if in prayer. Candles were lit all about.

In pairs, we took it in turns to sing psalms and prayers in vigil. At each of the offices, we raised our voices calling upon God's favour.

In chapter 4 of The Rule of St Benedict, we are called upon to, "Remember to keep death before your eyes daily." And yet, thus confronted it still came as a shock. I had not been ready to face mortality in such vivid detail. Tears were wrought from my eyes and my limbs did tremble.

Standing at Luke's side as we took our turn in the vigil office, he was likewise affected. Holding hands, we squeezed. And took deep breaths. There was duty to be done. With a nod, I took up the first reading. Before my eyes lay a lesson from the desert fathers.

I read, "*News spread that an elder father lay dying in the desert of Skete. The brothers came, stood around his deathbed, clothed him and began to cry. But he opened his eyes and laughed. And he laughed again, and then again. The surprised brothers asked him, 'Tell us, Abba, why do you laugh while we cry?' He spoke, 'I laughed at first because you fear death. Then I laughed because you are not ready. A third time I laughed because I am going from hard work to enter my rest – and you are crying about that!' He then closed his eyes and died.*"

Such comfort did I take from these words that I fell to my knees and gave thanks. I was thus reminded not to feel sorrow. My strength was renewed. For, as I had said unto Ralph just days before, death is not a punishment but a reward. Why should I now fear it so? Did I not believe my own words? Or those of God? Nay. I would not a doubter be.

Luke took a turn at reading. "*Let not your heart be troubled: ye believe in God, believe also in me. In my Father's house are many mansions: if it were not so, I would have told you. I go to prepare a place for you. And if I go and prepare a place for you, I will come again, and receive you unto myself; that where I am, there ye may be also. And whither I go ye know, and the way ye know. Thomas saith unto him, Lord, we know not whither thou goest; and how can we know the way? Jesus saith unto him, I am the way, the truth, and the life: no man cometh unto the Father, but by me.*" [John 14:1-6]

I held Luke's hand and shared a look of consolation.

"You see how it is? We shall rejoice that Brother Hector is taken to the house of the Lord," I whispered.

We prayed and chanted for the remainder of our vigil. With lighter hearts, we attended prime. Our lives were supposed to continue as normal, but we felt anything but. Because although our sorrow had lessened, the loss was still felt. It was sudden and sharp.

We felt not much like eating but went into breakfast even so and forced down the little bread and ale we could. Afterwards, Brother Maynard pulled us into the parlour.

"Brothers Luke and Paul. I see your wretchedness. This is the first time you have undergone such?"

"Nay, I lost a sister in my youth," I mumbled.

"And yet this feels different?"

"Aye."

"The loss of a loved one is always saddening. And I would remind you we are all family here. That loss of which you speak, it is alike after all. Where once you mayhap had the support of mother and father, you now have all the brethren here. You are not alone. Brother Luke, you were close with Brother Hector."

"I spent time with him daily, of course. He had been so very stern. But recently he..." tears stopped any further speech.

Wrapping an arm about Luke's shoulder, Brother Maynard said, "I knew him well also. He took his duty very seriously and sought to test you at every turn. However, you did not fail him ever. Not once. I would have you know he was so very proud of you."

"He declared as much," Luke managed to say, wiping at his eyes.

"And you will honour his memory in your every deed. For he has set you on your path well. Indeed, I may venture to say he must have waited until the very moment you were ready to take his place."

"Oh, no. No. I have not yet taken final vows. I am not ready."

"It would seem he thought different. As does God. And I, for all which that matters. In this too, you are not alone. You think me ignorant of the work?"

Luke shook his head.

"I have spoken with Prior Ambrose and agreed to take on Brother Hector's duties until such time as you take final vows. Although, I shall be giving you some of the responsibility. But your days shall be much as they are. It shall just be my hideous face you see of an afternoon."

"You are not so very hideous."

"Such flattery, Brother. I am all gratitude."

Luke managed a half-laugh at that.

Nudging shoulders, Brother Maynard told him, "You see. We shall get on well enough. Have no fear."

A rueful smile sat upon Luke's lips. "I am glad it is you, Brother."

After morning Mass, a funerary liturgy was celebrated. Through prayer, readings and psalms, we gave thanks to God for Christ's victory over death, and commended Brother Hector to God's eternal mercy and love. And we received the Eucharist to reaffirm our belief in and union with Christ. The church was filled with incense as we sang our brother to the Lord.

At the end of the service, Prior Ambrose called out, "In peace let us take our brother to his place of rest."

We all of us processed into the cemetery where a grave had been prepared. The church bells rang out as we committed the body of Brother Hector to his resting place.

Prior Ambrose spoke some more words. And we answered with antiphons. Until finally, we came upon the last, "*Suscipe me Domine secundum eloquium tuum et vivam, et non confundas me in expectatione mea!*" (Uphold me, Lord, according to your word, and do not disappoint me in my hope.) [Psalm 119:116]—as we enter our monastic life so too do we depart it.

Alms were then distributed in Brother Hector's name.

Chapter 27 - Cast Thy Burden Upon the Lord

At first, the added burden of additional responsibilities seemed to weigh heavily upon Luke. He was much subdued and threw himself too greatly into his work. So much so that within a fortnight he was brought into the infirmary.

"He fainted away, Brother Giles," Brother Maynard said, all but carrying a sorry looking Luke.

"Lay him upon this cot, and I shall see what we can do."

Luke fell more than laid upon the cot.

"I trust him unto your care," Brother Maynard announced before striding off.

"Oh, my, I do believe you have caused upset, Brother Luke," Brother Giles lightly reprimanded.

"I did not intend to. He shall receive my apology later. But first, prythee, am I taken so very ill?"

"Brother Paul, what say you?"

I raised a brow as I looked upon my beloved. "Hmmm...I would say it is over exertion."

"Indeed. And what would you offer?"

"I shall go and boil up some rosemary, lavender and thyme and mix it with some wine."

"Very good. Do so."

Turning to Luke, he added, "Now, must I tell you of your fault?"

"Nay, I pray you would not."

"You shall remain here and rest in between the offices for the remainder of the day. When you are able, you shall be escorted for short walks out of doors in the physic garden. But henceforth, you shall treat yourself with better care. I would not have Brother Paul upset by a repeat of this shameful behaviour."

Groaning, Luke laid a hand upon his brow, and I hurried off to make the promised preparation.

I returned and helped Luke sit up and sip the wine. "There now, this shall help you sleep," I soothed.

With pitiful eyes, he gazed up at me as his head fell back upon the pillow. "Thank you. I am sorry to cause such a fuss."

"You have heard Brother Giles?"

"Aye, I shall take on less. But there is so much to be done. Yet I see it does not all have to be achieved at once. I would not cause you any distress."

I kissed his forehead. "It gladdens me to hear it. Let Brother Maynard be your guide."

"I shall do better."

"Rest now. Sleep, my fairest of fair. May your dreams be of the sweetest nature."

Drowsily, he murmured, "My honey sweet."

He drifted off into slumber, leaving Brother Giles and myself to get on with our work.

"I fear Brother Hector instilled too much of himself in your Luke."

"Aye, so it would seem. He is intent on doing right by him."

"That should not be taken to such lengths."

"I agree. I feel awful for not having tried harder to stop him before."

"Nay, he would not be Brother Luke if he did not have to learn things the hard way. But let us hope he has now learned this lesson well. Other than over exertion, he seems to be doing well."

"Aye. But do not get any grand notions that I would do half so well without you. I do not give you leave to depart."

"Spoken with such vehemence, my young friend. Nay, I have no plan to put you to the same test. God be willing, I have some years in me yet." He encompassed me in one arm in a sideward embrace. "Come, let us see what more you can learn this day."

We left a sleeping Luke and read through some medicinal texts in the back room.

Luke was recovered and able to enjoy his birthday the week following. We were reading alone in the dormitory in the morning, lying upon my bed.

"Luke, what gift would you like for your birthday?" I asked, kissing his neck.

"We are not allowed possessions."

"Aye, but what would you like from me?"

"Oh."

"You may request anything of me."

"Hmmm...then we should get onto the floor, for there are a great many things I would like to do but may create a good deal of muck."

Knowing, or at least hoping we would not be disturbed, we disrobed with great eagerness. I laid out the supplies next to me as I lay myself upon the reed-strewn floor.

Luke lay atop me, kissing me with great fervour to the extent I thought I may spill from that alone. Especially when his body began to writhe and our pillicocks rubbed alongside one another. Groans escaped my lips.

Taking himself in hand, Luke pointed himself between my thighs, drawing up and down. His shaft ran up against my ballocks in teasing delight.

"Luke, that…is wondrous."

"Aye. Your milky thighs bring me pleasure beyond measure."

He continued to pump, his strokes becoming longer and faster.

"I need more," I whimpered, clutching at him.

"Show me."

As carefully as my fumbling fingers would allow, I drew our lengths together.

Luke bent down and kissed me. "I enjoy this too. Proceed."

I stroked us both in one hand. Then turned my attention to him alone, bringing his hood up and back down again. Looking down, I saw beads of creaminess at his tip and licked my lips.

"Would you like it in your mouth?" Luke asked.

"Aye."

Climbing his way along my body, Luke positioned himself so he could sink into my waiting maw. Hungrily, I took him as he slid in and out.

"Augh! he cried out.

I could do naught but moan around him.

Pulling free, Luke asked, "Might I place myself in a different hole?"

Vigorously, I nodded and reached for the oil but he beat me to it. I watched as he anointed himself until he glistened. My breath caught as he reached his finger and tapped my buttocks.

Drawing my legs up, I gave him the access he needed. His blue gaze didn't leave mine as his finger sank inside, his look growing ever more heated as he drew in and out.

"Prythee, Luke, I am ready."

Pushing my thighs apart, he aimed at my target and shot his arrow home.

"Oh," I exclaimed. "Ahh!"

"These are sounds of pleasure only?"

"Aye. Prythee, move and cease my torment."

Languorously, he drew back then plunged deep.

"Aye, this. This is all I need."

"Then permit me to give you all." With that, he thrust harder and deeper.

"Augh!" He had reached my most sensitive part.

Again and again he struck it like a bell clapper, and oh, how I chimed. Thrust after thrust, the heat grew inside of me. The familiar tension clenched my every muscle until I could only burst forth, my world igniting into Glory. With Luke following close behind.

"Oh, sweet mercy!" I gasped.

He kissed me. "That is the greatest gift I have ever received."

"I wish you the happiest of birthdays," I replied, kissing him in return.

By Brother Hector's month's mind, Luke seemed to settle into a quieter pattern of life. He came to the dormitory not so weary each night. And his eyes brightened once more. I made sure to reward his improved behaviour.

As I sat eating my food, listening to Luke's reading, I was greatly warmed. His dulcet tones spoke of '*de amicitial*' (friendship) from Cassian's *Collationes,* and my mind wandered through the monastery. How many friends I had made here. I had heard of rivalry and bitterness in such places. And there may have been a little of that. However, I felt mostly love and friendship—it was a beautiful thing.

Prior Ambrose had selected us all with the greatest of care. And it was reflected in us all. I supposed it was his privilege to have his choice, given the great houses we were associated with. Still, his diligence was to be commended.

Little news of the outside world reached my ears, but what I did hear seemed to suggest there was a fragile peace there too. King Henry VII seemed to have made steady progress in his one year reign. Just last month, the queen brought forth into the world little prince Arthur, and he was surely a blessing.

Yes, all seemed right with the world. I was content. Nay, more so, I was happy and filled with love.

Epilogue

By Martinmas, Brother Maynard had begun to leave Luke alone unless called upon. They each had agreed upon their allotted tasks and carried them out individually. This, of course, meant he had the cellarer's range to himself. And we did take advantage of that. After all, there was a bed in there, larger and more comfortable than the ones in the dormitory.

However, at night, Luke still opted to sleep in the bed next to mine. Nobody questioned it.

I did not forget my promise to Sybil. She had a fine, bound copy of all the approved medicinal notes I could offer along with her original ones. Brom conveyed it to her and informed me of her delight. Once again, she vowed to keep it secret.

Brom himself seemed happy with Ralph. And I was pleased for them both.

Edmund continued well, even if he did err rather frequently. Still, he continued to take his simple vows. A friendship grew between us. And other postulants arrived to fill Brother Barnabas' days. He did seem to relish the ability to reprimand each and every one. Yet I knew his heart to be good.

Four years passed in the blink of an eye. Mayhap, these were the happiest days of my life. Study, pleasure, work, pray became our habit. And we were all the better for it. Neither overworked nor slovenly. Thus, our minds, bodies and spirits were nourished. And we balanced our two kinds of love in harmony and respect. We were truly blessed.

Of course, all is transitory. All must come and go as we make our way through life. There are beginnings and endings aplenty.

Luke and I took our final vows, and our official time of study reached its close. Although there was still time allotted for reading, it was merely less intense and made more meditative.

I was exceedingly proud to see Luke take on the full mantle of cellarer. He had developed quite a skill for it. Our stores were filled with less expense, and we ate well.

It was a sad day indeed when Brother Giles went to be with God, some four years after my final vows. He was an old man by then and had ensured I knew everything he had learned. His passing was not over long or pained. We were all by his side; it was a good death.

But how I cried at the loss of so beloved a counsel and friend. The like of whom I have never met again. Yet, I know he is with God and must be happy for that.

I hope to have risen to his level in some small amount. His calm, rational thinking with an open, loving heart was a true gift to us all. And he is sorely missed to this day.

I became the infirmarer in his place, of course. But it was a title I would have put off as long as possible. I had not craved it. The price was too high.

The years seemed to pass ever quicker after that. Our year unchanging in its relentless routine.

Eventually, and with all humility, I was nominated to take the place of Sub-Prior Gervase when his health dwindled, and he too passed into God's hands. If I had not sought the position of infirmarer, that of sub-prior had been even further from my mind. It had not so much as occurred to me as a possibility. Mayhap, that was the very reason the brethren thought me best suited.

My new room was near the cellarer's range, where Luke still worked diligently. And I visited as often as possible. But my duties had me much in demand. It was a challenging period for many reasons.

When it was Prior Ambrose's time to return to his Heavenly home, I was elevated to prior. And Luke was voted my sub-prior. We became inseparable. His keen business mind and my studious, theological one seemed a marvellous union. And the abundance of love created between us was shared with all the community. We oversaw the brethren with the firm but fair approach my predecessor would approve of.

Often, as I walked about the precinct, looking upon the labours of the community, I felt satisfaction. We each prayed diligently and worked hard; *ora et labora*. As I then looked upon the large doors of the gatehouse, I saw how safely they held us all within, along with our secrets. The walls surrounded us with love, keeping the evils of the world outside. This was our home. Our sanctuary.

And, at last, patience was rewarded; Luke slept in my large bed almost every night. And we were mostly in one another's company throughout the day.

We were together in every way. And we gave thanks.

Final Word from Paul

Gentle reader - a word of caution here.
For our story is at an end. And the dictates of romance novels permit no other than a happy ending.

What follows is a bittersweet missive.
But Paul would have one final word.
And it is happy in its own way. For him, there can be no greater outcome.

Continue only if you are sufficiently prepared.
You may choose to end your reading here without judgment or reproach.

Herein lies my confessions. For I was born a sinner. And indeed, during my life, I have sinned. But I have repented. And I have loved. Surely, love is the most divine gift bestowed upon us. For does it not also lead to forgiveness, peace and harmony? It is the very thing which gives us humanity.

"Beloved, let us love one another: for love is of God; and every one that loveth is born of God, and knoweth God." [1 John 4:7]

I ask that anyone reading this judge me not too harshly. For, who amongst the living can claim to be entirely without sin? Even those who claim to be the holiest cannot claim such. For we within the monastery, sanctioned by the Pope himself, often dined upon flesh albeit in the misericord. But I fool myself not that such deeds were entirely without sin.

"Judge not, that ye be not judged. For with what judgment ye judge, ye shall be judged: and with what measure ye mete, it shall be measured to you again. And why beholdest thou the mote that is in thy brother's eye, but considerest not the beam that is in thine own eye?" [Matthew 7:1-3]

Seven times a day, I have praised Him, and God has ever dwelt within my heart. My life has been dedicated to His worship. And now I go to Him, with peace of mind and love in my heart. And to be reunited with Luke from whom I have been painfully parted for two long years.

In writing all of this, I have brought him closer to me once again. For when Luke was torn bodily asunder it was as if my heart and soul had been rent to pieces. I knew not at first how to live without him.

These happy memories have brought solace and helped me bear the rigours of my duty. Therefore, I have not included the more argumentative moments the brethren have shared, not that there have been over many. My aim was to share joy so my heart may feel not so lonesome. To heal some of the pain. To rejoice in happiness and forget despair.

"Why art thou cast down, O my soul? and why art thou disquieted within me? hope thou in God: for I shall yet praise him, who is the health of my countenance, and my God." [Psalm 42:11].

Luke came to me last night from Paradise, in a beautiful vision, surrounded by a brilliant light and accompanied by the ravishing scent of apples. He held his arms open, welcoming me Home. And I am not afraid.

By the comfort of God's presence and the kindness of brothers have I continued. But now I am ready, Lord, take me to thy embrace.

"Father, into thy hands I commend my spirit." [Luke 23:46]

What lies ahead is surely my happily ever afterlife. I take my leave with love and wish you nothing but gladness.

"The LORD bless you and keep you;
The LORD make His face shine upon you,
And be gracious to you;
The LORD lift up His countenance upon you,
And give you peace."
[Numbers 6:24-26]

"Suscipe me Domine secundum eloquium tuum et vivam, et non confundas me in expectatione mea." (Uphold me, Lord, according to your word, and do not disappoint me in my hope.) [Psalm 119:116].

Yours ever faithfully,
Prior Paul

Thank you for reading Love Habit.

I do hope you're delighted with Paul's tale, and that if you are you leave a review, post on social media and/or tell all your friends. Because, honestly, reaching out to find readers is getting ever harder, and I truly appreciate your help.

About the Author

TL Clark is an award-winning, best-selling, British author of love who stumbles through life as if it were a gauntlet of catastrophes. Rather than playing the victim, she uses these unfortunate events to fuel her passion for writing, for reaching out to help others.

She writes about different kinds of love in the hope that she'll uncover its mysteries. This has led to her hopping around the romance subgenres like a loved-up froggy.

Her dream is to buy a farmhouse, so she can run a retreat for those who are feeling frazzled by the stresses of the modern world. And to run writing retreats - authors are some of the most frazzled humans anyway.

Her loving husband (and mourned-for cat) have proven to her that true love really does exist.

Writing has shown her that coffee may well be the source of life.

If you would like to follow TL on social media, @tlclarkauthor will usually find her. She is most usually to be found on **Instagram** or **TikTok.**

Or simply scan this handy QR code to sign up to her newsletter:

Other TL Clark Novels You're Most Likely to Enjoy

Love in the Roses

Isabel is the daughter of a knight and is about to marry a man she's never met. Also set in 15th-century Kent, England.

Regency Love

Discover what Lady Anne really thinks as she enters the marriage mart in 1814.

A Haverton Christmas

A short story spin-off of Regency Love. Lady Caroline returns empty-handed from the Season, and her Christmas looks bleak.

Miss Georgiana Darcy's Quest For Love

A Pride & Prejudice variation novelette.
Discover what happened to Georgiana after her dealings with Mr Wickham.

Love Bites More

If you read this for the gay rep, then you may like this stand-alone m/m/m fantasy romance about elinefae. A polyamorous fated mates tale.

But do seek her other works out too. She hops around the romance subgenres like a loved up froggy.

You will find contemporary, inspirational, clifi, fantasy romances, and even a non-fiction 'how to' book amongst her plethora of offerings.

Acknowledgements

Thanks firstly go to Maldo Designs for this fab cover.

But also, a massive thank you to my beta reader who gave me the courage I needed to proceed with this book. My editor and proofreader always have my heartfelt gratitude.

And to Hubby, my everlasting love. Thank you for supporting me even in the face of adversity.

Extra hugs go to every reader who has ever read any of my other books, particularly if you left a lovely review - big gold shiny star to you.

And last but by no means least, thank you, dear reader for obtaining a legal copy of this unique book and taking a chance on an unusual tale.

Glossary

- **Affront** - early 14c., offend by open disrespect
- **Alackaday** – abbreviation of alack the day; used to express sorrow or dissatisfaction
- **Almonry** - a building where alms were formerly distributed
- **Antiphon** - (in traditional Western Christian liturgy) a short sentence sung or recited before or after a psalm or canticle
- **Aslant** - in a sloping direction
- **Attire** - c. 1300, equipment of a man-at-arms; became a general term for apparel, dress, clothes
- **Avaunt** - /əˈvônt/ away, begone
- **Ballocks** - "testicles," from Old English beallucas
- **Bawdy** - late 14c., baudi; soiled, dirty, filthy - became lewd, indecent, unchaste
- **Bellicose** - early 15c., inclined to fighting
- ***Bourbelier de Sanglier*** - roast boar with a spiced wine sauce (stew)
- **Braies** - /bɹeɪ/ breeches or trousers worn in aniquity, but as undergarments in the later Middle Ages
- **Bryndons** - Small cakes in a sauce of wine, fruit, and nuts. Red and yellow in colour.
- **Caitiff** - a contemptible or cowardly person
- **Calefactory** - a room in a monastery, warmed with a communal fire and used as a sitting room, aka warming house/room or common room
- **Canonical hours** - fixed times of prayer of the Divine Office, based on Psalm 118/119:164, "Seven times a day I praise you", and Psalm 118/119:62, "At midnight I rise to praise you".
- **Canticle** - a hymn or chant, typically with a biblical text, forming a regular part of a church service.
- **Carrells** - /ˈkær.əl/ (sounds like carols), also spelled carels - study area often found in the cloister or under the dormitory
- **Caudle** - a hot drink of ale, egg yolks, honey, saffron and bread consumed especially after severe illness or childbirth
- **Caustic** - c. 1400, capable of burning or destroying organic tissue, corrosive

- **Cemetery garden** - serene area of a monastery, planted with fruit trees; symbolic of Heaven / Paradise and supplied manual labor; an orchard
- **Chapter house** - meeting room where all the monks gathered daily to discuss the affairs of the monastery, hear confessions, and administer punishments
- ***Chireseye*** - a kind of bread pudding using cherry juice and wine for flavoring, decorated with flowers
- **Churl** - Old English, man without rank; villain - also fellow of low birth or rude manners
- **Clamour** - late 14c., a great outcry, utter loudly, shout
- **Cloister** - from the Latin word claustrum; meaning an enclosed space – central, tranquil communal space; an arcade, usually columned, around an open, green, square space (the garth) where access by outsiders was prohibited.
- **Comely** - late 14c., handsome, fair, graceful, pleasing in appearance
- **Copulation** - late 14c., a coupling, joining, uniting
- **Cumberworld** - from Middle English combre-world; someone who is an encumbrance on the world; a useless person or thing
- **Dalcop** - literally a "dull-head", a particularly stupid person
- **Dapper** - mid-15c., elegant, neat, trim
- **Decoction** - late 14c., creating an extract either from animal or vegetable substance by boiling it
- **Decrepit** - mid-15c., broken down in health, weakened, especially by age
- **Dejection** - early 15c., unhappy condition, degradation, state of being depressed or in low spirits
- **Disdainous** – Middle English, contemptuous, scornful, haughty
- **Doleful** - late 13c., from Middle English dole; emotion of grief, sorrow, lamentation, mourning
- **Dormitory** - sleeping area for monks - according to The Rule, a lamp was always kept on
- **Doublet** - a man's short, close-fitting padded jacket/vest (about hip-length), commonly worn over an undershirt from the 14th to the 17th century
- **Dulcet** - late 14c., sweet to the senses - also melodious, harmonious

- **Extremities** - early 15c., hands and feet, uttermost parts of the body
- **Folly** - early 13c., mental weakness, foolish behavior or character; unwise conduct
- **Fopdoodle** - (insult) a stupid person or insignificant fool
- **Four thieves vinegar** (aka Marseilles remedy etc.) - said to have been used during the black death epidemic of the medieval period to prevent catching the plague, but similar herbal vinegar recipes date back to Hippocrates.
- **Fundamewnt** - /ˈfəndəmənt/ anus, bottom or buttocks
- **Fusty** - 14c., stale-smelling
- **Fuzzle** - to make drunk, to confuse or befuddle
- **Gainsay** - c. 1300, contradict, deny, dispute
- **Garth** - square patch of green in the centre of a cloister
- **Grete Pye** - Or 'great pie', a yard across. Akin to a giant pork pie containing various minced meats, fruits and spices.
- **Halatafl** - a board game of Viking origin, aka Fox And Geese
- **Harlot** - during the 14th century, the term changed from 'vagabond' to 'whore'
- **Hearse** - a holder for several lit candles to be used in a tenebrae service
- **Hennin** - a lady's hat with a cone or steeple, worn with a veil, restricted to the wealthy
- **Herbarium** - a collection of dried plant specimens or a place that houses one
- **Horarium** - Latin for "hours", a daily schedule for monks
- **Hurtle** - early 14c., to crash together or to knock down
- **Hyperbole** - /haɪˈpɜː.bəl.i/ exaggerated statements or claims not meant to be taken literally. (Sounds like hi-PUR-buh-lee)
- **Hypocras** (there are various spellings) - a drink made from wine mixed with sugar and spices, usually including cinnamon and cloves. Named after Hippocrates as it was thought to be medicinal.
- ***Iesu*** - / yā z u:/ In Latin, Jesus is *Iesu* (sounds like yay-zoo)
- **Imbibe** - to drink or to absorb; soak into
- **Indubitable** - mid-15c., too plain to admit of doubt
- **Interminably** - endlessly
- **Irksome** - early 15c., annoyinng, troublesome
- **Jape** - say or do something in jest or mockery
- **Jester** - a minstrel, professional reciter of romances

- **Knave** – from late Old English, boy, male child; male servant. Became rogue, rascal c. 1200
- **Lascivious** - mid-15c., lustful, inclined to lust; lewd, frolicsome, wanton
- **Lash** - c. 1300, a blow, a stroke
- **Lavatorium** - also anglicised as laver and lavatory - from the Latin lavabo "I shall wash"; communal washing area in a monastery (handwashing before meals and entering the church)
- ***Lectio divina*** - literally "divine meaning"; contemplative spiritual reading of Scripture
- **Lief** - /li:f/ (sounds like leaf) - Middle English, beloved, dear; from Old English lēof
- **Misericord** – special room attached to the refectory outside The Rule, where the monks could eat meat (confusingly, also the 'mercy seat' to rest against in church)
- **Nether** - Old English niþera, neoþera; down, lower, below, beneath. In Middle English (and after) used also of body parts.
- **Office** - in the context of this book; the time monks attend prayer according to the canonical hours (office coming from *officium*, the Latin word for duty).
- **Onerous** - late 14c., burdensome, troublesome
- **Open-arse** - now called medlar; a fruit of the quince and crab apple family
- **Opportune** - c. 1400, seasonable, timely, convenient
- ***Opus Dei*** - "Work of God" - communal prayer (at Canonical hours)
- ***opus manuum*** - manual labour for communal bortherhood, which could be anything from gardening to copying manuscripts.
- **Oratory** - a small chapel, especially for private worship
- **Outer parlour** - room to hold meetings with people from outside the monastery
- ***Oystres in Cevey*** - a rich dish of oysters stewed in a spiced wine sauce
- **Parlour** (or parlor) - derived from the Old French word parloir or parler ("to speak") - room in cloister for monks to converse on serious topics
- **Physic garden** - a type of herb garden with medicinal plants (separate from kitchen garden)
- **Pillicock** - 14c., slang for penis

- **Pintel** - /ˈpintəl/ Old English; penis
- ***Poivre jaunet*** - a sharp, spiced, yellow pepper sauce
- ***Pourcelet farci*** - a grand banqueting dish of stuffed, roast suckling pig
- **Prattle** - foolish, inconsequential talk
- **Prepuce** - /ˈprēˌpyo͞os/ technical term for foreskin
- **Psalm** - a sacred song or hymn, in particular any of those contained in the biblical Book of Psalms and used in Christian worship
- **Quake-buttock quaffer** - (insult) a trembling, heavy drinker
- **Quire** - in the context of this book, Middle English form of choir; the area of a church with seating (stalls) where the choir sang, between the nave and altar
- **Ragamuffin** - mid-14c., demon; but became a ragged lout late 14c.
- **Rastons** - small round loaves made from sweetened bread dough and soaked with butter
- **Replete** - late 14c., filled (with something); completely full, filled to satisfaction
- **Saltarello** - a late 14th century dance, usually played in a fast triple meter and named for its peculiar leaping step, after the Italian verb saltare ("to jump")
- ***Sambocade*** - elderflower cheesecake/cheese-curd tart
- **Sard** - The original 'f word' for having sex - Bible quote "... don't sard another man's wife." [Matthew 5:27]
- **Selfdom** - Old English, independence or privilege
- **Sepulchre** - a separate alcove in some medieval churches in which the Eucharistic elements were kept from Good Friday until the Easter ceremonies
- **Silt** - mid-15c., fine sand or clay carried by running water and deposited as a sediment, especially in a channel or harbour (mud)
- **Sinister** - early 15c., sinistre, prompted by malice or ill-will; false, dishonest, intending to mislead
- **Solatium** (Latin) – solace, comfort in grief; that which brings consolation; also in Middle English to enjoy oneself sexually, and even to give (a horse) a rest – name of Paul's horse
- **Spleenful** - ill-humored, irritable or peevish, spiteful; the spleen being the seat of ill-temper
- **Stews** – (slang) brothels (from the public bath houses which had that reputation)

- **Tables** (game) - board game from which backgammon is derived
- ***Tart in Ymbre Day*** – a sort of onion and cheese quiche with herbs, currants and saffron baked for Ember Days
- **Tenebrae** - Latin for shadows or darkness; the Tenebrae service would be held on Maundy Thursday, Good Friday or Holy Saturday
- **The Rule of St Benedict** – A book of precepts St. Benedict of Nursia written c. 530 (guidelines for monastic life)
- **Timorous** - early 15c., fearful
- **Tisane** - medicinal tea (technically, *ptisan* in 14c.)
- **Variance** - late 14c., fact of undergoing change
- **Varlet** - an insult based on social class; a dishonest man, a rascal (from valet)
- **Vehemence** - c. 1400, forcefulness, violence, rashness
- **Vivacity** - early 15c., liveliness, vigor
- **Vivify** - late 14c., come alive or give life to
- **Wastrel** – (insult) a good-for-nothing
- **Whiff** - 13c., weffe; foul scent or odour
- **Winchester Geese** – term used for the prostitutes in Southwark, London, under the control of the Bishop of Winchester (and who were buried in the Cross Bones, unconsecrated graveyard there)
- **Winebibber** - a term used in the Bible to describe a person who drinks too much wine (or any alcohol) - habitual drinker / drunkard
- **Wretch** - Old English, a vile, despicable person / outcast